THE KRAMPUS CHRONICLES

COUNTESS OF CACHTICE

SONIA HALBACH

Red Sofa Literary
P.O. Box 40482
St. Paul, MN 55104
Tel: 651.224.6670
http://redsofaliterary.com/

© 2019 **Sonia Halbach**
http://www.soniahalbach.com

Cover Art by Maria Spada
http://www.mariaspada.com

ISBN 978-1-7343573-3-2 (ebook)
ISBN 978-1-7343573-2-5 (paperback)

For Evan, the historian

And for Erika, my support

Prologue

Something stirred in the cupola–something not human. Stephanus shook his head. Both his nerves and the heat of the day played with his senses, for when he gazed at the dome structure situated at the top of City Hall; nothing could be spotted. Placing a hand along his brow to shield his eyes from the glaring sun, Stephanus still saw little of interest. But when he looked downward again, a vision flashed through his mind like a lightning bolt illuminating a dark sky.

A beast!

A hairy beast with black horns and sharp teeth momentarily clouded his sight.

Stephanus had paused at the corner of Pearl Street where a crowd had gathered to see the Mayor with his five Aldermen swear their oath of allegiance to England. As the mid-June sun beamed harshly on the mass of people clustered in front of City Hall, Stephanus pulled down his tricorn hat, hoping to not only vanish the unwanted image, but also guard his identity.

The surrender of New Amsterdam to the English had support throughout the island of Manhattan, but Stephanus still worried about possible repercussions upon those responsible for the city's submission. And since his father had been instrumental in drawing up the terms for New Amsterdam's surrender, it would be best to avoid attention today.

But the small wish for anonymity did not last long.

"Stephanus," someone hissed through the throng of chattering voices. "Stephanus Van Cortlandt."

He froze. The voice was unfamiliar, and with the frightening vision still fresh in his mind, he felt no desire to discover the speaker addressing him.

"Stephanus," the voice repeated in a biting tone.

His interest piqued; Stephanus turned his head. However, he saw no one of importance while scanning the bodies adorned in vibrant suits and respectable dresses. The crowd was still focused on City Hall. The men of the hour had just entered the building, including Stephanus's father–Oloff Van Cortlandt.

At five stories–six when counting the cupola–City Hall towered over the surrounding buildings, particularly Lovelace Tavern to its immediate south. But Stephanus's attention wasn't on City Hall, or even the East River flowing on the other side of Pearl Street. A shift had occurred near Coenties Alley that wrapped along the north end of City Hall, and as the crowd swayed, he spotted a gray-cloaked man standing alone in the shadows.

Stephanus had never seen the individual before. Wiry blond hair hung over his strikingly young face. His pale skin was molded around the curves of his skull with chiseled cheeks and a defined brow.

No one else seemed to be paying attention to the stranger, and as he continued to stare, the young man gazed purposefully back. Unnerved, Stephanus weaved through the crowd until he stood in front of the stranger. In comparison, he was an imposing figure next to the lean young man. At twenty-two years of age, Stephanus was broad-shouldered with long, polished brown hair worn in a low ponytail, exposing his high forehead.

"Are we acquainted, sir?" Stephanus smoothed his cravat with one hand. The white linen knotted around his neck felt tighter than usual. The stranger looked up with ghostly gray eyes but gave no response.

"Are you to pretend that you weren't addressing me?" Stephanus said gruffly. His natural boldness had returned.

The young man remained quiet as Stephanus studied his alabaster

6

face. He was a curious looking fellow. Although he appeared in his early twenties, something about him seemed older. It wasn't anything in his physical nature that looked aged—rather something in his spirit—as though Stephanus was staring at a man whose heart had lived longer than his earthly years.

However, it wasn't until Stephanus began walking away did the stranger choose to speak.

"Poppel."

Stopping in the middle of Coenties Alley, Stephanus turned back to see the young man looking off toward the river. The stranger's voice carried an accent he could not quite place.

"I beg your pardon."

Showing little emotion, the stranger repeated, "Poppel—the three sisters of Poppel. This story is familiar to you, yes?"

Stephanus gripped his hips and straightened his back. "And who might you be, sir?"

The stranger twisted Stephanus's direction in one stiff movement. His face was expressionless, but his mouth slanted into something that almost resembled a smile.

"Laszlo. My name is Laszlo." The deep voice reached straight into Stephanus's body, filling it with a cold emptiness. "I know what became of Lily."

Minutes later, Stephanus pounded on the backdoor of Lovelace Tavern. A stout man with bushy hair and a finely trimmed mustache swung the door open with a bang. At first his beady eyes looked out harshly, but they quickly softened at the sight of Stephanus.

"Colonel Lovelace." Stephanus bowed his head.

"Why, Stephanus! To what do I owe this happy meeting? I would have thought to find you at City Hall with the others. No doubt an exciting day for your father."

"Yes, it's quite the occasion. But I have some business to attend to, and I'm afraid the crowds have made it difficult to secure a quiet space," Stephanus explained. "Would it be possible to use the tavern's cellar? I should not be long."

Colonel Lovelace spied the blond man standing behind Stephanus. The stranger avoided eye contact with the tavern owner. Even with the presence of the peculiar young man, Colonel Lovelace gave a permitting nod. "Of course, Stephanus. You are always welcome to use my tavern and cellar. For however long you need."

Colonel Lovelace stepped aside, allowing the two gentlemen to enter. As Stephanus and Laszlo retreated down the creaky cellar steps, a large man at the bar slammed down his tankard, causing dark ale to splash around its pewter rim.

"Allowing anyone into your cellar, huh, Lovelace?" The man punctuated the slurred words with a burp before wiping his moist mouth along the sleeve of his stained shirt. "You don't ever let me down there. No matter how often I ask."

Looking over at the drunkard, Colonel Lovelace stroked his mustache with a finger and thumb. "Archibald, that happens to be Stephanus Van Cortlandt. If your family owned one of the largest breweries in the city, as the Van Cortlandts do, only then may you and your bulbous gullet be granted unquestioning access to my cellar."

"Hear ye, hear ye! Let it be known across the land that on this day—the fourteenth of June in the year 1665—Susanne Leisler will henceforth be called Madame Welles!"

Casparus Houten let out a hearty chuckle while shoving a white disc into his mouth. Before the confection had even been swallowed, the chubby boy already brought another sweet up to his eager lips.

"Laugh all you want, Houten." Susanne crossed her arms. "But since New Amster—excuse me—since New York is now under the control of the English, it would be wise to consider embracing the situation by…"

"Changing your name?" Houten interrupted.

"It was just a thought!" Susanne snapped.

Across the cellar, a smaller boy with blond hair was examining the white confection in his hand.

"Are you going to eat that, Gerhard? Or just stare at it?" Houten remarked. He scratched his wavy brown hair that resembled melting chocolate, which was fitting for the aspiring candy maker.

Gerhard Hostrupp furrowed his brow. "What's this one, Houten?"

"Just sugar, cream, and butter," Houten replied. He popped another piece of candy into his mouth. "It's called borstplaat. However, we might need to rename it, since all Dutch words get butchered in America. *Heere Straat* becomes Broadway. *Breukelen* becomes Brooklyn. And now in Poppel they are spelling *Snoep* without the *e*! It's nonsense."

Hostrupp nibbled the confection and then shook his head. "That's terribly sweet, Houten. Terribly, terribly sweet."

Houten rolled his eyes. "Yes, Gerhard. That's what I strive to accomplish with my candies."

"Too sweet," Hostrupp added. "A bit too sweet this time."

Houten let out another robust laugh, which Susanne quickly shushed.

"Do you want Colonel Lovelace to hear you? He would not be pleased to see three Foundlings in his cellar. And we certainly do not want him to discover how we snuck in." Susanne nodded toward a crate in the corner that hid a tunnel opening. "Why did you insist on coming here in the first place? It doesn't seem worth the risk of getting caught."

Houten shrugged. "Until work ceases on the other areas of Poppel, we are limited in the places accessible by way of the tunnels. And I can only tolerate residing under the Van Cortlandt's mansion for so long."

"What's wrong with the Van Cortlandts?" Hostrupp asked. "Oloff and Annette are always so kind."

Houten scoffed. "And it becomes quite tiring."

"Yes, what a terrible family to open their home to children who have nothing," Susanne remarked dryly. "All they ask in return is assistance with developing an underground village." She paused and glanced around the cellar. "As you can see, we aren't even currently doing the one thing they request from us."

9

"There are other Foundlings helping," Houten mumbled with a mouth full of borstplaat. The creamy sugar threatened to dribble down his chin. "I don't see why we're needed as well. Nor do I understand the purpose behind building a hidden village."

"Do not forget, Houten—oh do not forget! The Van Cortlandts are originally from the Netherlands," Hostrupp said. "Poppel is reminiscent of the place where Annette grew up. And now that New Amsterdam, uh, I mean, now that *New York* is under the jurisdiction of England, I can see why they would be interested in secretly preserving their heritage. Why, yes, I quite see it, indeed."

"Well, whatever their reasons, I'm not interested in helping with Poppel today." Houten rubbed the excess sugar from his hands. "And we didn't come here just to eat borstplaats." Houten looked over at the stacked casks lining the cellar. He picked up a wooden tankard and went over to the barrel adorned with a faucet. Before he could fill the tankard with ale, footsteps sounded from the top of the stairs.

Immediately, Houten, Hostrupp, and Susanne scurried over to a corner and dropped behind a few discarded barrels. But when Houten peeked through the gap between the barrels and spotted Stephanus Van Cortlandt coming into the cellar, he released an audible sigh.

The Foundling sprang to his feet. "Stephanus, it's merely you."

Hostrupp and Susanne stood as well.

"Casparus, I cannot say I am pleased to see you down here." Stephanus glared at the three adolescents. "No doubt trying to steal some of Lovelace's ale."

Houten smirked, holding two fingers close together. "Just a bit." Then looking toward the shadows, Houten's eyes widened and his smile disappeared.

Stephanus glanced back at the stranger lurking behind him. He extended a hand, gesturing for the young man to come out into the open.

"Perhaps it's good the three of you are here. Laszlo appears to be carrying news that may be of interest to us."

Hostrupp and Susanne exchanged skeptical looks, while Stephanus went about introducing the group.

"This here is Casparus Houten, Gerhard Hostrupp, and Susanne Leisler."

"As of today, it's actually Madame Susanne Welles," Houten added with a sneer.

Stephanus's gaze narrowed on Houten and then shifted to Susanne who appeared flustered by the attention.

"Please pay Casparus no mind. He has recently consumed a great deal of sugar."

"What news does this man have?" Hostrupp piped in, trying to defuse Susanne and Houten's bickering.

Stephanus didn't respond. Instead he stepped aside to allow Laszlo access to the dull light of the cellar. The eerie young man slipped into the center of the room as the others curiously watched.

"Lily." The word seemed to carry tremendous weight as it passed Laszlo's lips.

Houten crossed pudgy arms over his chest. "What about Lily?"

Laszlo stood silently, making the others wonder if he was ever going to respond. He brushed a strand of faded blond hair away from eyes before casually replying, "I knew Lily."

Houten, Hostrupp, and Susanne all shared uncertain glances. But Stephanus's eyes narrowed on the stranger. "What do you mean you knew her? You must mean you knew *of* her?"

Laszlo shook his head, so Stephanus pressed on.

"You do understand that Lily was my grandmother's sister, and she has not been heard from for nearly sixty years. So, I have a hard time believing that you were in any way personally acquainted with her."

"Well, Mr. Van Cortlandt," Laszlo responded. "You better start believing."

The cellar was soon submerged in tense silence as Laszlo swept across the room and took a seat on a wobbly stool near the wall of casks. He folded his hands across his lap and watched the others expectantly.

"Since you are unable to offer any evidence for the implausible claim you are making, I remain skeptical." Stephanus approached Laszlo. "But I'm interested to learn how you know about Lily in the first place."

"I understand," Laszlo said with a nod. "Yes, I understand. I very much understand." He reached inside his cloak and pulled out a small chain. "And perhaps now you will start to understand."

Stephanus leaned over and stared down at the chain in Laszlo's hand.

"This once hung around Lily's neck," Laszlo explained. "I believe her sisters had similar chains as well."

Houten, Hostrupp, and Susanne eyed each other again before looking over to Stephanus. He seemed astounded at the sight of the chain. His mouth opened slightly, but no words came out.

"This looks familiar to you, Mr. Van Cortlandt," Laszlo observed. "No doubt one had been worn by your grandmother as well. Possibly passed through your family."

Stephanus still remained silent.

"Of course," Laszlo continued. "It's not the chain itself that was so very precious to the three sisters–but rather what had been carried on their chains."

Laszlo gazed around the cellar at the captivated faces. He now had their unwavering attention.

"I will not bother telling you the portion of the story you surely already know–Grace marrying Jan Loockerman and moving to Turnhout with her sister, Sarah."

"Yes, I would say you have no business educating me on my own family history," Stephanus snapped.

Laszlo's eyes narrowed. "But I would like to share with you the whereabouts of Lily after she departed Poppel with her wheel. Something, I imagine, you are less knowledgeable about."

Stephanus nodded so subtly that his head barely moved.

"I do not know the details of Lily's journey right after she left Poppel," Laszlo admitted. "But it was not long until she came to the outskirts of Vienna where the great Habsburg family had a mansion known as Katterburg. And that's where I first met her. The memory's so deeply set within my mind that it would take a hundred lifetimes to rid myself of it.

Chapter One

Countess Bathory

The Wien River coursed through Vienna with such energy that at times waves would thrash the walls surrounding Katterburg–a mansion standing at the bottom of a low hill just outside the city where wild game roamed freely. Since the Austrian nobility, who owned the estate, rarely visited, it was not unusual for pheasants and deer to be the only living creatures seen along the floodplain. So when Lily rode up to Katterburg in the late summer of 1608, she had not been expecting the mansion to be occupied.

But she was quite mistaken.

Matthias II had been on the far end of the mansion, reading in the library, yet he still heard the commotion brought on by Lily's arrival. Matthias flew through the halls, anxious to discover what had caused such a disturbance. He soon saw his most trusted confidant, Melchior, tousling with a cloaked intruder.

"You cannot barge into Katterburg," Melchior scolded. "Katterburg belongs to the House of Habsburg–the Holy Roman Emperor, Rudolf, and his brother, Matthias." Melchior firmly gripped the intruder's arms, but he struggled to restrain the flailing stranger.

"Melchior," Matthias's voice boomed. "What's the meaning of all this?"

Melchior's pointed face looked to the Archduke. The high collar of his red robe hid his wizened neck, leaving a receded hairline to indicate his many years. A silver mustache looped down to the whiskers on Melchior's chin, which didn't match the dark eyebrows widely situated on his brow. But the old man still managed to maneuver the intruder around with ease.

"She broke into the main gallery," Melchior snapped. "Charged right into the mansion as though she were an invited guest."

"She?" Matthias's gaze shifted to the veiled figure.

Melchior whipped back the intruder's brown hood, exposing a full head of long, thick hair the color of straw. The young woman's dark eyes fluttered toward Matthias. They were surprisingly strong, holding no trace of fear, and for some reason, also quite familiar. Although the woman didn't look like she could possibly be older than two decades, something about her reminded Matthias of someone he had met years and years ago.

"Archduke Matthias," said the young woman. While still within Melchior's hold, she attempted to bow.

"Have we met before?" Matthias studied the intruder's face.

She nodded but said nothing more.

"Please restore my memory. I cannot recall the time or place for such a meeting." Matthias stared at the stranger's full lips. Her olive skin glowed, having not been washed for some time.

"Do you remember the village of Poppel?"

Matthias's eyes grew in recognition. "Lily from Poppel!" He gestured toward his assistant. "Unhand this woman, Melchior. She's one of three sisters who helped me during my time as the Governor of the Netherlands. I was passing through the northern part of Belgium when I fell desperately ill. These sisters took me in without question and cared for me until my health returned."

Melchior released his grip on Lily and stepped to the side as Matthias approached the young woman.

"I cannot believe it is you. We crossed paths so many years ago, and yet, here you are in front me, looking as though no time has passed at all."

Lily smiled tersely. "Oh, how I wish that were true."

"Well, the years have certainly treated you far better than me," Matthias said. And Lily could not argue.

When Lily met Matthias more than a decade ago, he had been a spirited man on the brink of political prominence, even when overcome by illness. Although he still carried the same confident air, his features had become hollowed over time and his facial hair was now fully gray.

Matthias folded his hands across his front. "Now, I must ask, what brings you to Katterburg?"

Lily appeared hesitant. But finding her courage, she spoke steadily, "Before you left Poppel, you had instructed me and my sisters that if we were ever in the area, we should feel obliged to take shelter in your mansion, even if you were not there."

Matthias laid a hand along his chest. "Yes, I remember. Then am I to assume that you are in need of a place to stay?"

She nodded.

"May I inquire as to why?"

Lily locked gazes with the Archduke, but she did not respond. Matthias nodded at her silence before looking over at Melchior who was still distrustfully eyeing Lily.

"Melchior," Matthias directed. "Please show Lily to a room where she may get cleaned." Then he turned back to Lily. "A few guests are staying at Katterburg as well. I hope you will join us for a meal once you have rested." Matthias gently placed a hand upon Lily's shoulder. "It's very good to see you again. If you need anything, please do not be afraid to request it. The kindness you and your sisters bestowed upon me has not been forgotten."

Matthias started to leave the front gallery, but he stopped and turned on his heels in one sudden movement. "And where are your sisters? Grace and Sarah–I believe were their names."

"I am afraid they could not make this journey with me." Lily's tone was sharp.

"You are traveling alone?"

Lily nodded, and then changing the course of the conversation, she asked, "May I inquire as to who else is staying here?"

Matthias smiled. "Why, it is the great Bathory family from the Kingdom of Hungary–Countess Elizabeth Bathory and her children. I believe you will find them to be most fascinating."

Katterburg was a modest mansion when compared to the other palaces and estates belonging to the House of Habsburg. However, as Lily walked through the ornate hallways with mosaic ceilings and glass-paneled walls, she could not recall ever being surrounded by such grandeur in her rather extended lifetime.

Before entering the banquet hall, Lily paused at a large mirror near its doorway. She wore a dark blue dress with a thick white ruff that enveloped her neck. All of which had been borrowed. The only thing she wore that belonged to her was hidden beneath the ruff.

Lily gently fingered the small item resting along her breastbone as she continued to study her reflection. Others would have seen a remarkably beautiful woman, but Lily could only see time's gradual passing within the features of her face. The sight made her paw harder at the emblem resting against her chest. She choked back the sudden wave of sadness. But before she was overcome with emotion, Lily heard voices on the other side of the door.

The guests were anticipating her arrival.

There was a screech of sliding chairs as Matthias and another man stood to greet Lily when she entered the dining room. But Lily did not notice either. She was too captivated by the presence of an older woman seated directly across from the entrance.

The woman's raven black hair was swept up in a high mound on her head, and Lily could not stop staring at her flawless alabaster skin and rosy lips. Although the woman was probably twice her years of age, Lily felt unattractive and inadequate in comparison.

"You are gorgeous." Lily spoke the words without thought.

The woman smiled appreciatively at Lily's genuine remark while Matthias began the introductions.

"Lily, please allow me the privilege to introduce Countess Elizabeth Bathory as well as her daughters, Anna and Katalin, and son, Andras."

Anna and Katalin were pretty young women, resembling their mother with similarly dark hair and pale complexions. Lily curtsied toward Elizabeth Bathory and the daughters seated on either side of her. Andras was standing on the far end of the table, across from Matthias. Appearing to be the youngest, Andras's oily hair draped over his face as he bowed in Lily's direction.

Matthias looked around the room at his guests. "It seems, however, that we are missing..." The doors behind Lily shot open with a bang. "Ah, Laszlo," Matthias greeted. "We were wondering when you would join us."

Lily turned around to see a young man with shoulder-length blond hair and a pointed face standing in the doorway. He appeared startled at the sight of Lily and made no attempt to take a seat at the table.

"This is Countess Bathory's eldest son, Laszlo," Matthias introduced.

With a bowed head, she once again curtsied, but Laszlo remained unmoved. He continued to stare at Lily with a gaping mouth until Matthias finally directed him to an empty chair next to her, across from Countess Bathory.

Lily was quiet throughout much of the meal. But she could feel Laszlo's gaze on her from where he sat to her immediate left. Distracted by Laszlo's attention, she wasn't even listening to the table's conversation until Countess Bathory brought up a topic that could not be easily ignored.

"Matthias, I hear rumors about your brother. Is it true that Rudolf, the Holy Roman Emperor, has a great interest in the occult?"

Stiffly, Matthias set his fork down on his plate. Then he folded his hands on the table. "Why, yes, Rudolf has always been fascinated by the more magical things in life. It is not unusual to find alchemists and mystics frequenting the royal court."

"How strange," Countess Bathory remarked with a faint smile. "Now, what is the reason behind his fascination?"

"I believe my brother has a desire to uncover what some consider the elixir of life."

The Countess lifted a goblet to her lips, but she did not take a sip. Unconsciously, Lily mirrored the woman's actions by raising her own cup.

"Elixir of life?" repeated the Countess. "Am I correct in assuming you're referring to some kind of potion that grants eternal life?"

Matthias nodded as Lily struggled to keep the cup she was holding from crashing onto the table.

"Isn't that something?" Countess Bathory said in a wispy voice. "I never would have imagined such a remarkable thing could exist."

Matthias chuckled. "Oh, would it not be amazing if it did? However, I'm afraid my brother is under a misapprehension, for the existence of such an elixir is a myth that has circulated long before our time. I fear that Rudolf's passion for such a magical delusion hurts his ability to rule over our great empire. It may not be long until I am asked to replace my brother on the throne. Of course, I would not wish for such a thing. But if I were called to serve my people, I do not believe I would have a choice."

Lily could not help but notice that the words Matthias spoke did not match his rather pleasant tone at the thought of such an arrangement. Still, she was less concerned about Matthias's ambitions than her own, and she wanted the discussion of the elixir to continue.

"I would think that such an educated man like the Holy Roman Emperor would not fall for such an idea," Lily started to say. Out of the corner of her eye, she could see Laszlo completely twist in his chair, drawn by the sound of her voice. "If there was no evidence of its existence," she continued.

"That's certainly a valid point," Matthias replied. "It's true that stories have come to light about people who have achieved such lengthened lives."

"Oh?" Lily's mouth went dry as she tried to keep her composure.

"Not in this area," Matthias added quickly. "But by people who have come from more eastern lands, such as the Kingdom of Hungary."

"Oh, Matthias!" Countess Bathory waved her immaculate hand. "Surely, you cannot peg such silly stories on my region. If such myths were true, I would be the first requesting this unchanging youth."

Matthias smiled. "My dear Countess, you of all people do not require such nonsense. You look as beautiful and young as the day I met you."

Countess Bathory forced a laugh and then glanced across the table at Lily. Once again, the beautiful woman lifted her goblet, subtly gesturing the cup Lily's direction, before bringing it back to her lips.

"Oh, Matthias, if only your flattering words had the power to erase the years from my age."

"Tell me about the girl, Matthias." Countess Bathory leaned over the railing of the stairway that looked over the gardens of Katterburg mansion. The sun hung low in the sky, sending a pink glow across the green and blooming estate.

"Lily? Oh, she's an old acquaintance."

"Old!" Countess Bathory snapped. "Why, she looks like she was just born into this world."

"Yes, she certainly hasn't aged much since last I saw her." Then Matthias added with a grin, "Perhaps I should have her visit Rudolf. She would be quite a thing for his alchemists to study."

"Or perhaps, you should send her with me," Countess Bathory said earnestly. "We are heading to our castle, Lockenhaus, in the south. As you know, Lockenhaus belonged to my late husband. It's quite a large castle, and I do not possess as many handmaidens as I would like there. She no doubt would be of great use."

"You may absolutely offer her such a position. I am not privy to Lily's current circumstances to ascertain whether she would be interested. She's not from noble lineage, as far as I am aware."

Countess Bathory gleefully clasped her hands together. "Then that settles the matter. I shall ask Lily to escort my family to Lockenhaus. It would be such a great opportunity for any young woman of her status. Also, regarding my late husband, Ferenc Nadasdy." The Countess's tone turned solemn. "Although he passed away over four years ago, you are likely aware that there are some unpaid debts owed to him..."

"Yes, yes. We will straighten all of that out, of course," Matthias muttered with a dismissive wave. "But going back to the topic of Lily, it seems that asking her to join you would undoubtedly please one of your sons."

Matthias gazed over the railing where Laszlo could be spotted near the main fountain below.

Standing with his arms folded, Laszlo looked out across the estate to where Lily was taking an early evening stroll.

"There are very few things in life I am certain about, Countess," Matthias commented. "But I would wager the entire House of Habsburg that Laszlo's now a man in love."

Night had just crept across the land when Lily headed back to Katterburg mansion. Feeling uncomfortable in the presence of such a powerful family, she had tried to remain outside until the Bathory members retired for the evening.

Also, Lily could not seem to avoid the rather watchful eyes of Laszlo. The young man had yet to speak a word to her, but she still found his intense eyes following her every move. Even when she escaped to the outdoors, she could see him standing nearby, gazing out at her.

So when Lily returned to the mansion and saw a shadowy form waiting near the grand staircase, she assumed it was Countess Bathory's unusual son. But when the figure moved a candle up to his face, it turned out to be Melchior.

"I hope I did not startle you," he said drearily.

"Not at all," she snapped. "I was just going to retire for the night."

"I was not keeping an eye on you."

Lily scoffed. "I find it strange that you have not been around since Matthias approved of my staying."

Melchior took a step closer and lowered his voice. "It's not you I'm avoiding, madam. It's the others. The Bathorys are not people I care to cross."

"And why's that?"

"The Countess," Melchior began to say, but then glanced around nervously. "She's not a well woman."

"What do you mean? Is she ill?"

"In a way. She's sick over her quest for power."

"Political power?" Lily asked.

He shook his head. "She wants to obtain things that no human should. It would be best if you keep your distance as well."

"I do not understand. What is it that she wants to obtain?"

Melchior handed the candle over to Lily.

"Never-ending light, madam," Melchior responded. "Countess Bathory seeks that which can never be put out."

Chapter Two

The Crystal Palace

By the summer of 1857, Seneca Village was no more. As Maggie Ogden gazed out at the green lawn that once consisted of a church, cemetery, school, and wooden houses, she spotted the village's last residents pushing wheelbarrows filled with their meager possessions down the desolate dirt road.

And she could not help but feel responsible.

Of course, the reasons given by the city were justifiable on the surface–New York City needed a park, and Seneca Village's land happened to fall within the area designated for such a place. But Maggie knew the motives went beyond that.

Nearly three years ago, Maggie entered Seneca Village on Christmas Day, emerging from the hidden underground village of Poppel, while being chased by the clandestine authorities known as the Garrisons. Maggie–with the help of her brother, sister, cousins, and unusual children called Foundlings–had assembled the pieces needed to summon St. Nicholas's return and vanquish the Garrisons who had forcibly taken over Poppel thirty years earlier.

While Maggie did succeed in saving Poppel, and momentarily witnessing–so she believed–St. Nicholas's return, none of it would have been possible without the assistance from those in Seneca Village. Since the Garrisons had been well-connected officials, she didn't doubt that revenge played a role in choosing the new park's location.

"Maggie," a familiar voice called behind her.

She turned to see her cousin, Louis, scrambling up the hill to where she stood. His dusty brown hair glistened in the sunlight, while he shielded his freckled face with the palm of an outstretched hand.

"There you are," Louis panted. The eighteen-year-old came up alongside Maggie who was only a year younger than him. "I had an inkling I would find you here."

Maggie looked back toward Seneca Village, but there was nothing left to see as the final family disappeared from view. The village was now empty, perhaps forever.

"I never actually believed that it would come to this," she whispered.

"You cannot still think that you're to blame," Louis said. "The city had been planning the construction of this park for years—decades even!"

"They wanted to get rid of Seneca Village." Maggie's voice remained hushed.

"Even if that were so," Louis reasoned. "This land's ripe for development. It would have been considered regardless of what happened with the Garrisons."

Maggie shook her head. "They wanted to punish those who helped us."

"Us? Hey, don't bring me into this!" Louis raised his arms protectively in front of his chest. "You're the one responsible for destroying these innocent people's home and way of life."

She shot Louis a glare, but her eyes softened when seeing his teasing grin.

"You need to stop feeling guilty." Louis placed a comforting hand upon her shoulder.

With a frown, Maggie looked briefly at his hand. A moment later, she shrugged out of his touch and walked away. "It's not guilt I feel—it's vengeance."

"Where are you going now?" Louis asked with a sigh.

Maggie didn't respond to the question. She believed Louis already knew the answer.

The much-anticipated unveiling of the Greensward Plan was that afternoon. And Maggie had every intention of seeing that such an event did not occur.

The dome on the iron-framed Crystal Palace could be seen long before Maggie and Louis approached the front of the showing hall. The glass building sparkled in the summer light, casting a golden hue over the rather barren area that sat on the northern outskirts of New York City.

The Crystal Palace was the sight of the 1853 World's Fair and had since hosted hundreds of events showcasing to the public the newest innovations. But today was a special event–the grand reveal of the winning design for Central Park.

"I don't understand why you chose to come," Louis said. "It will only upset you."

They paid the fifty cents entrance fee at the main door.

Maggie huffed. "I want to see what monstrosity's being built upon the ruins of Seneca Village."

"Monstrosity?" Louis repeated. "You are aware that they are building a park–not a prison. Quite frankly, I do not find it to be such a poor idea. London has Hyde Park–it would be nice for New York to have a public outdoor space for everyone to enjoy."

"Everyone except those forced out of Seneca Village," Maggie grumbled.

She and Louis entered the main gallery of Crystal Palace. Although she had visited many times before, it was still a sight that left one momentarily speechless.

The Crystal Palace's layout was cross-shaped, heightened by soaring ceilings. The second level was connected by semi-circular staircases located at each of the four corners beneath the dome. The space was full of statues, plants, and exhibition booths that displayed everything from various minerals found across the country to the newest sewing machines. As the crowds wandered around the dozens of booths, people started drifting toward the back of the building. Maggie and Louis weaved toward the mob assembled near an indoor fountain on the other end of the palace. A group of gentlemen stood on a platform–above them hung a banner: *Greensward Plan.*

Maggie recognized two of the men, Frederick Law Olmsted and Calvert Vaux–the architects behind the winning Central Park design. The pair of thirty-year-old men proudly stood with overly stretched smiles plastered on their faces as they watched the mass of onlookers grow.

"Maggie Ogden!"

Turning around, Maggie saw Jervis McEntee making his way toward her. The young man with thick, chestnut hair was not alone–a stunning brunette followed closely behind.

"Catharine!" Maggie exclaimed at the sight of her older sister. "And Jervis. I'm pleased both of you came."

"When Catharine extends an invitation, it's impossible to pass up the opportunity." Jervis's smile expanded within his meticulously trimmed beard.

Louis looked between Jervis and Catharine before staring at Maggie, silently requesting an introduction. However, she was in no mood for formalities, so Louis reached out a hand to Jervis.

"I'm Louis Moore–Catharine and Maggie's cousin."

Jervis shook Louis's extended hand. "Jervis McEntee."

"Jervis happens to be Calvert Vaux's brother-in-law," Maggie quickly explained. She jerked her head the direction of the platform. "As you may know, Vaux is one of the winning architects."

"Ah," Louis said with a nod. "Then this must be an exciting event for you, Jervis."

"Quite honestly, I had no intention of coming today," he replied. "But I've never been to the Crystal Palace, and I was curious to take in the spectacle."

"There's more to see upstairs." Catharine seemed eager to escape the watchful eyes of her sister and cousin. "Let's venture up there before the presentation begins."

Jervis happily agreed. So with a polite smile, Catharine led Jervis away, leaving Maggie and Louis behind.

"What exactly is happening there?" Louis asked.

Maggie shrugged. "Jervis is a nice man. He's actually an aspiring artist."

"Catharine has befriended an artist?"

Maggie laughed lightly. "You give her too much credit. It was I who acquainted them with one another."

Louis arched an eyebrow. "And why would you do a thing like that?"

Maggie looked back at Calvert Vaux still standing on the platform.

"I believed it would be in my best interest to have a connection to those paramount to Central Park's success."

"You're using Jervis to get closer to Calvert Vaux?"

She didn't respond, even when confronted with Louis's pressing stare.

"Maggie…"

"Listen, Louis. We all know Catharine's an attractive woman with dozens of men lining up to call upon her. Unsurprisingly, Jervis was also eager to make her acquaintance. And if his family connections could potentially help me gain insight into the Central Park Commission, then the introduction was beneficial for everyone."

"How does your sister feel about being used like this?"

Maggie laughed more genuinely this time. "Catharine's so accustomed to men trying to court her that I hardly think she notices. And besides, I'm starting to believe she actually likes him."

"Catharine likes an artist?" Louis said doubtfully.

"He painted her a rather beautiful landscape." The corners of Maggie's mouth twitched. "He even sketched in a small silhouette of Catharine nestled under the shade of some trees."

"Oh, dear," Louis said with widening eyes. "If the branches of those trees cryptically form letters that spell out his undying love, this would truly be the worst story I've ever heard."

Maggie wasn't able to respond before one of the men on the platform started addressing the sizeable audience.

"Ladies and gentlemen, it's wonderful to see such an enthusiastic turnout. I'm Andrew Green, the president of the Central Park Commission. Today I am excited to share with you the Greensward Plan, designed by Frederick Law Olmsted and Calvert Vaux."

The distinguished president with gray temples and a toothy grin gestured to Frederick and Calvert. But Maggie was no longer focused on the presentation. With her neck stretched as far as it could go, she glanced about the space with a puzzled expression.

"Who are you looking for now?" Louis asked. "If it's Catharine and Jervis, I'm sure they're already halfway to St. Peter's for their wedding."

"Well, actually, no. It's not them I'm looking for," Maggie responded. "This may sound strange but…"

Maggie stopped speaking. She spotted Catharine and Jervis leaning against the banister on the second level. Catharine's alarmed eyes were directed on something in the crowd below. Maggie followed her sister's gaze and that's when she saw him.

Henry Livingston.

Maggie had not seen Henry in nearly three years. However, now with the young man standing across the crowded gallery, a stream of emotions returned to her. But Henry wasn't looking at Maggie–his eyes were locked on the second level where Catharine was staring back.

"I would like to present you all with the winning design for Central Park…" Andrew Green grabbed hold of the cloth covering the easel. "The Greensward Plan!"

As Mr. Green started to unveil the design, Henry looked Maggie's way and the pair met each other's eyes for the first time in years. Henry's lips curled at the sight of Maggie, but it wasn't a smile. Her face flushed with old familiar feelings. Meanwhile, a loud cry sounded throughout the Crystal Palace.

"Fire!" the voice screamed. "Fire! Fire!"

A cloud of smoke could be seen rising to the rafters from somewhere on the second level. The crowd swiftly reacted, and soon people rushed past, desperately trying to reach the exits. The charging bodies collided with Maggie, knocking her onto the ground.

Maggie recalled how the Garrisons had chased her through

Seneca Village. She had managed to unite the Sister Wheels, triggering a stampede of deer and horses, ridden by the Martyrs of Gorkum–deceased men who had disappeared with St. Nicholas centuries ago. Now as Maggie lay sprawled on the Crystal Palace's floor amid frantic feet and smoky air, she wished to be back on that cold dirt road instead.

While Louis struggled to pull her up by the arm, another individual appeared at her side. Henry had made it over to her remarkably fast considering he ran against the heavy stream of people. Quickly, he hauled Maggie to her feet, and then grabbing her hand, he led Maggie and Louis through the palace. The fire crackled above her head, but she didn't look up. She couldn't even if she tried. Although the Crystal Palace was made of iron and glass, a wooden frame fastened the dome, and chunks of the material began crashing down as Henry, Maggie, and Louis scurried below.

Soon Maggie became convinced they would never make it out of the burning palace, but eventually the bright sunlight blinded her eyes. Henry continued to lead them on, not stopping until they were blocks away. Maggie turned back to the Crystal Palace, the top of which was completely engulfed in flames and smoke.

"Catharine," Maggie cried with a cough. She looked through the flustered crowd for any sign of her sister.

Henry also scanned the sea of people with an expression marked by concern.

"Catharine," Maggie called again.

Her voice struggled to be heard through the noise of anxious people scattered throughout the area. But before Maggie's worry could grow, a body flashed in front of her, slamming into Henry.

"What did you do?" Catharine struck Henry's chest with her open palms.

Taken aback by Catharine's outburst, Henry quickly brought up his arms to protect his face.

"Catharine, what are you doing?" Louis asked. He tried pulling his cousin away from Henry. Jervis also reached out and touched

her shoulders lightly, a look of apprehension on his face.

"I saw you!" Catharine continued shouting, even as she received confused looks from bystanders. "I know you did something. You caused this!"

"What are you talking about?" Maggie stepped between Catharine and Henry. She lowered her voice so not to draw any further attention. "He was down on the main floor. I saw him."

Catharine shook her head, still glaring at Henry. "I watched you examining the second level right before the fire started. The expression on your face…you were expecting the fire to happen."

Everyone looked over to Henry who had been bracing for another attack from Catharine. Eventually, he straightened out his vest and adjusted his jacket.

"It's nice to see you, too, Catharine." Henry spoke steadily. "However, if I had known your greeting would be so…enthusiastic, I would have dressed more appropriately. Perhaps in a suit of armor."

Catharine crossed her arms over her chest. "What are you even doing here?"

"I invited him," Maggie said quickly.

Catharine stared at her sister in disbelief.

"You did?" Louis asked.

Maggie nodded. "I wrote Henry a month ago and asked if he would come to the Greensward Plan unveiling. I hadn't heard back, so I assumed he wasn't coming."

Henry gave her a pleasant grin. "I did receive your letter. However, until recently I was uncertain if I could make the trip. Also, it seemed like a fun idea to surprise you."

Maggie smiled back just as horse-drawn fire engines came bounding down the road toward the sizzling palace. The additional noise caused the group to grow quiet.

"I'm Jervis. Jervis McEntee." The young man stepped forward, reaching a hand out to Henry.

"He's an aspiring artist," Catharine stated.

Henry took Jervis's hand with a nod. "I'm Henry Livingston from

Poughkeepsie. And apparently, an aspiring arsonist."

Out of the corner of his eye, he playfully glanced at Catharine. She looked away.

"It just seemed like you were expecting something to happen. Something peculiar about the way you were staring."

"I was staring at you." Henry spoke so earnestly that Catharine's cheeks blushed. "But it seems as though my timing was poor…"

"Well, it's good to see you, Henry," Maggie interrupted. "How long are you staying?"

"I just came to the city for today," Henry replied. "With my luck, if I stayed any longer, New York would be burned down by Sunday."

The group looked back at the Crystal Palace. Most of the dome had been scorched, but it seemed like the fire department had now contained the blaze.

"You should stay until the end of the week," Maggie said. "We will be celebrating Grandfather Clement's seventy-eighth birthday."

Henry forced a smile. "I'm likely the last person Clement Clarke Moore would be interested in seeing on his birthday."

"Nonsense," Louis said. "All of that is in the past. You should definitely remain in the city until the party."

"I am afraid I have nowhere to stay," Henry admitted with a shrug.

Maggie didn't hesitate before replying, "You can stay at Chelsea Manor, of course."

"Maggie," Catharine admonished. "You cannot just extend invitations to Chelsea Manor without consulting Grandfather Clement…"

"Oh, don't be silly. Chelsea Manor has more empty bedrooms than Grandfather Clement can count. Also, Grandfather has become more senile in his old age. He keeps complaining of hearing noises, and items being rearranged throughout the house. It might be good for him to have Henry around for a while." Seeing that Catharine still wasn't convinced, she added, "And considering what we have all been through together, Henry should always be welcome there."

Maggie stared at Catharine pointedly, as though threatening to reveal the details about the events three years ago. Surely, she didn't want Jervis to know family secrets so early in their relationship.

Appearing to acquiesce, Catharine remained silent.

"Well, I would love to see the rest of the family," Henry finally said. "If you think Clement Clarke Moore would have me, I'd be happy to stay for the birthday party."

Maggie tried to repress her excitement at his response.

Catharine turned to Jervis. "Would you escort me home?"

"Of course." The man sounded relieved.

She draped her arm through Jervis's. "Are you coming with us, Maggie?"

"I'll go visit Chelsea Manor with Henry," she responded. "He might need an advocate."

Catharine nodded and then glanced briefly at Henry. "I expect I will see you again soon." Her voice was impassive, and her stoic expression was even harder to read.

After Catharine and Jervis walked away, Louis shook his head. "It's official, Henry. When the Moores and the Livingstons cross paths, only trouble ensues."

Before Henry could respond, an intense conversation broke out nearby.

Maggie glanced down the block. Andrew Green and the rest of the Central Park Commission were having a lively discussion with Frederick Law Olmsted and Calvert Vaux. Although Maggie couldn't make out what was being said, it was clear that all parties were quite upset, and rightfully so.

"The unveiling did not go as planned," Louis observed dryly.

"Hmm," Maggie heard Henry mumble.

She turned to him. "You think the fire will affect the construction of Central Park?"

"Just a funny thing about people." Henry stared at the group of men. "Confidence can be easily shaken."

Maggie studied Henry. The corners of his mouth were slightly turned up, as though he was pleased with the scene unraveling before his eyes. Although Maggie hadn't interacted with Henry in nearly three years, he still looked the same with his puffy bronze hair and penetrating blue eyes. Yet there was something different about him. Something that went beyond his appearance–something deeper–and for a moment, Maggie swore she saw what Catharine had tried to explain.

Perhaps Henry had been responsible for the fire.

Or he, at least, knew more than he would say.

Chapter Three

An Unexpected Messenger

Henry had visited Chelsea Manor twice–and neither was during the best circumstances. So he seemed pleasantly surprised when Clement Clarke Moore grudgingly allowed him to stay there. But Grandfather Clement was clear it would be for no longer than a few days.

Although Maggie had witnessed Grandfather Clement granting Henry permission to stay at Chelsea Manor, she still couldn't believe her eyes when the family's carriage pulled up to the mansion that Friday afternoon, and Henry appeared on the porch.

"Is that...?" Maggie's mother, Mary Ogden, started to say.

"What in the world is he doing here?" Dr. Ogden muttered from the front of the carriage.

"I invited him," Maggie said. "Strange, I thought I had mentioned it." Her mother scoffed. "I certainly would have remembered if you had." The Ogden family dismounted the carriage. Maggie's older brother, Clemmie, would be arriving later, and Catharine was coming with Jervis.

As Maggie approached the Manor's front porch, she could not take her eyes off Henry. Adorned in a dark jacket and square bow tie, she had never seen him dressed so formally. Even his bronze hair was parted and slicked to the side.

"Margaret," Henry greeted with a slight smile.

"Henry, you remember my parents, Dr. John and Mary Ogden."

Her parents acknowledged the young man from Poughkeepsie before entering the mansion, leaving Maggie and Henry alone on the porch.

Noticing Maggie's fixed gaze, Henry chuckled. "I suppose you're not used to seeing me cleaned up–and not completely covered in fireplace soot."

She hurriedly glanced away. "I'm just surprised that you even had a formal outfit for the occasion, since you'd only planned to stay for the Greensward Plan ceremony."

It was an innocent, even playful, comment, but Henry's smile disappeared, and his eyes narrowed. Before Maggie could ask him if she had said something wrong, Clemmie called from inside Chelsea Manor.

"By golly, is that Henry Livingston?"

Turning her head, Maggie saw her twenty-year-old brother standing in the foyer. He waved the pair inside.

Henry stepped into the mansion. "Clemmie, it's good to see you again."

Although it had only been three years, Clemmie had changed quite a bit in appearance. While still attractive, his boyish good looks had been replaced with a dashing man who had long ago entered adulthood. His upper lip and chin were now covered with dark hair, and his baggy eyes created a further resemblance to their father, Dr. John Ogden.

If Henry had any doubts that Clemmie's personality had also transformed over the years, it was soon clear that it had not.

"What family secret have you brought to endanger our lives this time, Mr. Livingston?" Clemmie asked.

"I thought you weren't coming until later," Maggie said to her brother. She then looked at Henry. "Clemmie has decided to become a recluse."

"I attend Columbia College," Clemmie clarified with emphasis on the institution's name. "And yes, I regret that when I am not huddled away in the Astor Library, pouring over stacks of medical volumes, I am mostly taciturn in my room, waiting for term to begin in a couple of months."

"So you can imagine the fun that's been had within the Ogden household this summer," Maggie said dryly.

Clemmie ignored his sister. "And what have you been busying yourself with? Still in Poughkeepsie?"

"Yes, actually..." Henry began before trailing off.

Maggie didn't understand what had caused him to become tongue-tied, but then she noticed Catharine and Jervis entering Chelsea Manor. On a normal day, Catharine could stop crowds with her beauty, but when an occasion called for elevating her dress and appearance, there was no point trying to compete with the attention bestowed upon her.

Catharine wore a lavender dress, and her glistening brown hair was laid ornately upon her head. Jervis proudly escorted her into the stair hall where she greeted family members, introducing them to her companion.

Maggie could see Henry sizing up his competition when Clemmie blurted, "Is she still seeing that artist?"

"It appears that way," Maggie said gloomily.

She didn't mind if Catharine and Jervis were together–particularly since she had introduced the pair–but she was bothered that after all these years, Henry was still enraptured by her older sister. Maggie understood it three years ago. At the time, she had been only fourteen and Henry nineteen. But now that she was seventeen, she found the age difference less significant, and she hoped he would perhaps see her in the same light he had once viewed Catharine.

Maggie wasn't sure why Henry had this jealous effect on her. They had been through a lot in a short amount of time, but she remembered feeling a strong connection to him the moment they met. However, as her fifteen-year-old cousin, Gertrude, swept over to the group with her eyes fondly planted on Henry, Maggie concluded that perhaps his appeal was simply surface level.

"Why, I remember you," Gertrude cooed.

Gardiner, Gertrude's twin brother, joined the circle.

"The Christmas Eve intruder!" Gardiner pointed his finger at Henry's face as though he was the only person who noticed the man's presence.

The party guests were mostly gathered in the Great Room, but Gardiner's exclamation easily reached them from the stair hall. Silence swiftly fell upon Chelsea Manor as those in the Great Room peered through the doorway at Henry Livingston.

"Yes, yes." Clemmie patted Gardiner on the shoulder. "Very well done, Gardiner. You are quicker than you look."

Maggie noticed Louis and his older brother, Francis, standing near their father and mother in the Great Room. Francis shifted uneasily at the sight of Henry; clearly remembering that they had been on opposing sides in Poppel after Francis had joined the Garrisons.

Pushing away the uncomfortable silence, Uncle CF cleared his throat while clinking his glass with a fingernail. "It's time for a toast!" Uncle CF raised his glass and the rest of the guests followed suit. "To my wonderful father, Clement Clarke Moore. Not only the greatest scholar the city has ever known, but also the greatest of all men."

Peeking into the Great Room, Maggie looked around for her grandfather. But then his voice boomed down from one of the staircases wrapping through the hall.

"Thank you, Clement Francis." Grandfather Clement nodded at his son in acknowledgement. He was positioned above the crowd where the staircase curved prominently.

Seeing the positive reception for Uncle CF's speech, Grandfather Clement's youngest son, William, pushed his way into the center of the crowd. Uncle William was a shorter man, so he projected his squeaky voice throughout the room

"As it is said in Psalm 4:7: *You have filled my heart with great joy... and lots of grain. And wine.*"

Maggie shook her head while Louis snickered next to her. Although she had grown up listening to Uncle William misquote biblical verses, it still never ceased to amaze her. When Maggie glanced back up, she tried to make eye contact with Henry and share a smile at her uncle's expense. But Henry was no longer standing nearby. After a second, she noticed that Jervis had momentarily left

Catharine's side, leaving Maggie's sister unattended next to a window in the Great Room.

"He sure doesn't waste an opportunity," Louis mumbled into Maggie's ear.

She couldn't find the words to reply. She had also noticed Henry's eagerness to take advantage of the artist's absence. So, after forcing a nod, Maggie dejectedly slipped away from the crowd before Louis could ask where she was going.

"Good to see you, Mr. Livingston," Catharine said distantly.

"That's certainly a much friendlier greeting than last time," Henry replied. "I didn't have to put my hands up for protection." He had hoped to garner a smile from Catharine, but his attempt proved unsuccessful.

"Yes, well, clearly that was under rather stressful circumstances."

He nodded. "Circumstances you accused me of starting."

Catharine opened and closed her mouth a couple of times as though the right words could not be found. "It…it was just so strange to see you again. I was not expecting to spot your face in the crowd. And you were acting most peculiar, staring purposefully toward the second level."

"I already told you. I was staring at you." Henry took an obvious step toward Catharine, closing the distance between them. "I was surprised to see you as well. Maggie had invited me to the Crystal Palace event, but she didn't say whether others in her family would be in attendance."

"Maggie can be almost as difficult as you to understand," Catharine replied. She turned her body away from the young man. "You two make quite the pair."

Feeling dejected, Henry gazed through the window. A moment later, he spotted a familiar brunette trudging across the back lawn of Chelsea Manor.

With her back pressed against the stone wall surrounding

Grandfather Clement's estate, Maggie closed her eyes and deeply exhaled. She didn't understand what was going on with her. A lot had changed in the past three years, but for some inexplicable reason, Henry's effect on her had not.

"We really should stop meeting like this."

Maggie recognized Henry's voice, but she hesitated to open her eyes. When she finally did, Henry was standing a few feet away with his hands in his trouser pockets. The sunlight flickered off his bronze hair.

"What do you mean?" The young man's sudden presence jumbled her thoughts.

Henry took a step closer. "Surely, you remember that this is where I first met you."

Maggie hadn't initially noticed, but he was right. She had crashed her sled at that very spot after flying over the wall that supported Chelsea Manor's hill. Although he had been a stranger at the time, Henry had rushed to her assistance.

"Things are different than they were back then." Wearing a slight frown, she stared at the uneven sidewalk beneath her feet.

Henry studied her dour expression. "Is something the matter?"

"I...I just..." Maggie started to say, but then trailed off as she looked over at Henry. However, this time it wasn't Henry that had caused her loss of words.

A boy walked down the road toward them. He was dressed in a green jacket, top hat, and white vest. Although a child, he moved with deliberate stealth. From his quick movements to his dodgy eyes, the boy seemed constantly aware of his surroundings.

"What is it?" Henry glanced back to see what had caught Maggie's attention.

"A Foundling," she whispered.

Throughout the past three years, Maggie occasionally spotted adolescents around the city who were, perhaps, Foundlings–workers from the hidden village of Poppel–but she never knew for sure. And even though she now felt certain that the approaching boy was indeed a Foundling, she could not begin to guess why he was there.

"Maggie Ogden!" The boy tipped the brim of his hat up.

"That's me." Maggie's voice failed to mask her unease.

Reaching into his jacket, the boy pulled out a beige envelope and handed it to her.

"Who sent this?" she asked.

Without offering an answer, the boy turned around and walked back down the street.

"Wait!" Henry called out. "What's happening in Poppel?"

Momentarily, the Foundling stopped moving, but just when Maggie thought he would respond, he took off running. They watched as he turned a corner near the seminary and disappeared completely.

"I guess he doesn't have time to talk," Henry remarked. He looked down at the letter in Maggie's hand. "Do you often receive mail from Poppel?

She shook her head. "I didn't even know they used letters. If they wanted to contact me, why not send a sugarplum?"

"Well, open it and find out."

Maggie tore a jagged slit in the envelope and pulled out the folded letter. With a furrowed her brow, she quickly read the note.

"What does it say?" Henry peered over Maggie's shoulder.

She glanced up from the paper. "Madame Welles requests that we return to Poppel." Maggie then dropped her eyes before adding quietly, "Both of us."

With evening's arrival, the last party guests filtered out of Chelsea Manor in a dreamy stupor. Maggie would spend the night at the mansion in order to visit with Henry before he headed back to Poughkeepsie in the morning. Or, at least, that's what she told her family.

"Do you need anything before I retire for the night?" asked Thomas, one of Grandfather Clement's servants.

Grandfather Clement had long ago gone to sleep. But Maggie and Henry continued to loiter in the Great Room.

"We're fine, Thomas. Thank you." Henry stood in front of the tall window. His fingers mindlessly flitted the curtains.

"At least allow me to light a fire for you." Thomas hobbled over to the fireplace, which held a pile of charred logs.

"No!" Maggie and Henry cried in unison.

Henry lunged toward the fireplace while she jumped up from the sofa.

Startled by their responses, Thomas took a step back, scratching his white beard that seemed to glow in the dim room.

"All right, Mr. Livingston and Miss Ogden. I will then just wish you both a goodnight." Thomas shuffled toward the far end of the Great Room. "I'll be right in the back if you need anything." Then he disappeared through the door that led directly to the kitchen.

Maggie and Henry both let out sighs before turning their attention to the fireplace. With hands placed behind his back, Henry peered down at the ornate andiron.

"Now that the Sister Wheel's no longer in the fireplace, how do we get down to the ash pit?"

Maggie approached the fireplace and crouched near the logs. "It wasn't the Sister Wheel that granted us entrance. There's a mechanism. It's all about hitting the right spot. Ward taught me…"

An uncomfortable silence hung in the air. Maggie hadn't spoken the Foundling's name for the past three years, even though she thought about him often. The Garrisons had killed Ward when the Foundlings rebelled. She owed Ward a great deal of gratitude for her and her family's survival.

Pulling the ends of her skirt aside while balancing on her knees, Maggie reached toward the back of the fireplace. She felt around the soot-covered ground. The trigger was located somewhere around there.

Henry watched Maggie struggle to find the switch that opened the ash pit.

"You really haven't been back to Poppel since that Christmas?" he whispered.

Maggie shook her head. "Not since that Christmas. We were told not to return, don't you remember?"

"You just always struck me as someone who disregarded rules."

Henry's comment seemed innocent on the surface, but it still rubbed her strangely.

Pausing her hand, Maggie twisted her head toward Henry and offered her most steely eyes.

"It was a compliment," he quickly added.

"You have a curious way with flattering," Maggie murmured before turning back to the fireplace. However, she lost her poise and slipped forward, landing awkwardly on top of the andiron and logs.

"Oompf," she moaned.

While attempting to steady her body, Maggie's hand pressed the brick that once held the Sister Wheel. The bottom of the fireplace shook slightly as an opening appeared; causing Maggie to almost fall straight down the dark abyss. But Henry latched onto her arm and tugged her back.

"Not so fast. You're not going down there without me."

"Oh, believe me. If I'm getting covered in ash and soot again–as are you."

Grinning, Henry gently took Maggie's hand. "Fair enough."

Henry stepped around the logs and andiron, and Maggie followed.

A moment later, they jumped into darkness together.

Chapter Four

Lockenhaus

Countess Bathory's head servant, Darvulia, flew through the halls of Lockenhaus castle. With graying hair and a heavier frame, she appeared older than the other servants. But she still moved quickly. So when Darvulia burst into the maid quarters, women gasped at her sudden presence.

"Darvulia? What are you doing here?" Lily's enthusiasm was evident in her tone. "Is the Countess leaving Lockenhaus again?"

The older woman nodded. "I'm accompanying her back to Cachtice this afternoon."

Lily tried to mask her excitement at the mention of Elizabeth Bathory's other coveted castle, located in the northern part of the Kingdom of Hungary. The Countess resided there half of the time. Lily had been a handmaiden for nearly a year, but she had yet to leave Lockenhaus. Although other handmaidens were taken to Cachtice, she was never picked to join the Countess on those trips.

It wasn't that Lily hadn't enjoyed her time at Lockenhaus. Since leaving Poppel, Lockenhaus was the only place she had felt somewhat content. She became well acquainted with the other handmaidens and had been treated kindly by Countess Bathory and her staff.

And then there was Laszlo.

Countess Bathory's son still watched her with the same intensity as he had at Katterburg. But while he gazed her direction with such unwavering adoration, Lily's body continued to uncomfortably age with each passing day. As someone who had spent the first thousand years of life lingering on the age of fourteen, the natural progression to eighteen had left her upset and bewildered, which is why she longed to be summoned to Cachtice.

Over the past year, Lily suspected there was more to Countess Bathory's beauty than could be seen. Each time the Countess returned to Lockenhaus, Lily noticed that she not only looked to be aging gracefully, but that she wasn't aging at all. However, her time at Lockenhaus would eventually wear on the Countess, and when the glow of her skin dimmed and her temperament weakened, she would run off to Cachtice for a month or two. The pattern was so noticeable that Lily believed Cachtice held the secret to the Countess's youth. And that was something Lily desperately sought.

"Is it just you and the Countess going to Cachtice?" Lily asked Darvulia.

"Well, no. That's why I am here," Darvulia explained. She clasped her hands together. "Countess Bathory would like another handmaiden to accompany us."

Lily's back straightened as her hopes grew. But her wishful thoughts were soon dashed.

"Ilona." Darvulia nodded toward the dark-haired girl standing next to Lily. "Please pack what you can. We shall be leaving within the hour."

Lily's stomach throbbed with a sudden ache. Once again, she would be left at Lockenhaus, watching her youth slip away. It particularly hurt that the Countess had chosen Ilona of all the handmaidens. Lily was rarely jealous of other girls, but something about Ilona deeply cut at her spirit. Unlike the other handmaidens at Lockenhaus, Ilona came from a family of high society. It was evident in her manners, dress, and a silver bracelet with a dark red garnet always worn around her petite wrist, usually hidden by her uniform.

While Ilona excitedly chattered with the other handmaidens, Darvulia glided back out the door. Without hesitation, Lily stormed down the tower steps after her.

"Darvulia," Lily called.

"Yes, Lily," Darvulia responded without stopping. Lily actually thought she noticed Darvulia's pace quicken.

"I'm curious why I'm never asked to travel with the Countess to Cachtice," Lily said sharply. She undoubtedly would be admonished later for her tone. However, Darvulia remained silent as they reached the bottom of the steps, so she continued, "Ilona has not been at Lockenhaus as long as I have, and she's also a bit younger."

"Precisely," Darvulia remarked listlessly. "You have already established yourself to be useful here at Lockenhaus. The positions at Cachtice require a younger, more malleable girl like Ilona."

Lily stopped walking as though a wall had appeared in front of her. Noticing her companion's abrupt change, Darvulia twisted around to see Lily staring dejectedly at the ground, looking like she had been struck in the face.

"Do not be disappointed, Lily," Darvulia said. "Cachtice is no more splendid than Lockenhaus. In fact, it is much quieter and less enthralling, which is why the Countess escapes to there every so often."

Lily didn't reply. She curtsied toward Darvulia and then disappeared down another hall.

Darvulia almost felt sorry for the girl, but unless something drastically changed in the Countess's thinking, Lily would never be invited to Cachtice.

But Lily did not know how fortunate it was that she remained at Lockenhaus.

"Did you notify Ilona of our departure?" Countess Bathory asked when Darvulia walked into the main chamber of her tower. The Countess sat at her vanity, brushing her dark hair.

Darvulia nodded. "She will be packed and ready to leave shortly."

Countess Bathory smiled to herself. "Very good. I have been admiring her for a while. She has such vitality. Her blood's no doubt rich and young. It's apparent in her silky skin."

"Lily was once again unhappy to hear that she had not been chosen to accompany you to Cachtice."

Countess Bathory twisted Darvulia's direction. "And what did you tell her?" The Countess's brush remained suspended in one hand like a sword poised to strike.

"I simply explained that she was needed here. And that she was not missing anything by not visiting Cachtice."

Countess Bathory's expression relaxed. With a sigh, she replied, "It is most unfortunate. How I would love for Lily to come to Cachtice. She has some of the most attractive features I have ever seen in a woman." The Countess resumed brushing her hair with thoughtful yet firm strokes. "There's something quite extraordinary about her. She is young and beautiful, yet she carries herself like a woman older than her years. And I would have her at Cachtice as soon as possible, if my own son hadn't fallen victim to her charms."

"Laszlo's certainly enraptured with that handmaiden."

"With Katalin and Anna both married off and Andras out on the battlefields, I do feel extra mindful of Laszlo's desires. If it's Lily he wants…" Countess Bathory paused and shook her head. "No, Lily will never come to Cachtice."

"What does Thorko have to say about all of this?" Darvulia asked.

Countess Bathory's eyes widened. "Thorko may be my most trusted adviser, but when it concerns the matter of Laszlo's heart, I am afraid it's something I do not discuss with him. Thorko's one of the most brilliant minds that has ever existed, with powers beyond what I can comprehend, but this is something he would not understand."

Armed with a lantern and book, Laszlo drifted through the lower chambers of Lockenhaus. He did not want to be seen going down to the dungeon, which is why he waited until the Countess's carriage disappeared into the horizon. However, as he entered one of the most secluded chambers in the castle, he was surprised to see it already had an occupant.

46

An old man, with dense white hair that hung past his shoulders, emerged from the shadows.

"Thorko," Laszlo greeted dully.

"Why, Laszlo," Thorko said, and then eyeing the item in the visitor's hands, he added, "Have you come to return the book you stole?"

Laszlo nodded. "I had hoped to steal another."

Thorko gestured to the stack of books teetering on a table against the wall. "Help yourself."

However, Laszlo didn't move. "I thought you were going with my mother to Cachtice."

Thorko shook his head. "I am not joining her this time. Too much to do here." He stared at Laszlo. "Why are you not going to Cachtice?"

Laszlo let out a hollow laugh. "You forget, Thorko. I spent most of my adolescence at Cachtice, while Katalin, Anna, and Andras grew up at the Nadasdy Castle in Sarvar. So, I've had enough of that place for this lifetime." He walked to the table and placed his book next to the stack.

"Ah, yes," Thorko mumbled. "I do sometimes forget how you were kept away for many years."

Laszlo shrugged. "It was the territory that came with being an illegitimate son."

A slanted grin crossed Thorko's withered face. "When you consider the punishment Ferenc Nadasdy unleashed on the peasant man who was your father, you undoubtedly see that staying at Cachtice was an agreeable alternative."

"I have always been grateful for the generosity Ferenc showed me, given the circumstances," Laszlo replied. "But if I were to never again lay a foot inside Cachtice, I would be quite content."

Thorko studied Laszlo with a knowing expression. "What was it about Cachtice that you found so unpleasant?"

Laszlo matched Thorko's questioning stare with his own. But soon he felt Thorko could read his thoughts, and he uneasily glanced down at the table. Picking up the book on top of the stack, Laszlo cleared his throat. "I will take this one."

As Laszlo turned to walk out of the chamber, Thorko called to him. "You should consider leaving Lockenhaus."

Laszlo froze in the doorway. "Why would you make such a suggestion?"

"The handmaiden, Lily," Thorko replied simply. "Your feelings for her have a strong hold on you. And such attachments tend to cause destruction over time."

Laszlo was silent, staring intensely at the book in his hand.

"Love is an illusion, Laszlo, and a dangerous illusion at that–particularly the unrequited kind. Am I wrong in that assessment?"

Laszlo hated that Thorko was aware of Lily's indifference toward him. But he would not give Thorko the satisfaction.

"I have no intention of leaving Lockenhaus," Laszlo whispered. Then to challenge Thorko, he raised his head and locked eyes with the old man. "Ever."

With the corners of his mouth curving up, Thorko appeared amused at Laszlo's defiant response. "I am only looking out for your best interests…"

But Laszlo was already storming out of the chamber. As with most encounters with Thorko, Laszlo was left unnerved by the interaction. The old man always had a way of pinching the tissue just beneath the skin. He seemed to know exactly where the most sensitive area was located and set his sights on exposing it. This time, however, Laszlo believed Thorko was not only quite accurate, but also sincere in his intentions.

Since Lily arrived at Lockenhaus a year ago, Laszlo had sulked around the estate, yearning from a distance. His melancholy demeanor was noticed by nearly everyone at Lockenhaus–including Lily. For the past year, Laszlo imagined the somber cloud shrouding him announced his presence before he even entered a room. It was like a dense fog, creeping across the grass in the morning.

While Laszlo had these thoughts, the rumbling of distant thunder shook the walls. He climbed the spiral stairwell to have a better look.

As predicted, when he glanced out the thin window halfway up the tower, he saw dark clouds pushing away dusk's pale sky.

Maybe the weather was trying to tell him something. Maybe it was a sign that it was indeed time to leave Lockenhaus. But he didn't know where to go. He would rather die than set foot in Cachtice again. The Nadasdy family did have the castle in Sarvar. But he never felt welcome there. Laszlo considered returning to Katterburg since Matthias had extended the invitation. The Archduke recently had replaced his brother, Rudolf, in controlling much of Austria and Hungary. So Matthias wouldn't often be at Katterburg now.

Suddenly, a horse could be heard galloping nearby. Laszlo looked down and saw a straw-haired girl riding low on one of the castle's stallions. He instantly recognized the handmaiden.

"Lily," Laszlo whispered. "Where are you going?"

Thunder rumbled again. He couldn't think of why Lily would be riding with a storm on its way. But he soon realized Lily wasn't taking a leisurely ride–she was leaving Lockenhaus.

Lily didn't hear the storm approaching in the distance. She was only focused on her destination–Cachtice Castle. She couldn't bear another day of watching her once permanent youth fade from her face. If Countess Bathory had somehow found a way to avoid aging, Lily was determined to do the same.

Unfortunately, Lily's horse did sense the impending storm. Before Lockenhaus was even out of sight, the gray stallion veered off the dirt path into the thick brush. The startled animal frantically weaved between shrubs and trees while Lily helplessly held onto to the reins until her hands turned numb.

Soon the woods grew dark around her, and when she believed her situation couldn't get more desperate, a strong shower washed over the area, blinding both Lily and the stallion. But before the horse had the chance to throw Lily to the ground, another set of hooves could be heard coming up fast. At first Lily thought it was just the sound of the storm, but soon another horse was running parallel to hers.

The rider had a rain-soaked cloak covering his head, so she couldn't see his face. A pale hand reached out toward Lily's reins and gripped them tightly. The horse jerked wildly to a halt, nearly flinging Lily off. But she locked her legs and managed to remain on top of the animal. When she looked over to the mysterious rider and saw familiar blond hair peeking out of the hood, Lily instantly knew the identity of the stranger.

Laszlo.

Tumbling down from her horse, Lily landed on her feet and took off running. She didn't know where she was going; she just knew she couldn't go back to Lockenhaus. And Laszlo would make sure she returned. She didn't know if he had followed her on his own or if he had been sent out after her. But knowing Laszlo, he probably had been watching her from the moment she left.

Swatting branches out of her face, Lily stumbled through the woods, trying to get away from the Countess's son. She wouldn't let him take her back to Lockenhaus. No matter what happened, she had to find a way to Cachtice Castle. Unfortunately, she didn't get far before a pair of hands grabbed her by the shoulders.

"Lily," Laszlo's voice echoed through the rain. It sounded miles away. "Stop, Lily!"

She somehow managed to slip out of his grasp, but she didn't make it far before Laszlo grabbed her once again. As the rain continued to pound down, Lily and Laszlo both struggled to stay upright. But before she could get away again, he locked his hands around her wrists.

"Let go!" Lily yelled hoarsely through the storm. "Unhand me!"

"Where are you going?" Laszlo said, but his words were mostly drowned out by thunder.

"I'm not going back!" Lily shouted. "I'm not going back!"

Lily nearly slipped out of his grasp, but a moment later she unexpectedly collapsed into his arms, crying. Even amid the storm, her sobs sounded through the woods.

"Whatever it is, I will help you," Laszlo said. He touched Lily's matted hair with soothing strokes.

"I can't go back. I can't get older."

Laszlo looked down at Lily's face. His eyes were full of concern and confusion. Her troubles were greater than he could have guessed. But whatever they were, Lily knew that Laszlo was determined to fix them.

The fire crackled next to Lily's body, its erratic flames nearly licking her exposed arms. A blanket was draped over her back as she sat next to the fireplace with arms wrapped around her legs. She had changed out of the wet clothes and now wore a floor-length nightgown. Although the current outfit was improper to wear with company, and more revealing than she wished to have on around the infatuated young man, Lily no longer cared. Laszlo's presence barely registered to her, even when he spoke.

"Will you talk to me now?" Laszlo asked with impatience coating his voice.

Lily had yet to say a word since Laszlo had brought her back to Lockenhaus.

"You mentioned in the woods that you didn't want to come back. You said that you didn't want to get older. What did you mean?"

Lily once again ignored Laszlo, choosing instead to stare into the fire.

"I know something's different about you," he continued, lowering his voice. "I noticed it when I first saw you at Katterburg. Something about your past."

But Lily remained silent.

Laszlo sighed, and then in a voice just above a whisper, he said. "Perhaps if I trust you with my story, you will trust me with yours?"

Lily looked back at Laszlo. Although she didn't say anything, she offered a slight nod, indicating a desire to hear what he had to say.

"I am older than I appear," Laszlo said. "Much older."

"How?" Lily asked. Her voice was hoarse.

"How much older?"

"No." She looked at Laszlo with intensity. "How have you achieved your youth?"

He walked to the other side of the chamber with his back toward Lily. She worried he was going to walk out of the room, choosing to leave rather than answer the question. But then she heard his voice.

"The Bathory family has a long history of mysterious youth and mystical powers. When Countess Bathory was a teenager, she was involved with a peasant boy. As a result, she gave birth to me. I not only retained the power of the Bathory blood but also my mother's own youth." Laszlo turned to face Lily as she tried to process what he was saying.

"So even though I have been alive for over thirty years, I have not aged past seventeen. I am not entirely sure why, but ever since my seventeenth year, I have physically stayed the same age," Laszlo continued. "This all had to be kept secret, of course. No one living other than my mother and Thorko know about this. But I believe I can trust you with this information. I don't know why, but I feel that you may understand."

Laszlo stared steadily into Lily's eyes, as though daring her to reveal whatever it was she kept hidden. But rather unexpectedly, Lily began to cry. "Why would you tell me this? How could you be so cruel?"

"Cruel?" Laszlo repeated. His eyes widened with confusion.

"It's not fair," Lily stammered through her tears. "Why would you be born with such a power? My youth was gifted to me and then senselessly taken away."

"What was taken away?" Laszlo asked. He still looked stung by her calling him cruel.

"The three wheels!" Lily sobbed.

She then divulged the entire story of Nicolas Poppelius, her sisters, Grace and Sarah, and their centuries of unchanging youth. She told about how Nicolas had saved the girls from being married off to horrible men and how they had all settled in Belgium. But Nicolas vanished nearly forty years ago. Then Grace married a young man, forfeiting not only her gift of youth, but Sarah and Lily's as well.

"My heart can't handle growing older. But I've already aged since leaving Poppel. And I will continue to age until I die." Lily's voice was laced with fear. Hugging her legs to her chest, she buried her face in her knees and continued to cry.

Laszlo kneeled next to her. Hesitantly, he placed a hand upon her shoulder. She shuddered at the touch.

"Don't cry," he whispered. He moved his hand to her cheek and caressed it gently. "I will see to it that you will not die. Not now, nor anytime in the future. I will help you maintain your youth."

Lily looked up. Uncertainty glazed her eyes. "How?"

"There are other ways," Laszlo replied. "Other means to not age. One doesn't need to be born with such a gift. It's something that can be gained."

Lily's eyes widened as her spirits visibly lifted. Motivated by her change in temperament and the attention she was giving him, Laszlo continued confidently.

"There are things found in nature that can be used to attain immortality. As long as you know how to use them," Laszlo said. "Thorko has vast books on the matter. With my help, I promise I can make you young like me. Forever."

For the first time that Laszlo could recall, Lily smiled at him. It was such a genuine and excited smile that he might very well fall into it, becoming eternally lost. Then something even more miraculous happened. Lily leaned over and pressed her lips against Laszlo's. Surprisingly, it was neither a gentle nor hesitant kiss like he would have expected. It was full of energy and hunger–and possibly a bit of gratitude.

At that moment, Laszlo would have promised her anything. But as they broke apart, and he could see the glow in her face, he considered that perhaps he had already promised her more than he could give.

Chapter Five

The Shattered Vial

As November approached, the colors of late autumn faded. The earth around Lockenhaus withered away, and the season's death knell sounded with the arrival of the first snow, layering the grounds in a white film.

Meanwhile, Laszlo was the happiest he had ever been. He spent entire days alone with Lily, roaming the Lockenhaus estate. Traveling through the woods and streams, they searched for ingredients that had not died off with the changing seasons, and also couldn't be found within Thorko's extensive, foreign supplies. During the night, they would huddle near the fire, reading over books Laszlo had snatched from Thorko's chamber.

It truly was the most satisfying time of Laszlo's life, and with the discovery of each promising antidote, Lily also seemed hopeful. Often, she rewarded Laszlo with much-desired affection, which prompted him to work harder at fulfilling the promise he had made.

"What is this?" Lily asked one morning when Laszlo presented her with a small, glass vial.

Laszlo had been waiting outside, bundled in a coat. His cheeks were pink from the cool air. Bouncing on his heels, he could barely contain his excitement when Lily finally arrived at the largest tree behind Lockenhaus.

"I worked on it for weeks," Laszlo said with a proud smile. "I wanted to surprise you. It took a while to gather all the items needed to properly prepare it."

Lily looked at the murky substance in the vial. "What's in it?"

Laszlo's mouth slanted coyly. "It's a special plant from the East. It must be fermented for a month and then placed outside on a night when there is no moon. It's said to dramatically slow the body's aging."

She looked at Laszlo with growing eyes. A moment later, she flung herself into his arms. After kissing the top of her head, he embraced her tightly.

"Thank you." Lily's words were muffled against his chest.

Laszlo kissed her head again. "Of course," he whispered. "I'd do anything for you."

Lily pulled away slightly so she could stare up at Laszlo.

"Is that so?" She continued to study his face as though searching for cracks in his sincerity.

"Yes," Laszlo said. "Of course."

With a small smile, Lily took Laszlo's hand within hers and then unexpectedly brought it up to her face. She took the tips of his fingers and brushed them against her temple, near the edge of her eye. At first Laszlo wasn't sure why she wanted him to touch there, but then he felt the tiny mark of time, a crease starting from the eye and extending faintly toward the temple.

"Is there something you can do?" Lily asked.

Although she didn't say anything more, Laszlo knew what she wanted. Lily now carried an imperfection across her once immaculate face. It was a sign of what time had already done, and she needed Laszlo to find a way to reverse the damage.

Silently, Laszlo bent down and laid a gentle kiss upon the wrinkle. It was his way of letting Lily know that if there were an antidote, he would find it for her.

The chamber door was suspiciously open.

Thorko had just arrived to Lockenhaus after traveling for the past three days from Cachtice Castle. The Countess always requested his presence at Cachtice as the winter season approached. There was much to do before the ground froze and the weather made it difficult to secure fresh help for the castle. Thorko always happily obliged assisting in the castle's less desirable tasks. In fact, he was so diligent in his work that he arrived back at Lockenhaus earlier than scheduled. Although he was exhausted from his travels, he immediately headed down to the castle's lowest chamber to drop off supplies. And that's when he noticed the opened door.

Thorko heard rustling coming from within the chamber. Instinctually, he reached for the dagger held in his belt's sheath. After slowly pulling the blade out, he slipped through the doorway.

A light floated on the other end of the chamber. It took Thorko only a moment to recognize the blond hair belonging to Laszlo. The young man had his back turned toward Thorko as he examined various books piled on the table. Although Thorko was accustomed to Laszlo riffling through his belongings, something about this particular encounter seemed unusual.

Thorko hid in the shadowy corner where he continued to observe the late-night thief. Laszlo had stepped over to a cabinet where he rummaged through the bottles and bowls. He pocketed a few items and then moved toward the door. Thorko pondered whether to make his presence known, but he was now curious about Laszlo's intentions. So when the young man disappeared out of the chamber, Thorko carefully followed.

Laszlo could hear crying before he reached Lily's chamber. Upon entering, he saw her sitting at the end of her bed, curled up with her hands cupping her bare feet.

"What is it?" Laszlo's voice was heavy with concern.

Lily looked up. Her cheeks were streaked in wet trails left by tears. A moment later, Laszlo was at her side, holding her tightly in his arms.

"Why are you crying?"

Lily sniffled as she sat up, while Laszlo kept his arms draped around her. He noticed that one of her hands was clenched. Slowly, she opened her fist. For a moment, Laszlo thought it was empty, but then he saw a strand of hair lying across her palm. Gently, he reached down and picked it up with a finger and thumb.

Unexpectedly, Lily started to cry again. "It's–it's gray!"

Laszlo held the strand up toward the glow coming from the fireplace.

"Nonsense," Laszlo said with a small smile. "It's light brown, nearly blond, just like all your other strands of hair."

"Look again. It's gray."

Laszlo stared at the bit of hair. Perhaps it was more faded in color, but it certainly didn't look gray to him.

"Lily," Laszlo said. "It doesn't appear to be gray."

But Lily wasn't listening.

"I'm aging! It's been months and nothing's helping."

"Don't forget about the potion I gave you earlier today. I worked hard on that. It will surely halt aging. Also, I discovered new recipes that are meant to maintain youthful skin."

Reaching over, Laszlo picked up a book he had dropped on the bed. He began flipping through the pages, but instead of seeming pleased, Lily sighed. "It never was this hard in Poppel. The wheels had provided immortality for centuries without us needing to do a thing. Can you understand how hard it is to have been the age of fourteen for hundreds of years just to have it taken away?"

"But you're still young," Laszlo pointed out. "A couple of years will not undo the centuries of youth you experienced. If anything, your blood's probably stronger and able to fight the effects of time on its own. And with the addition of the special antidotes I've created, you will not only maintain your youth, but also obtain immortality once again."

"You really think so?"

Laszlo smiled. "Of course." He spied the glass vial lying carelessly next to Lily on the bed. He picked it up and pulled off its lid.

"Drink a little of this." He handed the vial over to Lily. "It will help."

Lily took a sip of the concoction. She grimaced at its bitter taste.

"How was it?" Laszlo asked.

Licking her lips, Lily stared down at the half empty vial. "I think it's already starting to work." She laid a hand upon her chest. "Yes, it definitely feels like something's happening."

Laszlo rubbed Lily's shoulder. "I told you it would work. As long as you're here at Lockenhaus with me, I will help you to become as immortal as you were before."

But Laszlo knew there was something, or rather someone, who could get in the way of these plans.

Thorko.

If there was anything Thorko sought, it was beautiful, young girls for Countess Bathory. Discovering a girl that had been young for centuries was like a finding a rare gemstone. And if Thorko found out about Lily's secret past, he would do whatever it took in order to possess an extraordinary jewel such as her.

The morning sun had barely broken away from the horizon when one of Lockenhaus's handmaidens stormed into Lily's chamber.

"Thorko would like to see you," announced the girl sharply.

Lily had neglected her handmaiden duties since becoming close with Laszlo. With Countess Bathory's son as her companion, no one thought to confront her on the matter. However, Lily not only heard the resentment in the handmaiden's voice, but also a hint of optimism, as though the handmaiden believed Thorko finally intended to scold Lily.

When Lily arrived in Lockenhaus's lower chamber, however, Thorko did not appear angry. Instead he looked at Lily with grave concern.

"I am worried about you, Lily."

She had not expected Thorko to greet her in such a manner.

"As you know, I've been at Cachtice for the past month. Yet in the short time I've been away, I see that something terrible has happened here at Lockenhaus."

"What do you mean, Thorko?"

"You, Lily. You have changed. Before I left, you were a beautiful, youthful girl. But it seems during my absence you have aged considerably."

Lily stifled a cry. There was nothing worse she could imagine hearing.

"Is there something you want to tell me?" Thorko's voice was solemn, but his eyes danced with excitement as Lily told the entire history about Nicolas Poppelius, the wheels, and her immortality.

"I hoped that by coming to Lockenhaus, I might find a way to prevent aging. Laszlo has even been helping. He's created special antidotes to fight the effects of time."

"What has Laszlo given you?"

Lily pulled out the glass vial from the pocket of her skirt. She had not let it out of her sight since it had been given to her. She reluctantly handed it to Thorko who immediately stuck the tip of his finger in the vial. Bringing the finger up to his mouth, he dabbed the liquid against his tongue.

"Elderflower and gentian root," Thorko stated. "Neither will assist with much besides the easing of stomach ailments."

Lily's eyes grew wide with horror. "You must be mistaken. Why else would Laszlo say that the potion would help me?"

Thorko suppressed a smile as though it was the question he had hoped to receive.

"Laszlo has been obsessed with you since you arrived here, and he will do anything to keep you at Lockenhaus. He knows that at Cachtice…" Thorko trailed off. "I've said too much."

"What? What about Cachtice?" Lily asked firmly.

"I shouldn't say anything more. I'm sure Laszlo's intentions are nothing but honorable. It is awful of me to suggest anything less from Countess Bathory's son."

"What about Cachtice?" Lily repeated. The volume of her voice grew louder with frustration.

"I suppose you do have a right to know." Thorko forced a long sigh. "Particularly, with your current circumstances."

Anxiously, Lily waited for Thorko to continue.

"You see, there's a reason Countess Bathory often disappears to Cachtice. She, too, seeks longevity of life. And she has found success at Cachtice, with my assistance, of course."

"What do you mean? What have you done for the Countess?"

"I think it would be best if you came to Cachtice and experienced it for yourself. I can help you the same way that I have helped Countess Bathory."

Lily didn't say anything, but it seemed that Thorko could see her contemplating the offer. A second later, he added, "Of course, Laszlo wouldn't allow you to go."

Lily stiffened. "He doesn't make decisions for me."

"Then I think it would be in your best interest to head to Cachtice as soon as possible. I can make the arrangements."

Although Lily found it difficult to reply with words, she finally nodded in agreement.

Laszlo's face lit up when he spotted Lily gliding across the courtyard. He was so excited to see her that he didn't notice her darkened features as she aggressively approached.

"How could you?" She shoved Laszlo hard against the chest.

Caught by surprise, Laszlo stumbled backward, tripping over his feet and then falling to the cold ground. Looking up from his back, he finally recognized the anger on her face.

"You lied to me!" she screamed. "You don't know how to help me. You lied!"

Laszlo struggled to get up on his feet. "What happened?"

She opened her hand to show him the glass vial before throwing it at his face. He managed to catch the vial between his fingers.

"Elderflower and gentian root. How's that supposed to help me?"

Laszlo was surprised she had discovered the antidote's ingredients.

"I was following a recipe found in one of Thorko's books. I promise."

"Was it a recipe for indigestion?"

"No! The recipe was for aging. Why are you upset? Did someone say something to you?"

Lily sighed. "Do you actually know how to help me?" But she didn't get an answer.

"Laszlo?"

"I am trying," he said softly. "I am trying to figure out how to help you."

The response seemed to be what Lily had suspected. Without another word, she turned around and walked off, leaving Laszlo standing dejectedly with the vial in his hand.

Feeling a shadow of helplessness wash over him, he smashed the vial against the nearest tree, spraying the lawn with shards of broken glass. But Laszlo knew that even more than the vial had been shattered.

Over the next two days, Laszlo left Lily alone. He did not seek her out and she did not seem to have any interest in seeing him. Finally, on the evening of the second day, he headed to her chamber. After knocking on the door and getting no response, Laszlo entered.

However, Lily was not in the chamber. Instead Laszlo saw a handmaiden standing on the other end of the room, pulling sheets off the bed. She let out a muffled gasp at the sight of Laszlo.

"Sorry for startling you," Laszlo apologized. "I was looking for Lily. Do you know where I could find her?"

A strange expression appeared across the handmaiden's face. "Sir Laszlo, Lily left for Cachtice yesterday."

"What?" Laszlo cried. His outburst caused the handmaiden to jump again. "What do you mean she went to Cachtice?"

"That's all I know, sir. I saw Thorko packing a carriage for her."

Laszlo swept out of the room. By the time he reached Thorko's chamber, sweat was pouring down his face, and he was uncontrollably shaking.

"Thorko!"

"Why, hello, Laszlo," Thorko greeted. Seeming indifferent to Laszlo's presence, his back was facing the young man as he continued to grind powder with a mortar and pestle.

"Where's Lily? What have you done with her?"

"I have done nothing. She goes where she wants."

"To Cachtice?"

Finally, Thorko turned around. "Laszlo, you must calm down. There are things you need to consider."

"Is that where she went? What did you tell her?"

"We are not immortal, Laszlo. Neither you, your mother, nor I will live forever."

"Did Lily go to Cachtice?"

"I have spent years looking for a way to avoid death, and more importantly, to bring back those who have already died."

"Did she go to Cachtice?" Laszlo's loud cry shook the bottles on the table.

Thorko was silent for a moment. "Yes, Laszlo."

"Why?" he screamed.

"Because you can't help her. You can't offer her the immortality that you promised. And now she knows that."

"What are you offering her?" Laszlo's voice trembled. "Death?"

Thorko was silent.

"She will not become another of my mother's victims. I won't allow it."

"But, Laszlo, don't you see? If Countess Bathory had wanted Lily simply as another conquest, she would have been sent to Cachtice long ago. But Lily is much more important than that."

"How so?"

"Ferenc Nadasdy."

It was not the response Laszlo had expected. "What about Ferenc? Ferenc Nadasdy is dead."

"Quite right, Laszlo. But what if that were to be changed?" Thorko asked. "At the request of the Countess, I have spent years looking into how Ferenc could be brought back. However, I long ago concluded that the amount of life needed would be too great, making it nearly impossible to accomplish."

"What does this have to do with Lily?"

"She's the key that has been missing, Laszlo. Don't you see? She's not only vital to our continued immortality, but also rebirth."

For a moment, the chamber was drenched in silence. "And at what cost?" Laszlo's voice cracked with emotion.

"I believe you know the cost."

"Tell me!"

Thorko paused, knowing how his answer would be taken. "Her blood."

Without uttering another word, Laszlo was gone.

Chapter Six

Disappearances in Poppel

When Maggie and Henry first traveled on the mechanical sleighs below New York City, they entered Poppel in secrecy. That was three years ago. At the time, Garrisons patrolled the Sleigh Pit where the underground tunnels both originated and terminated, but now those black-coated officials were no more. Instead a familiar face greeted them as the sleigh pulled into the Sleigh Pit.

"Madame Welles!" Maggie exclaimed.

The tall, broad-shouldered old woman smiled faintly at the sight of Maggie and Henry. Dark gray hair stood upright on her head like feathers.

"The Van Cortlandt descendants have returned once again." The old woman's voice was strong and guarded, never revealing anything more than she allowed.

"But this time by invitation," Henry said with a grin. He jumped from the sleigh and then assisted Maggie down. "Don't tell me Poppel needs to be saved again."

Madame Welles hardened at Henry's comment. She turned and walked toward the arched doorway. "Please come with me to the Krog. I assume you remember the way."

Maggie and Henry exchanged uncertain looks. Apparently, something was indeed wrong.

They followed Madame Welles out of the Sleight Pit and up a flight of stone steps.

"Does this have to do with the construction of Central Park?" Maggie asked. Madame Welles didn't reply, so she continued. "Because I'm determined to see to it that construction will not commence. I have even befriended a relative of one of the park's designers..."

Maggie trailed off as the sign for Myra Lane appeared. A cobblestone road weaved between colorful shops, looking exactly like it did the last time. And while Maggie walked along the familiar road of Myra Lane, it seemed like nothing in Poppel had changed, including its emptiness upon their arrival.

"We really don't attract the crowds," Henry commented.

"Madame Welles, where are all the Foundlings?" Maggie asked.

"It's evening," Madame Welles replied. "The Foundlings are out in the city."

Something about her tone felt distant. Between her aloof demeanor and the absence of Foundlings, Maggie was beginning to wonder why they'd even been asked to return.

Madame Welles led Maggie and Henry through the large archway at the end of Myra Lane and then up a circular flight of steps. When they walked into the banquet hall at the top of the stairs, memories flooded Maggie's mind. From how she and Henry had hidden when chased by the Garrison, Augustus McNutt, to seeing Ward's dead body before the final battle. Eventually, Maggie had escaped Poppel by following the Foundling, Violet, who had been carrying the Horologe. And as her thoughts continued to wander, Maggie wondered how Violet and her other Foundling friends were doing now.

Maggie and Henry followed Madame Welles up to the banquet hall's mezzanine and then another short flight of stairs.

"Why are we going to the Krog?" Maggie asked.

She never received a response. Upon entering the Krog, she saw the space was no longer used as a tavern. Behind the counter, the shelves that once held rows of bottles were now crammed with books. The tables for card games were also gone and replaced with a single desk.

And sitting behind the desk was a familiar redheaded young man.

"McNutt," Maggie said without thought.

She didn't realize she had spoken out loud until Augustus McNutt glanced up from the paper he had been scribbling across.

"Please, Maggie, call me Augustus."

The former Garrison appeared out of place wearing a brown suit instead of the menacing black uniform. His red hair, previously cut short, had grown down to his ears, revealing its naturally wavy shape. But other than those particular changes, Augustus looked exactly the same. Maggie recalled Poppel's remarkable relationship with time, and in the last three years, Augustus would have aged just one year—making him eighteen.

"You remember Augustus McNutt, I see." Madame Welles gestured for Maggie and Henry to approach the desk.

"Quite difficult to forget," Henry said dryly. He no doubt remembered how Augustus had punched him squarely on the jaw during their first encounter.

Gazing rather uncomfortably at his guests, Augustus appeared like he hadn't forgotten the incident either. His fingers fidgeted and his eyes dropped down to study the various items on the desk.

Seeing that Augustus was in no hurry to talk, Madame Welles continued, "Augustus has been instrumental in running Poppel since the Garrisons were conquered. He has been our correspondent with the officials on the outside."

"Haven't they noticed that Castriot and the other Garrisons are gone?" Maggie asked.

Madame Welles looked over at Augustus. "No, I believe they know we somehow defeated the Garrisons. But since they are unsure how we could possibly overthrow dozens of armed men, they suspect we must have our own weapons. So they haven't sent anyone else down here."

"I'm glad to hear there hasn't been trouble," Henry remarked.

Silently, Madame Welles and Augustus exchanged glances.

"Has there been trouble?" Maggie added.

There was a long moment of silence before Augustus stated,

"Foundlings are disappearing."

"Disappearing?" Maggie blurted. "Where are they going?"

Madame Welles sighed. "It began earlier this year when a couple of Foundlings vanished. We assumed they had run away. It struck me somewhat as strange. In all the years of Poppel, we never had any Foundlings leave willingly, but that was before the Garrisons took over. And now even with the Garrisons gone, we live in different times."

"It didn't end with those Foundlings," Augustus added. "For the past few months, at least one Foundling has been disappearing every week or so. These are Foundlings we know would never run away. We believe they are being abducted."

"The Garrisons!" Henry exclaimed. "The Garrisons are obviously behind this."

Augustus shook his head. "I do not believe the city or the Garrisons have anything to do with this."

"Of course, you don't," Henry snapped. "Even after everything, you still don't believe the Garrisons were on the wrong side. Or more specifically, that *you* were on the wrong side."

Augustus glowered. "I do not believe the Garrisons would have any use for Foundlings. Also, clandestinely taking Foundlings one by one isn't their tendency. They are more likely to strike all at once."

"Then who do you think is abducting the Foundlings?" Maggie asked before Henry could respond again.

"That's why we have asked you here," said Madame Welles. "We have no leads. And we do not feel it's wise to have the Foundlings looking into this."

"But why us?" Maggie asked.

"You were once a great help to Poppel. I can think of no one else who could come to its assistance again."

"And you believe these abductions might be related to what happened last time." Henry's remark was more of a statement than a question. Before Augustus could insist again that it had nothing to do with the Garrisons, Henry added, "I'm referring, of course, to the Sister Wheels."

"We are leaving no possibilities out," Augustus stated.

Then Maggie realized that the missing Foundlings could be the same people she became acquainted with years ago.

"What Foundlings were taken? How are Wendell and Lloyd? And Harriet and Nellie?" Maggie inhaled sharply. "And Violet? Is Violet okay?"

"None of them were taken," Augustus said.

Although she felt relieved, it lasted just a moment. It could be only a matter of time before Violet and the other Foundlings were taken.

Before she could ask for further details about the situation, someone could be heard coming up the stairs to the Krog. Maggie and Henry both tensed, recalling how the Krog had been used as the Garrisons' tavern not long ago. But it wasn't a Garrison from the past. Instead a Foundling that Maggie didn't recognize entered the Krog.

"Elmer," Madame Welles greeted. "You've arrived just in time."

The Foundling looked a bit younger than Maggie. But she knew that only meant he was older in spirit. His curly, lemon-colored hair bounced on top of his head as he removed his blue cap. The brawny boy appeared muscular, which wasn't too surprising considering all the assignments Foundlings ran around the city.

"It's you." Elmer said with a wide grin. He hadn't stopped smiling since entering the room. "I remember both of you."

The Foundling looked so sincerely happy at the sight of Poppel's guests that Maggie felt bad she didn't know him. Elmer seemed to realize this as his smile slightly drooped.

"I suppose you don't remember me." Elmer's voice remained cheerful. "We weren't formally introduced that fateful Christmas Eve. But I certainly recall seeing you in the workshop, and when the Garrisons trapped us in the banquet hall, and then on Myra Lane before all of you left. I never thought you'd return to Poppel."

"I think we all did," Henry said. "Do forgive us if you've slipped from our memories. We were a bit occupied that night, having quite a lot on our plates."

"Of course," Elmer replied. "I'm just pleased for the opportunity to work with you both, especially since I wasn't as involved with saving Poppel back then."

"Working with us?" Maggie repeated.

"Yes," Augustus interrupted. "Although I want to keep the Foundlings away from this investigation, I still thought it would be useful for you and Henry to have at least one Foundling assisting. Someone who has knowledge of the tunnels and the Foundlings' daily schedules."

Elmer's face brightened. "Also, I can be used to capture the people behind these abductions. You just have to put me in a situation that makes it seem like I'm alone, and once they make their move, boom! We've captured them."

"How many times do I have to say it?" Augustus rubbed his brow with frustration. "We are not using you as bait."

"Yes, I know," said Elmer quickly. "I just wanted to reiterate that it's a plan I'm comfortable with executing. Besides, if anyone tried to take me, it would be the worst decision they ever made."

Elmer put his hands on his hips and tightened his arms, revealing the outline of muscles underneath his blue jacket.

"I'm hoping that together, the three of you can get to the bottom of these disappearances," Madame Welles explained. "That is, if you both are willing to help Poppel once again."

"Of course," Maggie replied immediately. "I feel I owe Poppel and the Foundlings as much as they owe me."

But Henry remained silent.

"And you, Henry," Madame Welles pressed. "Will you offer your services as well?"

Henry cleared his throat. "Unlike Maggie, I do not reside in New York City, and do not think I could be of any use from Poughkeepsie."

Maggie snapped her head Henry's direction. "Surely, you're not going back to Poughkeepsie so soon?"

Henry didn't respond to her. Instead he bowed his head and said softly, "I'm sorry I cannot be of any help. But I think my time with Poppel ended three years ago."

With those parting words, Henry disappeared down the steps to the banquet hall.

"That's most unfortunate," Elmer said. He shook his head with disappointment. "I was so looking forward to working with Henry Livingston."

"Maggie," Madame Welles said. "Please talk with him. Certainly, you can change Henry's mind."

"I'll try," Maggie said. She walked over to the stairs, but before disappearing from the Krog, she added, "Would it be possible to see some of the Foundlings, if they are around?"

"For the time being, we think it would be best if you do not have contact with any Foundlings," Augustus directed. "Except for Elmer, of course."

Obviously, Maggie wasn't eager to take orders from Augustus, so Madame Welles quickly added, "I'm sure in the near future, there will be opportunities to see them. But for now, it's in the best interest of everyone's safety that you are inconspicuous."

Maggie nodded. "Well, if there was anything Poppel taught me, it was how to sneak around."

"Maggie, I can't remain at Chelsea Manor indefinitely," Henry explained. "Even if your grandfather grudgingly allowed me to stay with him, it would be an uncomfortable situation."

Their underground sleigh clicked along the tracks, heading back to the Manor.

"So your hesitation to help Poppel is just a matter of not having a place to stay in New York?" Maggie asked. Her tone was disbelieving.

"Partly, yes," Henry replied. "Also, I don't think it would be wise for me to get mixed up with Poppel's problems again. And I don't think you should be involved either. Last time, it nearly cost us our lives on multiple occasions."

"What makes you think not getting involved will prevent that?"

Maggie asked. "If we learned anything, it should have been that we're connected to Poppel whether or not we want to be. There's no reason to think that if someone is taking Foundlings they won't come after the Van Cortlandt descendants as well."

Henry didn't reply, seeming to concede Maggie's point.

"I can't do this without you, Henry." She made one last plea as the sleigh pulled up to Chelsea Manor.

Henry helped Maggie out of the moving sleigh. Silently, they both walked through the dark tunnel to the ash pit. Then they ascended the ladder before climbing out of the Great Room's fireplace. While Henry watched the hole in the fireplace close and then disappear, Maggie stalked across the room.

"Goodnight, Henry."

Her tone was both sad and accusatory. But as she touched one of the doorknobs of the Great Room, Maggie heard Henry give a surrendering sigh.

"If I were to remain in New York to help, is there somewhere else I could stay?"

With a smile, Maggie spun around to face Henry. "The seminary's mostly empty in the summer. I'm sure Grandfather Clement would allow you to stay there."

Henry slid his hands into his pockets. "Well, I suppose we can ask him in the morning. Your grandfather's usually less irritable after breakfast."

Maggie ran to Henry and wrapped him in a tight hug. Then without thought, she placed a kiss upon his cheek. As she pulled away, she noted the surprise on Henry's face, which had flushed pink. At that moment, she knew there was more on the summer's horizon than the search for missing Foundlings.

Chapter Seven

General Theological Seminary

The hazy, blue light of an early summer evening shone through the stained glass windows of the General Theological Seminary's refectory. During the school year, the large room was used as the dining hall. With only a handful of students staying over the summer months, the tables were now stowed away, leaving behind an elegant yet empty tomb with its gothic-style vaulted ceiling, held in place by dark wooden rafters.

"Manners makyth man," Henry stated matter-of-factly.

Maggie spun around to stare at her companion. "What?"

Henry pointed across the hall to where a marble bust glowered down at them. "It's carved right above the mantel. I noticed it earlier."

Maggie turned back to study the bust. "That's John Pintard," she explained. "He was a wealthy and affluent acquaintance of Grandfather Clement. Pintard helped found the seminary's library."

"I imagine you've spent a lot of time there," Henry said.

She shook her head. "I've never actually visited the seminary until tonight. Grandfather Clement just used to say how John Pintard's bust in the refectory was hollow, much like the actual man."

"Really?"

"Oh, yes," Maggie said. "Even Grandfather Clement's friends couldn't avoid the wrath of the old scholar's sharp tongue."

"No, I meant that you really haven't been in the seminary before?"

"The seminary's for gentlemen only," Maggie remarked in a rather bitter tone. "I'm no such thing."

"Well, I've only been here for a few nights, but I can already attest that not all students staying at the seminary this summer are gentlemanly."

"The manners aren't makyth the men?" Maggie asked with a smirk.

"No, the men makyth a mess."

Maggie laughed, but then stopped when her voice echoed around the empty hall.

"I wonder why Elmer told us to meet him here," she whispered.

Henry shrugged. "Maybe so your grandfather doesn't become suspicious when his granddaughter and former houseguest start disappearing down his fireplace."

"You think Grandfather Clement knows that we returned to Poppel?"

"It's hard to say. Your grandfather is always more aware than he lets on. But I rarely saw him around Chelsea Manor, and I doubt he's too interested in our whereabouts."

"Well, it would be best if no one knows about any of this," Maggie said. "I don't want to get the whole family involved like last time."

"You need not worry about me telling anyone what we're doing," Henry said. "Because I'm not exactly sure what we're even doing. The whole situation's likely just a couple of Foundlings who decided to run away. We've been stuck in Poppel before. I would want to get out, too."

Maggie didn't feel the situation was as simple as Henry made it seem. Maybe it was the timing, but with the Crystal Palace fire, Henry's reappearance, and returning to Poppel for the first time in three years...the whole ordeal made her anxious.

Bang.

Maggie jumped nearly a foot in the air at the sound.

Henry chuckled softly. "The ash pit. Elmer's arrived."

She looked across the refectory at the fireplace under the brooding bust. Of course, Elmer would use the ash pit to meet them. She wasn't sure where else she expected him to enter. But as she intently watched the fireplace, she noticed that it wasn't Elmer. Instead a familiar curly-haired head poked out of the ash pit hole.

"Violet," Maggie called. She recognized the caramel-toned face of the young Foundling.

Grinning, Violet crawled out of the fireplace before running over to Maggie and wrapping her in a hug.

"I bet you weren't expecting to see me!" Violet beamed proudly.

"I sure wasn't," Maggie said.

"How did you know we were here?" Henry asked. His tone was less friendly.

"I was leaving the Boeken Kamer when I saw you enter the banquet hall with Madame Welles. I hid behind the curtains until you disappeared into the Krog, and then I listened to your conversation with Augustus and Elmer. But I'd already guessed why you were back. You're going to find the missing Foundlings."

"Well, we're just trying to help," Maggie admitted. "I'm not sure what we can really do."

"Oh, if anyone can find them, I know you can," Violet replied, still grinning.

"What do you know about the disappearances?" Henry asked.

"Only that a dozen or so Foundlings have mysteriously vanished over the past couple of months. Bickley, and Milton, and Rose, and…"

"Violet!"

Maggie looked at the fireplace and saw Elmer marching toward the group.

"What are you doing here, Violet?"

"I came to help," she replied simply.

"This is important business," Elmer said. "No other Foundlings are to be involved. It's top secret. How did you even know I was meeting them here?"

Violet rolled her eyes. "You're the worst secret keeper in the world. I could hear you across Myra Lane bragging to Lloyd about your important duties. And then in the next sentence, you asked if he'd ever been to the General Theological Seminary. It was a pretty easy puzzle to solve."

Violet giggled while Elmer flushed pink.

"That...that conversation was private," he stuttered.

"Violet's here now, so she might as well help us," Maggie said, trying to bring the topic back to the task at hand. "So, what exactly are we doing? And why did you want to meet at the seminary?"

Turning to Maggie, Elmer straightened his back and adjusted his blue jacket. "Because this is where the disappearances have taken place."

"At the seminary?" Maggie repeated in disbelief.

Elmer shook his head. "Not specifically at the seminary. Just in this neighborhood. All the Foundlings were working the nightshift in Chelsea at the time of their abductions."

Maggie's eyes grew wide. "They all disappeared in Chelsea?"

Now she understood why she'd been beckoned to Poppel. Although the events three years ago could be related to the disappearances, her family's intimate connection to the neighborhood was also important to the investigation.

Elmer nodded. "I'm hoping we'd look around the area to see if there's anything unusual happening. And being the largest building in the neighborhood, the seminary seemed like a good place to start."

The plan sounded logical to Maggie, but Henry was still doubtful.

"That's all you know?" he scoffed. "It's a pretty huge assumption to equate Foundling disappearances with the neighborhood they were assigned. If you consider it, Chelsea's near both the railroad and the river. It's more likely that the Foundlings were already planning to leave Poppel, and they waited until they could quietly slip away during one of their shifts. And Chelsea's the most convenient area to leave from undetected."

Elmer opened and shut his mouth a couple of times, clearly taken aback by Henry's suggestion. "I...I do not think Foundlings are leaving Poppel willingly. I see no reason for that."

"Well, just because some people in Poppel can't imagine such a scenario, doesn't mean it's not true," Henry defended. "Even with the Garrisons gone, Poppel might feel like a prison to some Foundlings. And the rest of you are in denial about it."

Maggie felt as equally upset by Henry's blunt speculations as

Elmer looked after hearing them. She was less concerned about Henry's apparent low opinion of Poppel, and more alarmed at the coolness in which he presented it. Although she hadn't seen Henry in three years, he was often on her mind. However, the memory of him seemed at odds with the person she saw now.

"I like Poppel, " Violet commented earnestly. "I don't think other Foundlings want to leave. Poppel's home for us."

Henry stared at the young girl but didn't say anything else. He'd already made his thoughts about the situation quite clear to everyone present.

Elmer uncomfortably cleared his throat. "We should still treat the situation as though the Foundlings went missing against their will. So we need to figure out why."

It was decided that the four of them would separate, exploring different corridors of the building. The General Theological Seminary stretched across a long block and would provide the best vantage points to examine any strange happenings within the neighborhood. Elmer didn't believe that the Foundlings disappeared inside of the seminary. Since the seminary was locked in the evenings, it wasn't likely the missing Foundlings had ventured into the building during their shift–even by way of the fireplace. Elmer was insistent upon this.

Maggie's corridor took her up a stairwell. Moonlight entered through a narrow stained glass window. When she crept across the hallway at the top, her shoes tapped its wooden floor.

Click clack. Click clack.

With the uneasiness brought on by the sound of her feet, Maggie paused at the nearest window. Staring out, she could see the seminary's courtyard below. In the windless night, everything looked frozen like a painting. Even the slightest rustling in the trees would catch Maggie's eye.

Could something out there in the night be responsible for the disappearing Foundlings, Maggie wondered. She wasn't completely convinced. And even though her experience in Poppel had been dramatic, it wasn't enough to make her believe that Foundlings would willingly leave the underground village. For many, Poppel was the only home they had ever known.

As Maggie continued to stare out into the night, an unusual feeling slipped through her body. She felt like she was being watched.

"Maggie?"

The voice behind her was both alarming and familiar.

She turned around and saw a candlestick floating in the air. It took an additional moment to recognize its holder.

"Francis," Maggie whispered.

Her cousin moved the candle up to his face. The boy's dense auburn hair glowed in its flickering light.

"What are you doing here?" he asked with genuine interest. His voice didn't carry its usual pretentious tone. Actually, since his disastrous involvement with the Garrisons three years ago, he had become less arrogant. But Maggie still didn't particularly trust him.

"I...I was just." Maggie searched her mind for any sensible reason that would lead her to the seminary. "I was looking for Henry. He's staying here for the time being. And I wanted to make sure that he got settled."

"Henry Livingston?" Francis arched an eyebrow. "Why's he staying here?"

Maggie shrugged, trying to appear calm. "Oh, he just wanted to spend more time in the city this summer. Grandfather Clement was kind enough to offer him a spare room in the seminary."

Francis still looked doubtful after Maggie's vague explanation.

"It's hard to believe Grandfather Clement would eagerly house Henry Livingston."

"A lot has changed over the years," Maggie replied.

"Indeed." Francis nodded. "But I don't trust him."

Maggie placed her hands on her hips. "Please say you're aware of how ridiculous that sounds coming from you."

Francis lowered the candlestick, sending shadows across his face. But Maggie could still spy his scowl.

"I'm not always so terribly wrong. You think you know Henry. But you didn't know him three years ago, and you certainly don't know him any better now."

"Well, I think I'm in a better position than you to judge his character. My perspective isn't as skewed."

Francis smirked but remained silent. He didn't need to speak. It was one of those rare times Maggie felt like her cousin saw through her. And she didn't like it.

"Have a good evening, Margaret." Francis turned around. "I hope you're successful in finding Henry. Or whatever it is that you're looking for."

Maggie watched the light from Francis's candle get smaller before it finally disappeared down the corridor, leaving her in darkness. Well, not complete darkness. The moonlight from the window still offered a soft glow, and she once again found comfort in the courtyard.

Then Maggie saw something move below. A recognizably small body walked casually along the trimmed green lawn.

Violet.

The girl had managed to slip outside.

Something in the corner of Maggie's eye took her attention away from Violet. The tree in the center of the courtyard swayed ever so slightly. She squinted toward the massive tree just as a shadow emerged from between its branches. The figure was large, but she couldn't tell whether it was human or animal.

As Maggie continued to study the creature, she noticed it setting its sights on the girl below. Its body tensed as though preparing for an attack. But before the creature moved again, a cloud intercepted the moon, casting the courtyard into darkness. Panic ripped through Maggie's chest as she heard Violet cry out from beyond the seminary's thick stone walls.

Without hesitation, Maggie bolted toward the stairway, stumbling down its steps at a record pace. Although she wasn't familiar with the seminary's layout, she didn't have difficulty locating the door that led out to the courtyard. With a loud *bang*, she crashed through the double doors just as Violet's screams evaporated into the night.

Undoubtedly, she had been carried off by the ghastly figure from the tree.

"Violet!" Maggie called out. "Violet!"

But only the wind bristled through the courtyard.

Maggie was about to shout again, but then she heard feet running up behind her. Frightened, she jumped aside, ready to fight the creature stalking her. But when she turned around, she saw Elmer's concerned face.

"It took Violet," Maggie blurted. "A monster took her."

She didn't know how else to describe what she had witnessed. And she didn't think she could muster enough strength to explain much more.

Elmer's eyes narrowed as he looked past Maggie into the ominous night.

"We should go back to Poppel," he said quietly. "The situation's worse than we feared."

Chapter Eight

Cachtice Castle

L ily sensed Cachtice Castle before seeing it. She didn't understand why, but as the carriage turned up the uneven, narrow road that extended a great deal from the village at the base of the hill, she felt a sudden sting of awareness.

She was being watched.

However, it didn't feel like a particular person was looking at her. It was as though *everything* had spotted her arrival. Then she knew Cachtice Castle was at the end of the road.

Her instincts were confirmed as the thick brush, which had enclosed the path, disappeared from view and high stone walls greeted Lily's carriage. She could see Cachtice through the iron bars of the gated entrance. The castle's slanted slate gray rooftops, varying in heights, loomed beyond the gate. Strangely, it wasn't until the carriage halted in the castle's main square that Lily considered her arrival as an expected one, instead of some intrusion, sneaking within Cachtice's boundaries in the middle of a cloudy afternoon.

A figure shuffled out from the shadowy crevice of two buildings. As the person neared, Lily recognized Darvulia.

"Lily," Darvulia crooned. "We have been expecting you."

"How could you have known I was coming?" Lily's voice was openly tense.

She felt foolish when Darvulia explained that Thorko had sent a message ahead of the carriage, alerting the castle of her arrival.

"Of course," Lily replied. Her cheeks flushed with embarrassment. The initial uneasiness was mollified as Darvulia took her arm and led her across the square.

"You must be exhausted from your travels," Darvulia remarked. "I will take you up to your chamber where you can rest. Then you can..."

A high-pitched wail screeched through the foggy air, drowning out the rest of Darvulia's words.

"Wha–what was that?" Lily stammered.

"Oh, just the wind," Darvulia replied as though she had been anticipating such a discussion. "It streams across the valley and up the hillside before sending that rather unpleasant sound throughout the castle. Do not let it alarm you. You will eventually grow accustomed to it."

Lily was about to say that she'd been alive for quite a long time and had never heard the wind make such a noise. But the topic had caused a noticeable shift in Darvulia. The woman seemed less welcoming than she had a moment ago, and Lily did not know what to make of the change in demeanor. Instead she allowed the uncomfortable silence to continue as Darvulia led her up a long stairwell. They soon reached an isolated chamber where Lily would be staying during her time at the castle.

"When will I see Countess Bathory?" Lily asked before Darvulia left her alone in the chamber.

Darvulia paused briefly in the doorway with her back toward Lily. "The Countess is away. She will call for you once she returns."

"Away?" Lily repeated.

"Just for the day," Darvulia corrected. "She had important business to attend to."

Darvulia started walking out the door, but Lily stopped her once more. "What about Ilona?"

Darvulia twisted around. "Who?"

"The handmaiden sent here from Lockenhaus a few months

back," Lily clarified. "Is she around? Or is she out with the Countess?"

Darvulia stiffened. "Ilona is no longer at Cachtice."

Surprised by the response, Lily immediately asked. "Where did she go?"

But Darvulia simply shrugged. "Her necessity here had expired."

And then she was gone.

Not since parting with her sisters years ago had Lily felt more alone. She thought about Laszlo and wondered how he had taken her sudden absence. Her anger toward him had softened, and she wished he were at Cachtice with her.

The shrieking wind forcefully returned, interrupting her mind's wandering.

That's not wind, Lily thought. But what it was exactly, she could not say.

Lily was allowed to roam Cachtice unaccompanied, but she never felt truly by herself. Even as she walked along the seemingly empty castle grounds, blanketed now in a layer of mist and light snow, she continually glanced over her shoulder. There was a presence that could not be ignored.

As the sun sank low in the sky, Lily turned away from the treacherous cliffs looking out across the valley and village below, and she headed back to the castle. As she neared the high wall surrounding Cachtice, a mound of undisturbed soil within the fresh snow caught her eye. Lily wondered if someone had been gardening, but the location seemed strange. The area didn't receive direct sunlight. Also, it was now early December, which was not ideal for planting.

Moving closer to the garden, Lily spied an unusual blemish on the otherwise perfect patch of dirt. It was as though a handful of seeds were already sprouting beneath the ground, creating a bumpy surface. Lily kneeled and lightly dragged a finger along the top of the soil. She was shocked when her finger snagged. Looking down, she saw a bit of pale blue fabric exposed in the dark earth.

"Hello! Hello! You there!"

Jumping up, Lily looked around for the strange voice addressing her. After spinning in a circle, she still didn't see anyone. Then out of the corner of her eye, she spotted a small figure running away with a shovel perched upon his shoulder. He disappeared behind the wall surrounding the castle grounds.

Lily ran after the figure, wondering what a child was doing outside of Cachtice. But upon turning the corner, she saw it was no child. Instead a short man, barely over three feet tall, was standing before her, the small shovel stationed between his legs. Lily gasped with surprise at the sight of him. His dark curly hair receded far back on his head while his olive skin was scarred and pockmarked. Gold rings dangled from his large ears.

"Lily!" the man bellowed. "Welcome to Cachtice."

Lily was about to ask how he knew her name, but then she recalled that Thorko had sent news of her arrival.

"And you are?" she asked.

"Ficzko. A longtime assistant to Countess Bathory." The man's tone didn't contain even the slightest trace of warmth. "You took it upon yourself to explore the castle grounds, I see."

Lily simply nodded. Her voice felt lodged in her throat. Ficzko was even more unnerving than Darvulia.

"You should stay within the walls of Cachtice." Ficzko's eyes darted from side to side. "The weather changes unexpectedly. It would be unfortunate if you were to become lost out here in the fog. And wind. And snow."

Ficzko guided Lily back to the main square of the castle. Lily looked forward to parting with the short and unusual man, but before she could politely slip away, Ficzko roughly grabbed her arm.

"Perhaps you would like me to show you around Cachtice. There are many areas of the castle you would not be able to explore alone."

There was nothing Lily wanted to do less than spend additional time with the strange man.

"No, thank you. I'm rather tired and would prefer to see the rest of the castle another day." Lily tried to pull away from Ficzko's grasp, but his grip tightened around her forearm.

"Ficzko," a silky voice called. "Is that Lily there with you?"

Lily turned to see Countess Bathory in the large arched doorway. Draped in a long, flowing black dress, Countess Bathory's porcelain skin looked striking, in addition to her rosy cheeks and blood-red lips. Darvulia, wearing a stern expression, stood beside the Countess as they looked out at Lily and Ficzko. Countess Bathory extended her arm toward the pair, gesturing for them to approach.

"Countess Bathory," Lily exclaimed, curtseying. She had never been more relieved to see the fearfully beautiful woman.

"Lily, I am so pleased to see that you made it to Cachtice." Countess Bathory turned to her handmaiden and then Ficzko. "Darvulia and Ficzko, excuse us momentarily while we reacquaint ourselves." The servants dutifully glided away, leaving Lily alone with the Countess.

"Walk with me," Countess Bathory instructed.

Obediently, Lily moved with the Countess around the main square. Shivers ran down her body, as though she just became aware of the cold temperature.

"You must pay no mind to Ficzko," Countess Bathory said. "He can be rather intense, especially with new arrivals."

"Of course," Lily said quickly. There seemed to be nothing she would disagree with when it came to Countess Bathory.

"I am aware that you are here not as a service to me," Countess Bathory continued. "But rather a service to yourself."

Lily was not sure how to read the Countess's tone, so she remained silent.

"I understand what you seek, for we are not so different." Countess Bathory stopped walking and twisted toward Lily. "I am willing to help you, if you in turn, help me."

Lily didn't know how she could possibly help the Countess, but she nodded her head in agreement. Countess Bathory smiled at the eagerly obedient girl.

"Very good," she remarked. "For I have important plans, you understand. Plans that can benefit both of us."

Lily once again nodded. Then in a fleeting moment of bravery, she asked. "And what specifically do these plans pertain to?"

"Why, everlasting life, of course." The Countess spoke softly, but her words struck Lily like a clap of thunder. Lily knew then that she would do whatever was asked of her.

Since the encounter with Countess Bathory, Lily had been unable to sleep. She didn't know if it was the excitement brought on by the Countess's proposition, or the eeriness of Cachtice that had yet to subside. Against her better judgment, Lily slipped out of her chamber in the middle of the night, hoping an exploration of the castle might cure her restlessness.

Carrying a candlestick for guidance, Lily moved through the shadowy corridors. The pale light of the moon offered some assistance. She passed numerous closed doors before walking down a curved stairwell. With each cautious step, Lily listened for the slightest hum within the castle. But not even the notorious wind was present that night.

When Lily reached the bottom of the stairs, she was greeted by an unusual smell. Something rotten filled the air, like an animal carcass decaying in the walls. Taking a couple hesitant steps forward, she suddenly collided with a knee-high statue. She fell to the ground, and with a faint clinking sound, the statue did as well.

"Oof!" Lily was surprised to hear the statue grunt until she realized it was actually Ficzko. He had been roaming the lower levels of the castle without a candle.

"Lily," he exclaimed. His deep voice was menacing as he scurried to his feet. "What are you doing down here?"

Ficzko did not extend a helping hand toward Lily, and she remained sprawled on the ground.

"I couldn't sleep," she replied.

"You should not wander Cachtice aimlessly," Ficzko scolded.

Lily started to stand up, but as she did, she noticed a silvery glint on the floor. While Ficzko went about fetching the candle Lily had dropped, she scooped up the trinket and clutched it within her palm.

"Yes, of course," Lily quickly agreed. "I know I should remain in my chamber. It was a careless mistake."

Ficzko stared up at Lily, his intense eyes studying her face. For a moment, she worried he'd caught her grabbing the item dropped during their collision. But then he forced a smile, causing his rough skin to tightly stretch in a rather unappealing manner.

"No harm done." His voice still held little warmth.

With much insistence on his part, Ficzko escorted Lily back to her chamber.

"Now stay put," Ficzko commanded as he shut the door, leaving her alone again.

Lily felt the coldness of the item still within her palm. Opening her clenched hand, she glanced down, and her heart skipped a beat. She recognized the red garnet embedded within silver—Ilona's bracelet.

The handmaiden would have never parted with the jewelry. Unless, of course, it had been taken. Lily concluded that Ficzko must have stolen the bracelet when Ilona worked at Cachtice.

Momentarily, Lily felt relieved she'd brought nothing to Cachtice Castle that could be taken by Countess Bathory's assistant.

At least nothing that she knew about.

Laszlo rode nonstop from Lockenhaus to Cachtice, knowing that it could already be too late. He had grown up with the horrors of Cachtice. Countess Bathory and her minions had tried to shield him from the dark events at the castle, but he still had been aware of the wickedness occurring around him.

With memories of Cachtice as fresh as the days they happened, Laszlo plowed on through the night until he spotted the cliffs upon which the castle was situated. The sight alone sent chills streaking down Laszlo's body, but he would not be deterred. He tied his horse on a tree near the bottom of the road and made his way up the high hill to the castle grounds.

Laszlo was halfway up the snow-laced hill when he felt it. He was being watched. And he instantly knew by what. The eyes following his moves didn't belong to his mother or a castle attendant–it was something less human. It was a shadow he usually only encountered in dreams. Laszlo did not utter a name for its identity was still unknown to him.

As the morning sun poured over the horizon, Laszlo had finally reached Cachtice's main square. Although it was deadly quiet, Laszlo knew the castle didn't sleep, and he hugged the wall near the entrance, trying to keep out of sight.

Laszlo suspected where he could find Lily. It sickened his stomach to know so. For if she had yet to be harmed, she would be kept in a particular chamber that was farthest from the dungeon, therefore, keeping her away from its horrific sounds. The chamber's location ensured that new arrivals wouldn't flee Cachtice in fear.

Familiar with the castle's layout, Laszlo knew how to get to Lily's chamber undetected. But when he reached the chamber's door, a new concern gripped him. There was a chance she was still angry and wouldn't listen to what he had to say. But he had no choice. She needed to be taken away from Cachtice–as soon as possible.

After the late night encounter with Ficzko, and discovering Ilona's stolen bracelet, Lily had eventually managed to fall asleep. However, she might have reconsidered doing so if she had known she'd be woken up hours later by a hand covering her mouth.

"Shh," a familiar voice whispered in her ear. "Lily, you must stay calm and listen."

Although Lily recognized the voice, she still instinctively fought against Laszlo's grasp.

"You're in danger," he hissed. "Please, listen to me."

Something in his tone made Lily stop fighting, and Laszlo removed his hand from her mouth.

"I know you feel like you cannot trust me, but you must," Laszlo said. "I will explain everything as soon as we're safely away from Cachtice."

"I'm not leaving with you," Lily snapped. "Not until I know what's happening. Don't lie to me again."

Laszlo released a shaky sigh. "In order to retain her youth, Countess Bathory lures young girls to Cachtice. She then has them tortured, mutilated, and murdered for their blood."

Lily's eyes widened with alarm. She hadn't expected him to be so direct. Upon seeing both the concern and disgust blanket his face, Lily couldn't help but believe him.

"After the blood's collected," Laszlo continued. "Thorko uses it in potions for the Countess's consumption. It's to maintain her youth. This has been happening for as long as I can remember."

Laszlo watched Lily's face, searching for signs of horror or disbelief. But she displayed neither in her expression. Instead a curious shadow emerged within her features, as she remained quiet, silently urging Laszlo to explain more.

"She wants you next. That's why you were brought here. Somehow Thorko discovered your history, and he believes your blood's more powerful than all the previous girls combined. You offer her more than just extended youth. With Thorko's help, she believes she not only could live forever, but also bring others back to life."

Lily's eyes widened with interest. She imagined Cachtice Castle offered things beyond her realm of understanding, but she never knew she was a target—or rather a vessel. As she began to process the unimaginable possibilities of Countess Bathory and Thorko, a scream thrashed the night's air.

Lily realized the price of what she sought.

Her life.

Chapter Nine

Broken Promises

I t was Krampus." Maggie braced her hands on top of Augustus's desk. "Years ago, Catharine told me about the creature from Van Cortlandt Manor. And it was Krampus."

Augustus glanced over at Henry for confirmation. Both of the men had also come face-to-face with the monster in the orchard on Christmas Eve.

"I didn't witness Violet being taken away," Henry admitted with his hands clasped behind his back. "But if Maggie's description's accurate, there's reason to believe it was that creature."

Augustus looked back at Maggie, and then over to Elmer who had been quiet since the group entered the Krog. Undoubtedly, he was depressed another Foundling had disappeared on his watch.

"What do you think, Elmer?" Augustus finally asked the taciturn Foundling.

Elmer dropped his head, restlessly shifting between feet. "Why would Krampus want to abduct a bunch of Foundlings?"

"That's also what I'm wondering," Augustus admitted.

"I know what I saw," Maggie said firmly. "I saw Krampus."

Augustus's eyes widened at her directness. "No one is doubting you, Maggie. I believe everything you told us to be correct. This just raises other questions we weren't ready to answer." Staring down at his desk, Augustus absentmindedly straightened some papers. "I had not prepared to hear that the Foundlings are being taken by something…"

Augustus paused. "Something not human."

"Well, they are," she snapped. "And the sooner we alert all the Foundlings to what's happening, the better chance they have to protect themselves."

Augustus didn't respond, so Maggie glanced at Henry. But he avoided her eyes. She was surprised to find him having no opinion on the matter.

"It would be best to keep what you saw tonight between us," Augustus said. "At least until we know more. Telling everyone in Poppel about Krampus will only scare them…"

"They should be scared," Maggie interrupted.

Augustus cleared his throat. "Or worse," he continued, ignoring Maggie's outburst. "It might rouse their own curiosity and desire to capture the creature. We don't need a bunch of vigilantes running around the city, putting more Foundlings in danger. That will not serve any good."

"So your plan's to do nothing?" Maggie was still addressing Augustus, but she stared at Henry, hoping her pressing gaze would stir some kind of emotion in him. To her disappointment, however, he remained quiet.

"The plan's to keep the Foundlings safe while I figure out the next course of action." Augustus's voice was rigid. "Of course, I would appreciate your continued assistance, as well as your silence."

Maggie stiffened. "I can promise you my help. But I can't guarantee your second request."

Realizing he wasn't going to get far with convincing Maggie to see things his way, Augustus forced a terse smile. "Do at least try."

"Krampus is snatching Foundlings and Augustus McNutt won't do a thing about it," Maggie exclaimed before Catharine and Louis were even seated in the Great Room of Chelsea Manor.

As her sister and cousin stared back with puzzled expressions, Maggie realized she probably should have added a bit more exposition. When inviting Catharine and Louis over to Chelsea

Manor earlier that day, she hadn't outright explained the topic of discussion. Maggie had only insisted that it was a matter of urgency.

Distracted by her remarks, Louis nearly missed the sofa when he awkwardly toppled down onto its green cushions. "Huh? What's happened to the Foundlings?" he asked.

"Are you still in contact with Poppel?" Catharine's tone was disapproving. She then looked over at Henry who, like earlier in the Krog, was standing quietly off to the side. Catharine no doubt assumed any troublesome news from Maggie was linked to Henry's reappearance into their lives.

"I should probably explain more properly," Maggie admitted while tangling her fingers together. Then she relayed everything that had happened since she and Henry received the letter from Poppel, requesting their return. From the initial meeting with Augustus regarding the vanishing Foundlings, to Krampus abducting Violet in the seminary's courtyard, Maggie tried to include every detail.

The room was quiet as Maggie finished her story. However, her sister soon arched an eyebrow Henry's direction.

"You were present for all of this?"

"I was at the seminary but did not see Krampus. Unlike Maggie, I thought we shouldn't get involved. I still feel that way."

Catharine looked surprised by Henry's response. She then turned toward Maggie.

"For once, I agree with your Poughkeepsie friend," Catharine said. "I appreciate you telling me what happened. But if you're doing so in hopes of recruiting help, I'll save you the trouble. I refuse to get involved with the plights of Poppel. It nearly cost us our lives last time. So I must insist that you remove yourself from their current problems as well."

Maggie looked down at her feet, trying to avoid her sister's pressing stare. The conversation was not going as planned.

"Maggie," Catharine said in a gentler tone. She stood from the sofa and approached her sister. "You must promise to end your involvement with Poppel. Their affairs are no longer ours."

She shook her head, still avoiding Catharine's intense green eyes.

"Whether we like it or not, our family will always be connected to Poppel. We shouldn't be too quick to turn our backs on their problems, thinking it doesn't concern us."

"Maggie…"

"Krampus is taking Foundlings," she snapped. Maggie lifted her face to finally meet Catharine's gaze. "You can't guarantee that we won't be targeted next. It could come after Gertrude or Gardiner. Or Louis." Maggie sent a sharp look her cousin's way, wishing he would take her side.

"Why do you naturally assume I'd be an easy target?" Louis asked, clutching his chest in mock offense. She could see a smirk forming at the corners his mouth. "You couldn't at least list Francis and Clemmie before me? I could outrun either of them. And I definitely scream louder."

Louis's attempt to lighten the tension in the room failed.

Instead Maggie and Catharine ignored their cousin while Henry remained standing silently near the fireplace. Maggie glanced over at him again, feeling betrayed by his lack of support as well.

Henry just stared blankly back, which only infuriated her more.

"I encountered Krampus three years ago." Catharine's voice held genuine fear. "And it's not a creature I wish to ever see again. Even after everything, I don't think you realize that the dangers of Poppel go farther than we can comprehend. So I need you to promise that you'll not get involved again."

"And if I don't make such a promise?" Maggie asked, wondering how Catharine planned to push her hand. Their parents were unaware of Poppel's existence and going to them about Maggie's involvement would just cause additional conflicts.

Without turning her head, Catharine eyed Henry, still hovering off to the side. Maggie then knew what her sister had in her arsenal. Now she actually wished Catharine would resort to telling their parents.

"Henry and Louis," Catharine said. "Could you kindly give us a moment in private?"

After the boys disappeared from the Great Room, Catharine shut the double doors and turned back to Maggie.

"I don't think it would be difficult to convince Grandfather Clement that Henry's continued presence is detrimental to our family's safety," Catharine said in a hushed voice. "I suppose that would force him back to Poughkeepsie, if Chelsea Manor and the seminary were not available. From what you've told me, Augustus also wouldn't want Henry staying in Poppel. That would only stir up rumors, inciting the Foundlings' suspicions."

Maggie could barely hide her surprise. She opened and closed her mouth without saying anything. She wasn't sure what caused more alarm; Catharine using Henry against her or knowing such a threat would work.

She narrowed her eyes. "You wouldn't."

"Oh, wouldn't I?" Catharine huffed. "I don't like that Henry has returned to our lives. I do not doubt that part of this trouble is his doing, even with his insistence on wanting to stay uninvolved. I also don't like your attachment to him. It's always been too strong. It clouds your judgment."

Not only did Catharine's words hit a nerve, but it also bothered her that they were similar to the comments made by Francis the other night.

"This has nothing to do with Henry," Maggie replied curtly.

Catharine gave her an inquisitive look, but then changed tactics. "Promise me you will stay out of Poppel's affairs." When she didn't respond, Catharine sharpened her gaze.

"Maggie..."

"Fine. I will stay out of Poppel's affairs," Maggie agreed, frowning. "I promise."

Catharine studied her face closely, looking for signs of dishonesty. Finally, with a satisfied nod, she reached out and embraced Maggie. "I just don't want anything to happen to you."

Loosely patting Catharine's back, Maggie returned her sister's hug halfheartedly. She was still bitter that Henry had been used against her. It was unusual for Catharine to take such a ruthless approach to get her way. Clearly, her sister was more concerned for her safety than Maggie would have predicted.

And that made the promise she couldn't keep taste all the more unpleasant.

"Precisely, what did Catharine say until you agreed to not get involved?" Louis asked.

The sun had recently set, shading the neighborhood in gray. They crossed the road that separated Chelsea Manor and the General Theological Seminary. Maggie was already a step ahead of Louis, so he didn't see her flush at the question. She still didn't appreciate that Catharine was acutely aware of her feelings for Henry, and she wasn't in a hurry to make them known to Louis as well.

"Who said I agreed to anything?" Maggie remarked. She slowed her pace so Louis could catch up.

"Catharine sure acted like you had," Louis said. "It was hard to miss when you two emerged from the Great Room. She kept sending you knowing smiles. And yet..."

"And yet what?"

Louis smirked. "And yet here we are, sneaking over to the seminary."

They had just reached the seminary's front entrance. Louis looked at the double doors and then to Maggie with an eyebrow arched.

"We're not sneaking anywhere," she said. "I don't recall Catharine making me promise not to visit our dear grandfather's seminary. This outing has nothing to do with Poppel."

"Really?" Louis asked doubtfully.

Maggie didn't respond as she lightly rapped on the door with her knuckles.

"If you want to lie to Catharine, that's your choice. But don't start lying to me, Maggie. I wouldn't be standing here if you didn't have my support."

Maggie glanced over at her cousin. His normally playful eyes were regarding her earnestly. She sighed under their mounting inquisition. "I'm just visiting Henry," Maggie replied before mumbling, "If I happen to run into any Foundlings who are searching for Krampus, it's purely coincidental."

She knocked on the door again. This time it opened a moment later. Henry's face emerged from the dull light of the seminary. Without a word, he moved aside, allowing Maggie and Louis space to enter. Quietly, Henry led the pair to the refectory where a familiar Foundling awaited them.

"Elmer," Maggie said.

She was unsurprised by the Foundling's presence. Louis, however, seemed taken aback. His shoes screeched to a halt on the wooden floors, while he curiously gazed at Elmer. Maggie could tell memories from Poppel had returned to his mind.

"Elmer, this is my cousin, Louis." She turned to Louis and placed a reassuring hand on his forearm. "Elmer is leading the search for the missing Foundlings."

"It's now a search for Krampus," Elmer corrected. "Krampus is the best chance we have at finding them."

"You're not going to try and fight the creature, are you?" Henry asked steadily. He unsuccessfully tried to mask his anxious tone.

"Fight? No, of course not." Elmer's face appeared alarmed at the notion. "My plan's to carefully track the monster down, allowing it to unknowingly lead us to the Foundlings."

Figuring out why Foundlings were vanishing seemed like a simple task in hindsight–now that they knew what they were actually up against. Elmer laid out his strategy as a palpable tension weaved throughout the room. Unlike the previous night, the group would not remain in the seminary. Elmer decided that they would split up into pairs and discreetly comb through the Chelsea streets, looking for any sign of the horned creature.

Maggie instinctively wanted to partner with Henry, but she was responsible for dragging along Louis, and her cousin preferred sticking with her. Also, Elmer was insistent that Henry would accompany him. However, before they separated in the seminary's foyer, Maggie hugged Henry. He seemed genuinely shocked at the gesture, lightly touching her lower back in response. Even Louis stared at them with a quizzical, if not amused, expression.

"What was that all about?" Louis whispered. He and Maggie

clandestinely walked down the faintly lit road running south of the seminary. Elmer and Henry had ventured in the opposite direction, agreeing to meet back at the refectory in no more than a couple of hours.

"Do you think we should head toward the river?" Maggie asked, ignoring Louis's question. Of course, Maggie's obvious avoidance of the topic would only increase her cousin's curiosity.

"Do you have feelings for him or something?" Even coming from Louis, Maggie was surprised at the remark's directness.

"Who?" Maggie said. She tried to sound disinterested, even though she felt her body's temperature rise a few degrees.

"Who?" Louis echoed with a chuckle. "Oh, I don't know. How about the dashing young lad you nearly affectionately squeezed to death back there in the seminary?"

Maggie's face flushed a deeper shade of red. "Henry's my friend. I care about him," she muttered.

"Indeed," Louis replied simply. He knew Maggie quite well. So not only was Louis already aware of the words she kept locked away, but he also knew when he should stop prying.

"I think heading toward the river would be a good idea," Louis said, indicating that he had willingly changed the topic.

Maggie and Louis crossed the railroad tracks that ran along Tenth Avenue. As they moved further west, the neighborhood became less residential. Distilleries soon replaced row houses, and the smell of sour milk, turpentine, and charcoal filled the air.

"The last time anyone saw Krampus was at Van Cortlandt Manor," Maggie said as they approached the banks of the Hudson River. The masts of docked ships stood erect along the horizon like soldiers. "It's possible that it came down to New York City by boat. Perhaps it's still using the river to transport Foundlings."

"But why would this creature want to take Foundlings anywhere?" Louis asked. "The way you described it made it sound like an animal. How do we know it's not, like, eating them or something?"

After seeing the pained look on Maggie's face, Louis seemed to immediately regret the insensitive comment. The idea of Violet, or any

Foundling, being harmed by Krampus was terrible enough. Maggie didn't need the additional imagery of them being consumed as well.

"Ignore me. I'm just spouting nonsense," Louis recoiled. "You're right in your thinking that the Foundlings could be transported by boat. Maybe back up to Van Cortlandt Manor."

"It could be revenge for taking away the Sister Wheel," Maggie said stiffly, still trying to calm her nerves. "Krampus had guarded Sarah's wheel at Van Cortlandt Manor. Catharine and Henry made it clear that it was not pleased when they took it."

Louis nodded. "That's a likely possibility."

Maggie could tell he was being purposefully agreeable, and she somewhat appreciated it. Louis usually covered his softer side with cynicism. But she suspected the prospect of a mysterious creature attacking them at any moment weakened his derisive exterior.

They walked along the riverfront for about a half hour. Nothing seemed out of the ordinary. And that was the problem. The western industrial end of Chelsea was already unsettling after nightfall. Large desolate brick buildings loomed around them and the dark streets were particularly foreboding. Any extra presence from Krampus would be hard to detect. And Maggie believed the likelihood of Krampus stalking them was much greater than the pair skillfully tracking down the creature.

So, when Louis suggested returning to more familiar surroundings, Maggie agreed without hesitation. She also was curious as to how Henry and Elmer were faring.

Maggie and Louis hurried back toward the seminary, hardly speaking a word to each other. They both were eager to be in the vicinity of Grandfather Clement's Chelsea Manor estate, a neighborhood they knew only too well.

They had just crossed Tenth Avenue when a stifled cry cut through the air. Its brief–but anguished–tone reverberated through Maggie's body.

"What was that?" Louis's voice trembled.

Maggie didn't respond. The scream sounded like it came down Twentieth Street, so she took off running in that direction with Louis trailing right behind.

As the emptiness of the street echoed under their thudding feet, Maggie considered that she had been mistaken. But upon nearing Ninth Avenue, a large silhouette emerged from the night. From its arched, hairy body to the twisted horns spouting out of its head, Maggie immediately recognized Krampus. Her breath halted in her throat.

"What is it?" Louis asked, stopping alongside Maggie. She heard him gasp as he spotted the creature up ahead.

"Krampus…"

At the sound of its name, the creature's head snapped their direction. Surprisingly, Krampus did not attack, even while they remained frozen in fear. In a swift, violent movement the creature vanished between row houses. Maggie felt compelled to follow the creature, in hopes of finding the Foundlings. Before her feet could move, however, Louis gripped her arm and pointed to a form in the middle of the road.

It was a body.

A motionless body.

Worried it could be Henry, Maggie's stomach painfully tightened. But as she cautiously approached the body–nervous that Krampus was lurking nearby–she recognized the lifeless face, twisted in a horrified expression.

Krampus had killed Elmer.

Chapter Ten

An Unspeakable Crime

That's not good enough!" Maggie voice shook with rage as she stormed around the Krog.

Augustus had finished explaining that until Krampus was captured, he would forbid the Foundlings from leaving Poppel.

"I just carried a dead boy all the way down here." Maggie continued pacing from wall to wall. "Meanwhile, your grand solution's to keep the Foundlings locked up when they should have been out tracking down Krampus in the first place."

After finding Elmer's body, mauled and bloodied, Maggie knew they needed to get the deceased Foundling off the road before any suspicion arose in the neighborhood. Louis wrapped the body in his jacket while Maggie considered the options for returning Elmer to Poppel. She worried they'd have to take him through Chelsea Manor, but fortunately, the seminary door was unlocked. They used the fireplace in the refectory, saving them an additional block, and possibly unwelcome questions from Grandfather Clement's servants.

When it came to carrying a body, any amount of distance felt endless. For it wasn't just the physical toll of dragging Elmer down into the ash pit, it was also emotionally taxing. However, focused on the difficult task at hand, Maggie kept her emotions confined until she confronted Augustus in the Krog.

"It was my decision to keep the Foundlings uninvolved,"

Augustus defended. "I still do not think it was the wrong thing to do."

Maggie came to a halt in front of Augustus's desk, squaring her trembling body toward the young redheaded man.

"Except now you have a dead Foundling," she said in a frightfully quiet voice.

Louis was waiting down in the banquet hall while Madame Welles tended to the arrangements of Elmer's body. It was just Maggie and Augustus in the Krog, tensely debating the next steps to take.

"How do you know they'll be any safer in Poppel?" Maggie snapped. "Krampus could be anywhere. The Foundlings are possibly more vulnerable trapped down here together."

"Then what are you suggesting? That I let all the Foundlings loose in the city?"

"I'm suggesting that you give them the opportunity to fight Krampus head on. Sneaking around seems to serve the creature's strengths."

Augustus eyed Maggie intensely, appearing to gather his thoughts before responding, "What does your friend, Henry Livingston, have to say about all of this? I noticed he wasn't with you and Louis tonight. Has he returned to Poughkeepsie, abandoning us once and for all?"

Maggie bit her lip and looked down. She hadn't told Augustus that Henry had been with Elmer earlier and now there was no sign of him. At first, she feared the worst. Then she realized it was likely Henry had escaped when Krampus attacked Elmer. She had hoped he would have gone to Poppel. However, it was clear that he hadn't.

Augustus stared at Maggie, who was avoiding his eyes. After taking a breath, she explained that Henry was partnered with Elmer, but Maggie hadn't seen him since the pairs separated outside the seminary.

"Do you think Krampus captured Henry or..." Augustus trailed off, not wanting to alarm Maggie.

She shook her head. "I'm not sure what happened to him."

Augustus nodded. He undoubtedly didn't want to push the topic of Henry's absence, especially when emotions were still high. "I'm sure he safely got away," Augustus murmured. He turned his attention to the papers scattered across the desk.

"We have to recruit the Foundlings to help," Maggie said. She tried lessening the anger still present in her voice. "Everyone credits me and the other Van Cortlandt descendants with saving Poppel from the Garrisons. But without the Foundlings, we couldn't have done it. I fear it's the same for defeating Krampus."

"Until we know the reason for Krampus's actions–" Augustus started to say, but Maggie cut him off.

"The Sister Wheel. This is revenge for taking the Sister Wheel."

Augustus glanced up momentarily, and then returned to digging through his papers.

"Sarah's wheel was seized from the creature nearly three years ago," he stated. "It seems strange it would take that long for Krampus to come looking for it. And enacting some kind of vengeful ploy is not in its nature."

"How do you know about the nature–"

Now it was Maggie's turn to be interrupted.

"Right here." Finally finding the paper he sought, Augustus victoriously held up the yellowed page next to his face before extending it over the desk to Maggie.

"What's this?" Maggie examined the cursive writing sprawled across the old document.

"From Stephanus Van Cortlandt's personal journal. Nearly two centuries old."

Maggie looked at the paper again and then back at Augustus, curiously. "Just the one page? What's so important about it?"

"I came across the page a while ago, stuffed inside a book in the Boeken Kamer. It didn't seem important at the time, other than being from Stephanus's journal. It chronicles some monotonous activities in what was once known as New Amsterdam. I thought it was left in the book by mistake. But over the past few months, I've come across more pages, belonging to the same journal. It's as though someone had hid them, hoping they would be safe if separated."

"But why?" Maggie asked. "What do they contain that's worth

hiding?"

Augustus looked down at the fragile page in his hand. "I didn't know at first. Again, most of the writings seemed of little value. But then I came across a particular passage not long ago. It had to do with Krampus. And Laszlo."

"Laszlo?" Maggie repeated. She recalled the odd man who ran Poppel's workshop.

Augustus gazed back at Maggie with widening eyes. "Laszlo and the creature's pasts, it appears, are greatly entwined. Krampus followed Laszlo to New York centuries ago, in an effort to take Lily's wheel from him. As you know, the Foundlings fought Krampus away, and he remained hidden near Van Cortlandt Manor where he could keep an eye on Sarah's wheel."

The story was familiar to Maggie. All of it she had heard at least once before, with the exception of one particular detail.

"Laszlo had Lily's wheel?"

Augustus stared at his desk, rummaging through more papers. "Laszlo became acquainted with Lily after she left Grace and Sarah. I've only been able to assemble bits of the story from the journal pages. Laszlo was even less forthcoming with any additional information. Apparently, his past is something he keeps quite private." Augustus glimpsed Maggie's face before looking away. "Of course, I didn't tell him I'd discovered these pages throughout the Boeken Kamer. As of now, you're the only other person who knows. It seems easier that way."

"Laszlo should still tell us his history concerning Krampus," Maggie insisted. "I don't care if you think it seems easier. We should tell him about the journal, if he can help fill in the missing pieces of the story. Where's he now?"

Augustus cleared his throat, uncomfortably. "I no longer know where to find Laszlo. After you saw Krampus abduct Violet at the seminary, I secretly sent Laszlo off to find the creature. I thought his knowledge would lend itself to capturing Krampus. However, he has yet to return, and I have not heard anything from him."

"He couldn't have been gone for more than a couple of days,"

Maggie observed. "That's not too unusual, is it?"

"Perhaps not," Augustus said. "But now with Elmer's death, I'm starting to wonder."

Silence fell over the Krog. Maggie's anger had subsided, but she still wanted to pressure Augustus into letting the Foundlings help. Before she could make her case known again, she heard him mumble something.

"Pardon?" she asked.

"Will you help me?" Augustus repeated. "Finding the rest of Stephanus's journal is imperative. I do not wish to recruit the Foundlings—at least not yet. But perhaps you would be willing to help search the books in the Boeken Kamer for journal pages?"

Maggie didn't know how to respond. As much as she wanted to help Poppel, she didn't think the place to do so was in the underground village's library. Also, she still needed to find Henry. Until she heard his version of what happened that evening, it would be hard to focus on anything else.

Augustus noticed Maggie's hesitation. "You've had a long night." His tone was uncharacteristically sympathetic. "We can discuss this later."

A long night was one way to describe it, Maggie thought. Elmer was dead. Henry was missing.

And even with the few scattered notes from Stephanus Van Cortlandt, Krampus was still a mystery needing to be solved—and quickly.

The late July sun steadily dangled over Manhattan the next few days, its rays only broken up by the occasional cloud. Yet Maggie felt nothing but gloom as she compulsively navigated the streets of Chelsea, searching for any sign of Henry.

While weaving through the summer crowds as horse-drawn omnibuses packed the avenues, Maggie desperately tried to spy familiar bronze hair and piercing blue eyes. But she was unsuccessful.

Day after day, she returned to the Chelsea estate, sweaty and tired. Still, she would make one last stop at the seminary before heading home, always hopeful that Henry would finally turn up.

"What are you doing here, Maggie?"

She spun around and saw Francis standing in the refectory's entrance. It was the first time she had encountered anyone in the seminary since Henry disappeared. The door was usually unlocked during the day, but the building always appeared empty.

"Francis, I was just looking for..." Maggie paused. She didn't know if she should mention Henry. Francis wasn't particularly trustworthy, and she feared revealing more about the troubles at Poppel than she intended.

But Francis had already guessed the reason behind her visit.

"You're searching for Henry." Not only was Francis commenting with certainty, but Maggie also detected unease in his tone.

"Yes," she admitted. "I haven't seen him for a couple of days, and I was hoping he might be around."

Francis slowly walked into the refectory, as though thinking if he approached Maggie too quickly, she might scatter like an unwelcome household pest.

"Have you seen him?" Maggie tried not to sound too anxious. "I would have looked in his room, but I am not sure which one he's staying in."

"I haven't seen Henry since..." Francis started to say, but then trailed off.

"Since when?" Maggie pressed, no longer hiding the urgency in her voice.

"Four nights ago," he replied reluctantly.

Maggie sighed, wishing it had been more recently.

"That's the last time I saw him as well. He was probably on his way to see me."

Francis raised his eyebrows. "I don't think so."

"Why do you say that?"

"Because Henry came back to the seminary, a little after midnight.

And he was..." Francis paused once again. "He was covered in blood."

Maggie couldn't suppress the gasp that slipped from her mouth. She imagined Henry injured while trying to save Elmer from Krampus. She wondered if he was in a hospital somewhere in the city. Or had he already succumbed to his wounds? Maggie's stomach dropped at the thought, and she bit her bottom lip to quell the tears forming in the corner of her eyes. Francis must have spotted her sudden onslaught of emotions, for his nervous expression quickly turned into concern.

"Henry was fine, Maggie," Francis remarked. "It wasn't his blood."

"What do you mean not his blood?" Her trembling voice was louder than she had intended. But she found its volume difficult to control.

Sighing, Francis rubbed his auburn hair, as though contemplating how to communicate to Maggie without upsetting her further. When he spoke again, she could tell he was carefully choosing his words.

"I'd heard someone entering the seminary. The hour was late, so I was curious about the visitor's identity. I snuck down to the first floor and peeked around the corner near the foyer, and that's when I spotted Henry.

"He was standing in the entryway with his hands bracing his knees and his shirt covered in blood. Momentarily, I thought he had been injured somehow, but before I could make my presence known and offer assistance, he ripped his shirt off. He was panting, having trouble catching his breath, as though he had just witnessed something terrifying. But I couldn't see any wounds on his bare skin. He looked unharmed.

"That's when I realized the blood on his shirt was not his own. So I stayed in the shadows, waiting for him to pass. But he did not go back up to his room. Instead he headed toward the refectory, and I silently followed. He lit a fire and then burned the bloodied shirt, as though ridding himself of evidence to an unspeakable crime."

Francis nodded to the large fireplace on the far end of the refectory. "I have not seen him since that night."

Maggie continued to stare at the fireplace as though expecting

Henry to materialize from its ashes. But he did not appear. For the first time, she hoped that he never would.

"I'm not sure what happened to Henry that night." Francis's voice was barely above a whisper. "And I do not know where he disappeared to…"

She turned sharply and looked at Francis. Reading her thoughts, he waved a hand and added, "His room's empty. I checked. Any belongings he brought with him are long gone."

Maggie's mind returned to finding Elmer's dead body in the middle of the street. Her stomach lurched at the memory and water stung her eyes. However, she wasn't entirely sure if it was the loss of Elmer or Henry that affected her most.

"You might not believe what I say," Francis said. "But I think Henry has secrets. Dark secrets."

"No, Francis," Maggie said weakly. "I believe you." And she did. She really did.

Chapter Eleven

A Bloody Proposal

On the outside, the solid walls of Cachtice Castle looked impenetrable. But that didn't prevent a cadence of screams from flowing within the hallways. As Lily trailed Laszlo through the castle's passages, it sounded as though the agonized cries were following their steps. Lily tried blocking the terrifying noises from her ears, while Laszlo gripped her hand tighter, leading her on. Occasionally, he would glance back, but his eyes were not reassuring.

Lily expected Laszlo to immediately take them outside. However, it seemed as though he was avoiding obvious exits. Instead he directed them deeper into the bowels of the castle. Since the screams eventually ceased, she trusted his instinct. After all, he was raised at Cachtice.

When they entered another passage, completely void of light, Laszlo stopped walking. With firm, yet gentle hands, he pressed Lily to the cold wall.

"There's a secret tunnel that leads out of the castle," Laszlo whispered. "I do not feel safe using another way. It's not just the Countess and Thorko we must be concerned about..."

Laszlo's voice dropped as another cry drowned out his words.

"What was that?" But she didn't need an answer.

Even with limited visibility, they were clearly now in the castle's dungeon. And if what Laszlo said earlier was true, the Countess's victims were possibly detained nearby. As the cellar's bone-chilling air swept over her body, Lily felt conflict bubble under her skin. A strong urge to seek out those being held prisoner fought against the tingling in her legs to flee the castle. Before she could be forced to choose, a chilling voice greeted them.

"Why, hello!" Ficzko stepped out from the shadows. "Going for another stroll, are we?"

Lily watched as Laszlo's face changed from worry to rage. He shoved Lily aside, and with a guttural noise, he lunged at Ficzko. Swiftly, Laszlo tackled the man to the ground.

"Don't touch her," Laszlo grunted. He smothered Ficzko's scarred face with his palms. "Don't you ever touch her!"

Laszlo's advantageous position was short-lived. Although small in size, Ficzko was unusually strong, and once he freed his arms from Laszlo's grasp, he threw Laszlo off his body with ease.

"Oh, Laszlo," Ficzko snarled, as Laszlo tumbled along the uneven stone floor. "What a silly, foolish boy you are."

Laszlo crouched on the ground as he watched the small man slowly approach.

"I'm no longer a child, Ficzko. You can't hurt me now like you could back then."

A sneer crossed Ficzko's lips. "As you know, Laszlo, things do not change here at Cachtice."

Ficzko rolled each of his sleeves up to his elbows. A moment later, the small man slammed Laszlo into the nearest wall. With his neck pinned under Ficzko's thick arm, Laszlo let out a choked groan.

Frozen in fear, Lily remained in the shadows. She wanted to go to Laszlo. She wanted to fight Ficzko away. But she didn't know how. Quickly, she scanned the area around her, desperately searching for anything of use. The only object she spotted was a bit of stone that had crumbled from the wall. She picked up the jagged piece of rock, and without hesitation, she hurled it at Ficzko's head. The fragment struck above the nape of the neck with enough force to cause him to momentarily lose his grip on Laszlo. As Laszlo stumbled

away from the dazed man, he locked eyes with Lily.

"Run," Laszlo mouthed. "Please. Go."

Seeing the fear boiling in his eyes, she heeded his words. Her lone footsteps shuffled along the corridor, but the tearing of flesh and the piercing scream that followed soon masked the sounds of her feet.

Ficzko had produced a curved blade, and before Laszlo could defend himself, the knife had been unabashedly stuck into his side. With an agonizing yell, Laszlo collapsed to the ground, grabbing right below his ribs.

Laszlo's last image was of Ficzko towering over his slumped body. A lopsided smirk moved across his lips.

"Nothing changes at Cachtice, Laszlo. Nothing."

Then everything went black.

Lily didn't know where she was running. Even if she had, it would have been hard to see in the darkened corridors of Cachtice's dungeon. Also, her nose hadn't adjusted to the sour and rotten smell permeating the halls. Whatever evilness had been committed within the castle, Lily was nearing its source.

Grazing the wall with an outstretched hand, Lily blindly guided herself through the corridor. She no longer heard the yells of Laszlo, and she shuddered to think what Ficzko might have done to him. But she couldn't turn back now. She wouldn't even know where to go.

With each foot carefully placed in front of the other, Lily continued down the corridor. Silence had now enveloped the castle. All she heard was her own staggered breathing. As stale air moved stiffly through her throat and chest, burning with its heaviness, it soon became impossible to regulate. Troubled by this lack of control, she momentarily paused, hoping to regain the ability to steady her breathing. But even when her feet stopped, the labored breaths continued. Lily placed a hand above her breast, feeling her thumping heart. However, its rhythm didn't match that of her breaths. Feeling a chill run down her spine, she hesitantly took her other hand and covered her lips. She listened.

Breathing.

She still heard breathing. And it wasn't hers.

Swallowing a gasp that threatened to escape her mouth, Lily scanned the shadowy surroundings. Her eyes had slightly adjusted to the darkness, but still not enough to decipher the forms around her. But it was clear she wasn't alone.

Feeling more vulnerable, Lily started walking at a quicker pace. However, it wasn't long before her feet collided with something solid on the floor, releasing a weak grunt into the air. Once again, the sound didn't belong to her.

Lily struggled to stay upright, but her body awkwardly tumbled to the ground. Fortunately, she avoided landing on the object that had tripped her. Upon realizing its identity, she was even more relieved by the spot she had fallen—or at least she would have been relieved if the sudden sensation of nausea hadn't spiked through her system.

Two ghostly gray eyes stared up at her. They belonged to a pale young girl, no older than thirteen. Although it wasn't a corpse, indicated by the hollow and labored breaths still seeping out of her cracked lips, Lily wasn't sure the girl's current state was any better than death. Part of her actually wished that it had been a corpse. The terror in the girl's eyes was unlike anything Lily had seen before. Her bruised face was shaped into an expression of pure agony. The girl had been tortured, beyond what Lily could even imagine.

Acting on reflex, Lily reached a shaking hand toward the young girl. Carefully, she touched the girl's shoulder, only to snap her hand back a moment later, as though she had grazed fire. It wasn't that the girl's body felt hot. Rather something burned beneath the skin—something that couldn't be seen by eyes. Lily glanced down at her throbbing hand and noticed that a faint layer of blood now stained her palm.

"Leave her." The voice was accompanied by a candle's glow. Lily glanced up as the silhouette of Darvulia came into view. "There's nothing that can be done for her now. She has served her purpose. Let her go."

When the young girl took a frail breath, rattling the air within her dry throat, Lily realized Darvulia had been right. A moment later, the girl stopped breathing completely.

"Who… who did this to her?"

Lily had trouble pulling her eyes away from the girl's body, which became more illuminated as Darvulia approached with the candlelight. She wasn't sure if it was the woman's deliberate and looming footsteps that struck each nerve of her body, or if it was the full sight of the tortured girl. Now captured in an orange glow, Lily spied raw flesh, marbled with bruised and scabbed skin. The girl had been mutilated and abused for quite some time.

"You must come with me." Darvulia's stern voice made it clear that it wasn't a request.

"Did you do this to her?" Lily stood up. Her voice was steady, but her hands weren't. She had to clench her fists to still the trembling. "How many others have seen her fate?"

Darvulia took another step toward Lily, causing her candle to nearly graze Lily's chest. Lily brought her hand up, as though to shield herself from the older woman.

"The girl fulfilled a great service for Countess Bathory, but her necessity had come to an end." Darvulia was not defensive. Instead she spoke like she was explaining the most trivial and mundane matter related to handmaiden duties—and not murder. "The amount of girls needed in the future is entirely up to you, Lily. Countess Bathory does not wish to harm you. She has heard of the glorious gift bestowed upon you so long ago, and she wishes to return you to that extraordinary state of immortality. However, she would need your help. Perhaps you would be willing to help her, if she, in turn, helps you?"

Lily stood in silence. She tried to disregard Darvulia's words, but the offer—echoing Countess Bathory's own proposition—was hard to ignore. She didn't doubt Countess Bathory had abilities that would give Lily what she so desperately sought, and the prospect of retaining the youth she had held for centuries was difficult to dismiss.

But when her eyes once again took in the sight of the dead girl, she knew nothing could be that simple.

Trying to respond to Darvulia, Lily opened her mouth, but no words came out. It became clear that she could neither accept such an offer–nor reject it. Instead Lily brushed past Darvulia, believing that leaving Cachtice was the only true option. She still needed to reunite with Laszlo. He might already be waiting for her outside the castle grounds, injured and alone.

Lily expected the dungeon to get darker the farther she got from Darvulia. However, she soon discovered a well-lit cellar. Torches lined its stone walls, exposing the odd wooden devices and glass jars filling the chamber. She was so mesmerized by the various objects that she barely noticed the blood smeared across the floor. It was clear the chamber's purpose was nothing short of evil. But soon her attention was solely focused on the figure standing before her.

"Countess Bathory," Lily choked out in both fear and admiration.

Even with the knowledge she now carried about the Countess, Lily was still in awe of the woman. Countess Bathory's hair was worn down, and its dark waves flowed all the way to her chest. Her elaborate purple gown gave the Countess an additional air of royalty, and Lily felt her shoulders bow in reverence.

"Lily, I am so pleased that you are here." Countess Bathory's voice was smooth like velvet. "Together we can do miraculous things. Things thought to be impossible."

Countess Bathory reached her jeweled hand out to the girl. Lily felt hypnotized by the immaculate and silky skin. Without even a fleeting glance behind her, Lily took the offered hand within her own–still carrying remnants of the dead girl's blood upon it.

Laszlo snapped his eyes open and sat up with a gasp. A searing pain shot through his side. He recalled the image of Ficzko gleefully looking down at him, a blade grasped in his small hand.

"Stay still," a voice directed.

Laszlo's blurred vision finally settled on the old man kneeling next to him.

Thorko.

"Save your energy," Thorko murmured. "This should offer you some relief."

He watched as Thorko dipped his fingers into a bowl filled with green sludge. The old man then applied the ointment onto his open wound. Instantly, Laszlo let out a hiss as his side burned like fire. But a moment later, the pain subsided, and his injured abdomen felt remarkably better.

"It will heal," Thorko observed simply. "Others things, however, are not as easy to fix."

Laszlo locked eyes with Thorko. "Where's Lily? What happened to her?"

"She remains at Cachtice Castle," Thorko replied. He lifted a withered finger up toward Laszlo's face. "Unfortunately, you must stay here."

Laszlo looked around. A large wooden door with a small barred window was the room's only opening to the outside world. He appeared to be imprisoned within one of the dungeon's cellars. As Laszlo shifted his body, a chorus of jangling chains greeted his ears. Both his arms and legs were bound. Immediately, he worried that Lily was being kept in similar conditions.

"Lily's not held captive," Thorko stated, reading Laszlo's thoughts. "She remains at Cachtice. Willingly. She's a guest of the castle. No harm will be brought to her—at least, no harm that she does not agree to. The Countess is taking care of Lily. You need not trouble your mind."

Laszlo's eyes darkened. "I am well aware of my mother's hospitality toward her guests, as you may call them."

Thorko shook his head. "Lily is not like the others. Surely, you must realize this."

Laszlo didn't answer. Lily was indeed special in more ways than he could name. But he didn't dare give Thorko any more information than the old man already knew.

"Yes, I know about Lily's past and her miraculous youth." Again, Thorko saw straight into Laszlo's head. "I also know that is something you cannot return to her. No matter how much you may want to help. Only I can truly bring Lily what she seeks." Before Laszlo could protest, Thorko added, "And I can bring you what you desire, Laszlo. With my help, you and Lily can be together. Forever."

Laszlo's eyes grew wide with intrigue, but then quickly clouded over. "You have been in the services of the Bathory family for a great deal of time, Thorko. And you have undoubtedly extended the Countess's youth, with methods too atrocious to name." Laszlo did not bother to hide the bite in his tone. "But no one in the Bathory or Nadasdy lineages have ever been immortal. Even with my delayed aging, I will also reach death like the others before me."

Thorko smiled knowingly. "The Nadasdy house is weak. But luckily, it is not Ferenc's blood that courses through you."

"I'm not sure how that makes me fortunate. My blood is even weaker due to my commoner father. My mother's Bathory side is what preserves me."

"No," Thorko said. "It is not your mother's blood, and it certainly isn't that of any peasant man that grants you this power—it is mine."

Thorko looked to the boy for a reaction, but Laszlo remained silent, his eyes searching the old man's expression for signs of dishonesty. But in Thorko's face all he saw staring back was his own features. Laszlo then knew the claim to be true.

"It can't be." Laszlo's voice held little conviction. "You can't be my father."

"It was a long time ago," Thorko explained. "Before the Countess was to marry Ferenc. The pregnancy was blamed on a man of little importance. I don't remember his name. But Ferenc had him killed immediately. As you know, your illegitimate status was hidden, and Ferenc raised you as his own son."

Laszlo felt a heaviness grow across his chest. The pressure made it hard to breathe, and he took a large gulp of air.

"Calm down," Thorko said. His voice was anything but soothing.

"Surely, this news cannot be too upsetting. This means your father was not actually killed by your stepfather, and instead exists right before you. Also, I do not believe this can be too surprising. Search your feelings, and I think you'll find that you have known longer than this moment."

It was possible that Laszlo could have known the truth all this time. But he felt in no hurry to journey through any emotions about the matter.

"This changes nothing," Laszlo muttered.

"Oh, I believe it changes a great deal," Thorko insisted. "Now you know why you are the way you are. And now you know why Lily is instrumental to our future. Her blood is unlike any other. What would normally have taken the lives of many young girls can be achieved through a drop of her blood. It can sustain us. And not just you, me, and Countess Bathory–but Lily as well."

Laszlo opened his mouth to speak, but then closed it. Once again, he didn't need to say anything for Thorko to know his thoughts.

"Lily does not need to die, Laszlo. No one does."

But he had never trusted Thorko. And even if the old man was truly his father, Laszlo didn't believe him now.

Chapter Twelve

Foundling Pairs

Chelsea Manor was quiet in the mornings. Even with occasional locomotives running along the Tenth Avenue tracks, and distilleries churning to life as workers arrived for their shifts, the neighborhood still emanated a calm not found in the lower sections of Manhattan. One morning, alone on the hill where Chelsea Manor stood, the lanky silhouette of Jervis McEntee could be spotted. With a brush suspended between his fingers, the young man thoughtfully paused, looking down at the canvas propped upon an easel. He had worked hard to find a place on Chelsea Manor's hill that was flat enough to balance the contraption, and yet still provided a good view of the General Theological Seminary across the road.

Jervis studied the building with one eye squinted, and then brought his brush to the canvas, applying delicate strokes. The morning sun was particularly flattering against the stained glass windows and red brick of the seminary, and he wanted to expose the distinct characteristics. When his gaze returned to the building, a voice sounded behind him.

"Jervis!"

He turned to see Catharine walking out the backdoor of Chelsea Manor. Her confident, long strides reached him in a matter of moments.

"Catharine," Jervis said, unable to suppress the smile stretching across his face. "I wasn't expecting to see you. Were you looking for me?"

"I was looking for Maggie," Catharine corrected flatly. "She didn't return home yesterday, and the servants sent word that she'd spent the night at Chelsea Manor. However, it appears she has already taken off for the day."

He nodded. "Yes, I saw her briefly when I arrived. She was in the Great Room. She must have left soon after. To where, I do not know."

A meaningful look crossed Catharine's face, indicating to Jervis that she knew the whereabouts of her younger sister.

"So what are you doing out here, Jervis?" Catharine asked, changing the topic. Her tone was more pleasant, but he detected that she was asking merely as a courtesy. Even with Catharine's thoughts seeming elsewhere, Jervis still thought he'd indulge her.

"Mr. Moore has requested paintings of the Chelsea neighborhood." Jervis gestured with his brush toward the easel. "I thought I'd start with the General Theological Seminary."

"That sounds lovely," Catharine replied with a smile, but it quickly vanished from her face as she looked past Jervis.

Turning the same direction, Jervis followed her line of sight. He spotted a man crossing the avenue.

"Who's that?" he asked.

When he looked back to Catharine, she was no longer standing nearby. Instead she had swiftly marched down the hill to where the steps led out to the street.

Jervis glanced back toward the stranger on the road. A moment later, he recognized the young man.

It was Henry Livingston.

Henry must have assumed the occupants of Chelsea Manor were not outside as he passed. For when Catharine glided out from the hill's steps, quickly intruding upon his path, Henry stuttered in his walking.

118

"Catharine," he huffed. His face flushed slightly. "I was not expecting to see you."

"And I was not expecting to see you without my sister," Catharine commented. When Henry gave her a puzzled expression, she added, "Maggie spent the night at Chelsea Manor but has already left. I imagine she has gone to Poppel. But you are not with her, clearly."

"I...I had a change of heart," Henry said. "About my involvement in Poppel. I think it would be best, for everyone, if I were to keep my distance."

"Oh," she said, somewhat taken aback. "Does Maggie know about this *change of heart*?"

Catharine hadn't intended her tone to be biting, but she could tell from Henry's hesitation that it had been. She wasn't sure why she took such a harsh attitude with him. He hadn't really done anything to her. Considering what they'd been through in Poppel, she should have felt a stronger connection to him than others in her life. And, perhaps, that was precisely the reason for her hostility.

"No, I haven't talked Maggie about it," Henry said. Glancing away, his eyes eventually settled on the seminary. "She wouldn't understand."

Henry's explanation was simple, but she sensed the deeper meaning attached.

"No," Catharine agreed. Her voice softened. "No, I don't imagine Maggie would. She can be a bit single-minded at times. It's one of her few faults."

"And also, perhaps, her greatest strength," Henry replied earnestly.

His genuineness surprised Catharine, and she found herself unable to respond.

Momentarily, Henry looked down at the ground, as if carefully planning his next words.

"Please do not tell Maggie that you saw me." Henry glanced back up, staring right into Catharine's eyes. "I know she wants my help, but I fear that I will only bring additional trouble."

"How so?" she asked.

He sighed, clearly hoping that Catharine wouldn't push the issue further. He seemed in no hurry to explain himself. Forcing a small smile, Henry replied with raised eyebrows, "Don't I always?"

Catharine was going to call out Henry's inability to give a direct answer, but the words were lost in her throat as he stepped toward her.

"I need to go away for a while." Henry's voice was quiet and tainted with notes of regret. "It seems that my presence continues to be a distraction." Then unexpectedly, Henry took Catharine's hand into his own. "I'm…I'm not a bad person, Catharine. I'm not."

She couldn't tell if Henry was trying to convince her of that, or rather, trying to convince himself. But she remained silent as he continued.

"I promise to return if needed. I will not be far."

There was an emotion buried in Henry's eyes that Catharine could not quite name. It was a conflict of some kind, as though an internal battle raged behind his stoic exterior.

"Where will you be?" Catharine finally managed to ask.

But Henry didn't respond. Instead his eyes glanced to hers, sadly. In a final gesture, he brought her hand up to his mouth, grazing her knuckles lightly against his lips. Then he walked away.

For a few moments, Catharine stood alone on the sidewalk after Henry's departure, fighting the desire to defiantly wipe the back of her hand against her blouse as though it would erase Henry's lingering presence. But she didn't.

It had little to do with her feelings regarding the encounter. For the more Catharine considered Henry's parting gesture, the more she believed it was less about affection. It was as though Henry had been asking for help. But help with what, she couldn't even begin to guess.

It had been three years, but unsurprisingly, none of the Foundlings looked different than they had Christmas Eve 1854. As Maggie glanced around the backroom of Kleren–Poppel's clothing shop–she could almost convince herself that she was simply in a memory.

120

Lloyd and Wendell had greeted her with unexpected hugs while Harriet, with her dark hair and almond-shaped eyes, hesitantly patted Maggie's shoulder, as though she wasn't quite sure what to make of her reappearance.

"Gerhard's sleeping, so we won't be bothered here," Wendell said.

Unfamiliar with the name, Maggie asked, "Gerhard?"

"Oh, I'm referring to Hostrupp. Gerhard's his first name," Wendell explained and then adding with a smidge of pride, "I'm the only Foundling who calls him Gerhard. I've been taking over a lot of the duties here at Kleren. Since I'm able to run the place alone, Hostrupp's not around as often."

"Good for you," Maggie said, feeling genuinely happy for Wendell. She knew the position had been his dream. However, she couldn't help but feel disappointed that she wouldn't see the unusually energetic older man who ran Kleren. Still, it would be best if Hostrupp, Houten, and Madame Welles weren't included for the time being. It would only complicate matters.

"Where's Nellie?" Maggie asked, noticing the absence of the beautiful blonde Foundling.

Harriet let out a guttural noise as though clearing her throat. But she didn't say anything.

"Nellie moved back to Furnace Brook," Lloyd explained. He pushed his round eyeglasses further back on his tiny nose. Then glancing over at Harriet, he added quietly, "With Albers."

The additional information wasn't needed. Maggie knew that if Nellie had gone back to Furnace Brook, a village on the Hudson River that provided Poppel with food and supplies, it would have been for her former love, Albers. Love sounded like the most justifiable reason for giving up the extended time offered in Poppel. But by the agitated look on Harriet's face, some Foundlings seemed to disagree.

"You're probably wondering why I'm here," Maggie finally said.

"Violet's missing, Laszlo's gone, and we aren't allowed to leave Poppel," Harriet said bluntly. "It's really not too big of a mystery that you've returned."

121

"Although creeping in the alleyways of Myra Lane was a bit of a surprise." Lloyd pushed his eyeglasses up his nose again. "I'll admit that you scared me quite thoroughly when you grabbed my arm."

Maggie winced. "Sorry, Lloyd. I had been waiting there for an hour until I spotted a Foundling I recognized. So I may have been a little overly excited."

"Excited?" Lloyd rubbed his arm sorely. "I'm going to have a bruise from your excitement." But Lloyd's teasing smile gave him away.

"Did you come with a plan?" Wendell asked. "As Harriet already mentioned, we aren't allowed leave Poppel until the missing Foundlings are found. So I'm not sure how much assistance we can offer."

Maggie nodded. "I'm aware. Augustus has actually recruited me to help get to the bottom of the disappearing Foundlings. I was working with Henry Livingston and Elmer…"

She trailed off as strange expressions crossed the Foundlings faces. She realized that hearing Elmer's name would still be upsetting to them.

"Where's Henry now?" Harriet asked.

"I, uh, I don't know," Maggie admitted. "I haven't seen him since the night Elmer was killed."

The Foundlings exchanged knowing looks. This time it did not seem like sadness brought on by the mention of Elmer. There was something else not being said.

"Is there something you wanted to share with me?" Maggie asked.

Lloyd spoke up first. "We heard some rather peculiar things from Edwin, who used to be Elmer's Foundling pair…"

"Foundling pair?" Maggie repeated.

"Oh, all Foundlings are paired with another Foundling," Lloyd replied. "When we're on duty, Foundlings travel through the city in twos. Didn't you know that?"

Maggie shook her head.

"My pairing used to be Milton," Harriet said. "So I would travel the tunnels with him before, you know, he disappeared. He was the second Foundling taken, right after Bickley."

"So Edwin was Elmer's pairing. And they were rather close," Wendell said. "And Elmer confided in him some interesting information."

"What did he say?" Maggie asked hesitantly. She already had a feeling that it wouldn't be good news.

"Elmer apparently saw Henry..." Wendell started to say but he couldn't finish the sentence.

"Henry did something rather questionable," Lloyd supplied.

"What?" Maggie asked. Her voice grew louder in frustration. "What did Elmer see Henry do?"

Before Lloyd could respond, Harriet blurted, "Henry helped Krampus capture Violet."

A thick silence fell over the room. Maggie could hear her own throat gulping as though it was now difficult to swallow.

Seeing the ghostly expression on Maggie's face, Lloyd added gently, "That's not *exactly* what Elmer said happened." He cleared his throat. "Apparently, when everyone had been exploring the seminary, the night Violet had been taken, Elmer saw Henry with her. They were talking, and Elmer heard Henry suggest to Violet that she should go out into the courtyard to look for you."

Maggie's mouth became even drier. "I wasn't in the courtyard." Her voice was barely a whisper.

Harriet sighed. "We had figured as much."

Henry's betrayal was bad enough, but Maggie could not process the thought of him using her friendship with Violet in such a way.

"Elmer started to wonder if Henry could be trusted. His plan was to use Henry to lead him to Krampus and the missing Foundlings. As we all know that didn't work out so well."

Maggie felt ill. She remembered how Elmer seemed rather adamant that he should be paired with Henry on that fateful night. Although she hadn't given it much thought at the time, everything now seemed pretty clear.

However, Maggie still had trouble believing that Henry was somehow working with Krampus. Then she thought about what Francis had told her in the seminary, and how he'd watched Henry return that night blooded yet unharmed. With Henry not around to justify his actions, there was only a single conclusion that could be drawn.

Elmer had been right.

Henry Livingston could no longer be trusted.

When Maggie went to the Krog and found it empty, it didn't take long to figure out where Augustus had retreated. After slipping behind the maroon curtains in the banquet hall, she quietly walked through the hidden door that led to the Boeken Kamer, the location of Poppel's books and records.

Maggie saw Augustus right away, but he didn't seem to notice her. With his hands braced on the table in front of him, his eyes were fastened on an open book. Hypnotically, he turned the pages with a purposeful yet gentle touch. Maggie watched for a few moments, studying the young man's profile. His pale skin was dusted in freckles, causing him to maintain a boyish quality. Yet with hunched shoulders, his back stood perfectly erect, a posture exposing a manner older than his years–even older than his Poppel years.

Eventually, Augustus sensed his visitor standing in the doorway, and he slowly turned to look at Maggie. His face remained expressionless, but he couldn't hide the surprise in his eyes. Maggie approached the table and picked up a book. She carefully turned the pages, one after another, as she searched the space in between the paper for something that wasn't meant to be there. Although she continued to scan the inside of the book in silence, Augustus seemed to understand her actions. With a content sigh and a somewhat concealed smile, he eventually turned his attention back to his own book.

For once, Maggie and Augustus seemed in agreement. They both knew it'd be best to not ruin such an odd occurrence with words.

Chapter Thirteen

The Curious Bickley

While the summer reached its burning height at the end of July, Maggie spent her days and occasional evenings below the heated streets of New York City. By the dim glow of candlelight, Maggie shared a table with Augustus in the Boeken Kamer, huddled over mounds of books, searching for the yellowed pages that once belonged to Stephanus Van Cortlandt.

The air in the Boeken Kamer was pleasantly cool, but Augustus still kept a handkerchief close at hand, periodically dabbing his freckled face. Although the pair rarely exchanged words, Maggie would sometimes peer over at Augustus. It didn't take long for Maggie to become familiar with her acquaintance's habits.

"Is something on your mind?" Maggie asked one afternoon.

He seemed confused by the question before mumbling, "Why do you ask?"

Suppressing a grin, Maggie looked up from the book she had been scanning. "Because you haven't turned the page for over a minute."

In response to Maggie's blunt observation, Augustus uncomfortably cleared his throat. "I guess I have a few things on my mind."

"Anything you'd like to tell me?" Maggie pressed.

She had learned that Augustus needed to be nudged in order for him to share his thoughts. When it came to the other people in her life, especially family members, Maggie rarely had to deal with

125

such introverted traits. So it was almost refreshing.

"It's nothing particularly interesting," Augustus admitted after a few long moments of silence. "I'm just reviewing all we know so far."

"So you aren't thinking about much then," Maggie said. She lightly prodded Augustus with her elbow.

Maggie wasn't usually playful with him, but the tedious work they had been doing in the Boeken Kamer sometimes called for such an approach. Even Maggie couldn't help but gain satisfaction from the occasional smile she forced from her taciturn partner.

"No, it's not much then," he agreed with a crooked grin. He set the book he was holding down on the crowded table. "We haven't come across any new pieces of Stephanus's journal for days. I'm beginning to wonder if maybe we've already found all the hidden pages, and now we're just wasting time."

Maggie shook her head. "That can't be all of them. We're missing too many. These pages are the best chance we have at learning about Krampus and why it's taking the Foundlings. We have to keep searching."

Augustus glanced over at Maggie briefly before looking back at the table. He murmured something, but even sitting a few feet away, she couldn't make out the words.

"What did you say?"

"Maybe there are other ways," Augustus stated carefully. "Other ways to find out more about Krampus."

"How?"

Augustus continued to avert his eyes. "Henry Livingston. He clearly knows more about that creature."

Maggie stiffened at the mention of Henry. "You know I haven't seen him since the night Elmer died."

"You and Henry used to be close..." Augustus started to say but Maggie cut him off.

"I barely know him. I didn't meet Henry until that Christmas Eve we snuck into Poppel. And prior to this summer, I hadn't seen him once in the past three years."

Augustus's eyes widened with surprise. "Really? I always assumed you had been acquainted for years. You two seemed to share a strong bond."

Maggie shook her head, struggling to find the words to explain how Henry had showed up at Chelsea Manor one Christmas Eve, insisting that his grandfather, Major Henry Livingston, and not Clement Clarke Moore, was the true author of the poem, *'Twas The Night Before Christmas.*

"Henry was just a strange young man who broke into Chelsea Manor on Christmas Eve. We both happened to watch Wendell disappear down the ash pit in the fireplace. So we followed him. You already know about the rest of that night."

Augustus simply nodded, seeming to have no additional thoughts on the matter. His silence left Maggie alone with her memories of that fateful Christmas Eve. As her mind remembered spying Wendell in the Great Room of Chelsea Manor, and then watching him vanish down the ash pit in his burgundy jacket and top hat, she realized something about that evening.

Wendell had been alone. Or at least, she had always believed he had been alone.

"Augustus." Maggie spoke quietly, but he immediately snapped his attention back to her. "Who was paired with Wendell?"

Augustus raised his eyebrows, clearly confused by her question.

"Foundlings are always paired together, right? Who was Wendell paired with that Christmas Eve? Do you remember?"

Augustus opened his mouth and then closed it again. He scrunched his brow, as though deep in thought. Just as Maggie was about to give up on receiving an answer, his eyes popped open.

"Bickley. Wendell was always paired with Bickley."

Maggie gulped. "Bickley," she repeated. She recalled hearing the name before. "Wasn't Bickley the first Foundling taken by Krampus?"

Augustus stared at Maggie, pondering her question, until his expression intensified. "Yes, he was. He most certainly was."

Maggie had been staring at the fireplace in the seminary's refectory for the past half hour. She now knew every intricate detail of the mantel, including its inscription *Manners Makyth Man*. She had asked Grandfather Clement about the saying weeks ago, after Henry had pointed it out.

Startled, Grandfather Clement had glanced up from the book he was reading. It was uncommon for his granddaughter to address him directly–even stranger for her to approach him in Chelsea Manor's library in the early evening. Grandfather Clement hadn't known that Maggie was biding time until she snuck over to the seminary with Louis. And Maggie hadn't known that it'd be Elmer's last night alive.

"I beg your pardon," Grandfather Clement answered, seeming to not quite understand the question.

"Francis told me about the inscription," Maggie lied. She didn't want to reveal that she had been in the refectory. "I was curious as to its meaning."

Grandfather Clement cleared his throat, annoyance evident on his face. He answered rigidly, "The refectory is a gentlemen's dining area. And manners are of the utmost importance to any gentlemen. It's rather simple."

Maggie hadn't replied to grandfather, choosing instead to appreciate the rare and arguably pleasant exchange. But as Maggie now stood in the seminary's refectory, reliving the short interaction in her head, she felt herself responding to Grandfather Clement.

"It's a rather stupid saying," Maggie grumbled out loud.

"What's that you say?" A familiar head of blond hair popped out from the ash pit.

"Wendell, you made it." Maggie let out a relieved sigh. "I wasn't sure you had received my message."

Skillfully, Wendell pulled his body out of the fireplace in one fluid motion. "Yes, I was quite surprised to receive your sugarplum. I didn't even realize you had any."

"Augustus had given me a few."

"Ah, well, I'm sorry I didn't respond," Wendell said. Then he solemnly added, "Since we found out that the Garrisons had poisoned your grandmother, Catharine, and aunt, Margaret, decades ago using arsenic dusted sugarplums, Madame Welles had forbidden Foundlings from sending sugarplums to people outside of Poppel."

Maggie wanted to point out that such a rule seemed futile since Madame Welles hadn't instructed her and her family members not to eat any sugarplums that came their way. However, she instead focused on the reason she had called Wendell to the refectory.

"Was Bickley with you?" Maggie blurted.

Wendell raised his eyebrows. "No, Maggie. Bickley's been missing for months…"

"Not tonight," she interrupted with a wave of her hand. "Was Bickley there when Henry and I caught you in the Great Room on Christmas Eve?"

Wendell seemed unsure about the question, but he finally replied with a timid nod.

"Where was he then? Why didn't we see him?"

Wendell cleared his throat, anxiously. "Bickley heard you and Henry outside of the Great Room before I did, so he dashed toward the fireplace. He disappeared down the ash pit just as the two of you burst through the doors. Bickley assumed I would follow, but I was so startled that I froze in place. And that's when you saw me."

"Then you did disappear through the ash pit moments later. Did you see Bickley down there?"

Wendell shook his head. "I didn't see Bickley again until the end of the night, after the Garrisons were gone."

"But you must have eventually discussed his whereabouts?" Maggie asked. Seeing Wendell's hesitation, she added, "This is important, Wendell. Bickley was the first Foundling to be taken by Krampus. I know it might seem insignificant now, but I really need to know what happened that Christmas Eve. If you remember Bickley saying anything to you about it, please tell me."

Wendell's whole face seemed to perk up. "Bickley and I have been paired for years. Of course, we discussed what happened that night.

Foundling pairs are important bonds. Bickley had been waiting in the ash pit for me, but I must have run right past him, on my way to the sleigh tunnels. Before he could follow, he heard the two of you trying to open the ash pit. So he hid in the shadows until you and Henry also vanished into the tunnels."

A cold shiver trickled down Maggie's spine. "Bickley had been in the ash pit with us?"

Wendell nodded, but he didn't seem to carry the unease Maggie felt with the revelation of unknowingly being watched three years ago.

"Soon he made his way back to Poppel, but all the chaos happened with the rumor of the missing Sister Wheel. Then Ward hid you in the backroom of Snop. A little bit later, Harriet had gone to the Sleigh Pit to look for her Foundling pair, Milton, and that's when she spotted Bickley leaving Poppel on a sleigh. It was right before she ran into Lloyd who was about to send sugarplums to Catharine, Clemmie, and Louis at Chelsea Manor."

As Wendell spoke, memories of that Christmas Eve vividly returned to Maggie. Before getting lost in all the details of that unforgettable night, she pressed Wendell further. "Leaving Poppel? Where was Bickley going?"

Wendell looked down at his feet.

"You did ask him," Maggie said matter-of-factly. "I know that you did."

Wendell nodded. "Yes, I asked him much later. But I did ask him. He said he was returning to Chelsea Manor."

"Why would he do that?" Maggie still felt anxious about how Bickley had spied on her and Henry. It was unnerving that she didn't remember seeing the Foundling.

"Bickley was concerned about how we left Chelsea Manor. He was worried the ash pit had been kept open, or that there were other signs of our presence. Bickley's one of the oldest Foundlings, and he's always been in charge of Chelsea Manor. So he felt strongly about seeing that everything was as it should be. By the time he got there, Catharine, Clemmie, and Louis had just received their sugarplums. Once again, he had to hide in the ash pit and wait for them to leave."

"And then what?"

Wendell shrugged. "Bickley realized that things in Poppel were a mess, and he stayed away until everything was over. There's not much more to it. I don't see how any of that has to do with why Bickley was the first Foundling taken by Krampus."

Maggie wasn't completely sure either. But she still felt wary of Bickley.

"Where did Krampus abduct Bickley?" Maggie asked. She noticed that Wendell seemed to wince at the question. "You were with him, weren't you?"

Wendell looked down at his feet in dejection. "No, I wasn't with him that night. He was all alone."

"Alone? But I thought you were Foundling pairs."

Wendell frowned. "We were. But for the past couple of years, Bickley had started to become more distant. He would go off on his own, usually to the Chelsea neighborhood. Sometimes secretly visiting the Manor. At least that's what he told me. He was going to Chelsea Manor the night he disappeared."

Maggie muffled a gasp. "Are you sure?"

Wendell's eyes widened. "Bickley wasn't often forthright with information. But if I asked him something directly, he would tell me the truth. The night Krampus took him he had been going to Chelsea Manor. I know this to be true. We weren't best friends. We were Foundling pairs. That demanded honesty."

Maggie could see the resoluteness on Wendell's face before she finally asked, "Did Bickley mention why he was going to Chelsea Manor?"

Wendell shook his head. "Unfinished business. That's all he said. He had unfinished business at Chelsea Manor."

Maggie tried not to obsess over what Wendell had told her in the refectory. But it was hard to focus on other things as the question of what unfinished business Bickley had at Chelsea Manor loomed over her. However, she needed to push her curiosity aside. Similarly to Bickley, Maggie had unfinished business at the seminary. Meeting with Wendell had only been her first task of the night.

The evening air was warm as Maggie stepped into the seminary's courtyard. She hadn't ventured out there since Violet had been taken. The fear that Krampus could be lurking among its trees had kept her away. Over the past few days, however, the circumstances surrounding the abducted Foundlings had become more complicated. Between Stephanus's journal, Laszlo's disappearance, and Bickley's clandestine work, Krampus now seemed to be just another piece in a rather deep and mysterious plot.

Although the August night was humid, Maggie felt chilled while walking across the courtyard. She kept her eyes to the trees as her feet crunched along the dry grass. She had only made it a dozen feet before something in the corner of her vision moved. Immediately, Maggie turned and captured a pair of yellow eyes piercing her own.

Krampus.

Maggie had mentally prepared for the possibility of such an encounter, but she still found her breath catching in her throat at the sight of the creature. Its bony face, horned head, and gray hairy body was as she had remembered. Old, rusty bells hung over its haggard and matted chest, but they were silent as the creature's body crouched low on the branch.

While Maggie debated whether to remain standing still or run, she watched as Krampus darted to another branch. For such a large beast, Krampus glided from branch to branch with surprising grace. She could barely tell which direction it was going. When it finally stopped on a nearby tree, she expected it to launch at her. Maggie braced her body in preparation, but instead of attacking, Krampus scurried farther up the tree, and dashed away, disappearing into the night.

Feeling exposed in the vacant courtyard, Maggie saw her chance to run back to the seminary. Twisting around, she nearly collided with the form of someone she knew only too well.

"Henry!" she gasped. However, when her eyes focused on the young man, she barely recognized the person standing before her.

Henry's typically handsome face looked gaunt and discolored as though he had not adequately slept and eaten for weeks. His bright blue eyes were now dark and gray. As he stood in front of Maggie, with his arms outstretched to impede her path, his dirty hands trembled. An anxious energy stirred between their bodies, and she felt the urge to get away.

"Maggie," Henry said quietly. Even his raspy voice sounded unfamiliar. "What are you doing here?"

Had Maggie been able to regain her composure, she would have laughed at Henry's question, for he was the one needing to explain his whereabouts–not her. But she still managed to give Henry a halfhearted sneer.

"I'm searching for the missing Foundlings, of course." Maggie wanted to maintain a cold exterior toward Henry, but as she studied his nervous face, she spotted a look of concern within his expression. "Where have you been?" Maggie's voice quivered as she spoke.

Henry relaxed his arms, allowing them to drop by his sides.

"You need to go home," he instructed.

Maggie felt her defenses starting to return. "I'm not going anywhere until you tell me why."

"I can't explain," he replied. "But you need to leave. Krampus will get you."

Maggie studied Henry for a moment before slowly asking, "How long have you been working for it?"

"I'm not its servant," he snapped.

"You led Violet to it. You helped it murder Elmer," Maggie stated steadily, trying to suppress the emotion rising in her throat.

"Elmer fought back. That's why he died," Henry said adamantly.

Horrified by such a dismissive excuse, Maggie snapped, "How long have you been helping it? What does it want?" Maggie paused before adding, "What is it that *you* want?"

A sudden rattling from within in the trees briefly broke their eye contact, which had been constant up until that moment.

"You need to leave, Maggie," Henry hissed. "Please, just go."

Ignoring Henry's pleas, Maggie continued, "It has control over you. I can see it. You're not the same person. What's happening?"

"This no longer concerns you!" Henry's voice cracked in frustration. "Poppel, Foundlings, and the Sister Wheels are no longer your concern. You shouldn't even be involved!"

The ominous noises behind Maggie continued to grow louder, but before she could turn around and confront the disturbance, Henry reached his shaky arms out and gripped Maggie's face. She didn't realize what was happening until he pressed his lips roughly against her own mouth. Although she had hoped to experience such a kiss for the past three years, it was not what she had expected. His mouth was dry, and his chapped lips tasted bitter.

Also, Henry's intentions were quite clear. He was trying to control her.

When Henry pulled back from Maggie, she knew her expression showed disgust, for it was reflected in his own face.

"I'm so sorry," he whispered. He released Maggie's face from his uncomfortable grasp.

With a look of both sadness and regret, Henry dashed past Maggie. She could hear his frantic footsteps disappear down the empty road and into the night.

Chapter Fourteen

Istvan Magyari

A burning sting ran through Lily's arm as a sturdy needle pierced her flesh. However, it didn't hurt with the same intensity that greeted her the first time. After weeks of having the needle routinely stuck into her arms and legs, the pain was starting to dull. Instead Lily was left with a steady soreness resonating across her skin.

A rosy red streak slowly dripped down her arm, eventually spilling over into a crystal bowl. Initially, the sight of that much blood leaving her body caused Lily to panic. She imagined a dark abyss spreading throughout her insides, emptying her of all life. However, Thorko and the Countess insisted that every individual had more blood than was imaginable, and it even regenerated. But Lily didn't like being reminded how they knew so much about the body's relationship with blood.

"Very good, very good," Thorko muttered while gripping the bowl with both hands. He nodded at Darvulia. The woman walked over and cleaned Lily's arm with a wet cloth before bandaging the small wound. Then she took the bowl from Thorko and disappeared out of the room.

Lily had not returned to the dungeon since Countess Bathory and Darvulia caught her trying to escape. She was housed in the same tower as before, but now she felt particularly watched even when no one else was in sight. A few times a week, Lily was summoned to a chamber on the ground floor, located on the far end of the castle. The room had a vaulted ceiling and stained glass windows, which caught the sun throughout most of the day, sending cascading colors across the wooden walls. Some moments when the chamber was perfectly still, Lily swore she heard the faint sound of a flowing stream.

Of course, Lily was not brought to the chamber to enjoy its serenity. Obediently, she would take a seat on the maroon-cushioned chair that was situated in the middle of the room. The first few occasions, Countess Bathory had been present as Darvulia pricked Lily's skin with a needle. Once the bowl was nearly full, Thorko would take it out of the room, and then with a satisfied smile, Countess Bathory would follow, leaving Lily with a severe-looking Darvulia.

Recently, Elizabeth Bathory had stopped coming to the chamber. In fact, Lily hadn't seen the Countess in over a week. Also, Thorko now sent Darvulia off with the bowl while he stayed behind, never saying much but not remaining silent either.

"Very nice," Thorko continued to mumble. He organized the stained needle on a tray of utensils. "Very well done."

"Where does it...?" Lily's voice cracked and she cleared her throat. "Where is my blo... where is it taken?"

Thorko turned to Lily with an expression impossible to read. "I've told you. Your blood is taken away where it will be added to other elements in order to form the substance needed for the special elixir. Once everything's ready, you'll be given the tonic in addition to the Countess."

"How much longer until it's ready?"

"One cannot predict such things, for these matters take time," Thorko said. "Unlike the silly concoctions Laszlo prepared for you, my tonics are complex but effective. Therefore, they take an unspecified amount of time."

Lily winced at the mention of Laszlo. She had learned from Darvulia, and later confirmed by the Countess, that on the night they had attempted to escape Cachtice, he had fought Ficzko. Fearing for his life, the small man had pulled out a knife and stabbed Laszlo. Hours later, Bathory's eldest child had succumbed to his injuries. He had been buried before Lily even learned about his death.

Initially, Lily doubted the claim. But Darvulia produced Laszlo's torn and blood-soaked shirt. And with the Countess corroborating the tale, Lily felt no choice but to trust it. Although Countess Bathory had committed terrible acts over the years, Lily could not see the woman lying about her son's death. There seemed no point in such dishonesty.

Also, Lily believed that if Laszlo were still alive, he would have found her again. For the past year, he had been an impossible presence to shake, and he had been determined to take her away from Cachtice Castle. It may have been an opinion partly conceived by arrogance, but Lily truly thought that if Laszlo was alive, she would know by now.

Laszlo was dead. It was hard to believe differently. The reality of his death left Lily feeling more hurt than the countless cuts that had been made across her body in order to access her valuable blood. When Lily thought about Laszlo dying while attempting to save her from Cachtice Castle, unwelcome moisture formed in the corners of her eyes.

Never missing a detail, Thorko quickly observed, "Do not waste your tears on him. Laszlo was not a well man. Clearly, you saw how obsessed he was with you. I'm afraid his mental instability went beyond amorous fixations. He knew how Cachtice Castle would benefit you, yet he tried to make you leave. Laszlo wanted you under his control. Without provocation, he tried to kill Ficzko that fateful night, and Ficzko did what he could to protect himself. Lily, do not cry for Laszlo. Instead be relieved that he no longer suffers within the prison of his mind." Thorko put a comforting hand on Lily's shoulder. "Be relieved he does not suffer at all."

Laszlo wanted to scream out in pain, but his lungs no longer moved with ease. A constant pressure now resided along his chest, and he couldn't decipher whether his emotions were the culprit. Or perhaps, he truly was dying.

Whack.

Feeling like his cheek had been hit with a stone, Laszlo collapsed to the ground. Although dazed from the collision, Laszlo still recognized the voice hovering above him.

"You are getting weaker," Ficzko said dully. "What happened to your mystical youth that had served you so well these many years?"

Laszlo wasn't sure how long Ficzko had been in the cellar. It wasn't the first time the small man had struck him during his imprisonment, but the moments were starting to run together. Laszlo no longer could tell when specific incidents began or ended. He didn't even know how long he'd been in the dungeon. He hadn't seen Thorko for quite some time. And the Countess had never paid him a visit.

Unfortunately, it seemed Ficzko had been charged with his care.

Whack.

Ficzko's fist struck Laszlo again, but this time he took an open palm and pressed it against Laszlo's cheek, pushing his head into the cellar's hard floor.

"You are nothing but a peasant boy dressed in royal garb," Ficzko grumbled with a hand still weighing down Laszlo's head until his vision blurred. "The girl you so desperately love will never return your feelings. Lily has already forgotten you. It made no difference to her whether you lived or died. You are nothing more than a meaningless memory to Lily now."

Lily.

Lily was still alive, Laszlo remembered. Ficzko had mentioned it before and Laszlo couldn't help but believe him. The man could have lied and claimed she was dead in order to observe Laszlo's unimaginable pain. Unless, of course, Ficzko thought implying that Lily was alive and indifferent to him was more devastating than thinking she was dead but in love. In many ways, that would have been an accurate conclusion to draw. But Laszlo felt that Lily was indeed alive and what Thorko had said about needing her blood–her living blood–was true.

Laszlo no longer heard Ficzko's voice. For a moment, he wondered if Ficzko had successfully killed him. But feeling the aches of his human form, he hadn't been brought such relief. He didn't open his eyes, but he sensed it was later in the day–perhaps even night. Still, there was no point in getting up. Eventually, his evening meal would be dropped through a slot in the door. And that would be the only indication of the time.

Laszlo allowed his thoughts to drift back to Lily. He imagined Lockenhaus during those autumn months when life had been seemingly perfect. Although Lily had been distressed about aging, she had trusted Laszlo. At times, she had looked at him with such adoration in her eyes that he felt certain he could do anything.

Laszlo envisioned how the sun stroked the lighter strands of Lily's hair, bringing the blond to its surface. He saw the way her cheeks would flush, even in the cool air, and then how Lily's mouth would turn into a knowing smile each time she caught Laszlo's gaze lingering. But just as the image of Lily formed in Laszlo's mind, it started to change. Lily's carefree face was no longer bright with joy. Instead her features twisted, as she seemed to spot something beyond what Laszlo could see.

In his mind, Laszlo turned to locate the object of displeasure. But an ominous shadow darkened his sight. Something large and frightening was approaching him. That's when he heard it.

Bells.

The clanking of rusty bells filled Laszlo's ears, causing him to sit up with alarm. But the moment he opened his eyes, the sounds disappeared. Laszlo once again was alone in the dark cellar. He brought his palms to his bruised cheeks, cupping them gently. The combination of Ficzko's beatings and the imaginary bells had brought on a stinging headache.

However, the silence that had greeted his waking ears soon vanished.

"No, no. I've told you no more," an irritated voice said from somewhere outside Laszlo's prison door. "I will no longer play a role in this wickedness."

"This is the last one," Ficzko hissed. "The very last one."

"How can I believe that? You and the Countess have put me in a compromising situation for decades. The tunnels are lined with the remains. There is no more room."

138

"This wouldn't be an issue if you had just followed the Countess's wishes about burying the others, Istvan."

Istvan Magyari.

Ficzko was speaking to the village's minister. The church was located at the bottom of the hill, not far from Cachtice Castle. As Laszlo looked around at the walls, he realized that he wasn't being imprisoned in the castle–he was in the cellar of the church. When he was a boy, he often had traveled the length of the tunnels that connected the castle with the church. The brown and gray stones of the cellar matched the church's foundation.

"It's evil," Istvan said. "And I cannot be part of it any longer."

"But this will be the end of it," Ficzko insisted. "That's what I'm trying to make you understand. The Countess does not wish to require the..." Ficzko paused momentarily before continuing. "Require the services of any more girls. Lily will be the last one."

Laszlo's throat clenched.

Lily was not as safe as Thorko had led him to believe.

Lily knew someone was watching her.

She was always being watched.

Countess Bathory and Thorko pretended to trust Lily, granting her permission to freely roam the castle grounds alone. But Ficzko, or another assistant, was constantly monitoring her movements. Although it was only on rare occasions when she actually spotted them spying on her, she always felt their eyes. Still, Lily refused to stow herself away in the tower–and especially not on Christmas Eve.

Since coming to Cachtice Castle nearly a month ago, Lily had stopped tracking the days. It wasn't until she took a walk along the castle's hillside that she realized the holiday season had arrived. A thin layer of snow crunched under her feet as she walked down the frozen path that led to the stone church at the bottom of the hill. She had done the walk a few times before. Each occasion she sensed Ficzko trailing her within the trees. Today was no different. The woods bordering her path rustled, even though there was no wind.

Upon nearing the church, Lily started to turn back around. She had never gone past the building. Countess Bathory and her assistants certainly wouldn't appreciate her getting close to the village. But before she could walk back up the hill to the castle, the church's door opened, and a man walked outside.

Judging by his robe, Lily assumed he was the church's minister. He didn't notice Lily at first, but when he finally turned away from the church, he looked at her with alarm. His eyes widened, deepening the wrinkles that weaved across his face. The wisps of hair, circling his head like a crown, matched the snowy ground.

"I'm sorry to have startled you," Lily said. "I was just going for a walk. Your church is beautiful."

The man nervously nodded while his eyes darted toward the woods. A moment later, his gaze returned to Lily. "Yes, it is. Thank you. My name is Istvan Magyari. I'm the minister here. Please come by this evening for the service. Most of the village attends."

Lily furrowed her brow. "There's a service tonight? Is that common?"

"For Christmas Eve? Of course."

Lily opened her mouth and then closed it again, momentarily puzzled by the response. "It's Christmas Eve?"

Istvan stared at the girl with a baffled expression.

"Where are you from that you don't even know it is Christmas?"

Lily stuttered, debating how much to reveal to the minister. Finally, she decided there was no reason to hide her identity or whereabouts.

"I am working at the castle for Countess Bathory. My name is Lily."

Once again, Istvan couldn't conceal the emotions settling his face. After he heard Lily's name, his mouth twisted, and his eyes expanded. He looked eager to slip away. And even though Istvan seemed like he wanted to speak, his eyes darted back toward the woods, and whatever he wanted to say to Lily was quickly lost.

"I should be going now," Istvan said. "Errands to run in the village. It's a busy time."

Noticing that the man was carrying nothing in his hands and wasn't dressed for a walk to the village, Lily sensed he was lying. But Istvan seemed like he no longer wanted to carry on with the conversation.

"I also need to go back to the castle," Lily said. "But I will try to attend the evening service."

"Don't!" Istvan nearly barked, causing Lily to jump. The minister calmed himself a moment later. "I shouldn't have mentioned the Christmas Eve service, for it's really more of an intimate gathering. We don't usually include outsiders. Perhaps another time."

Then with a farewell nod, Istvan disappeared down the trail to the village. He moved at such a rapid pace, Lily was certain there was more than just a handmaiden he was trying to leave behind.

As Lily started walking back toward Cachtice Castle, her eyes were drawn to a barrier of evergreen trees lining the path. A few branches swayed, as though something had been positioned between the trees before swiftly departing.

A vision of yellow eyes lingered in her mind.

Cachtice Castle gave no indication of the holiday. If Istvan hadn't told Lily it was Christmas Eve, she wouldn't have discovered its arrival. She thought back to her time at Poppel with Nicolas and her sisters. Music and decorations always filled the village, and the festive atmosphere was even heightened on Christmas Eve. But when Lily returned to Cachtice, she found it cold and empty.

Lily didn't see a single individual around the castle. She quietly ascended the tower stairs to her chamber where she planned to reside for the remainder of the night. A peaceful snow had started to fall, and Lily tucked herself upon the window seat. The large flakes floated on the other side of the paned glass. Her eyes latched onto a snowflake and followed its wavering movement through the air. As it passed by the window and continued its downward path, Lily's gaze caught something moving in the castle's courtyard below. Even in the dark, she could see a shadow dash across the ground with surprising ability. The shape looked both human and animalistic.

Fascinated, Lily watched the figure leap to one of the lower rooftops surrounding the courtyard.

Soon Lily's curiosity turned into fear as the creature continued along the rooftops, seeking higher vantage points. In very little time the shadow had landed on the roof right below Lily's tower window. And then she lost sight of it.

Slowly, Lily pressed her face to the window. She still couldn't see where the creature had gone. Hesitantly, she unlatched the window and pushed it open. Lily leaned over the ledge, peering into the darkness below. Coldness licked her cheeks and she rapidly blinked, pushing the icy air away from her eyes. Yet she spotted nothing on the rooftop underneath the tower's window. She wondered if she'd simply imagined seeing such a figure. Perhaps the weeks of allowing her blood to be stripped from her body had finally affected her mental state. However, as she started to pull the window closed, a shadow dropped from above, filling the space with darkness as it blocked out the light from the moon. Startled, Lily stumbled back into the room, nearly falling to the floor as she worked to regain her footing.

Lily recognized the yellow eyes staring at her. Not only were they the same ones she had spotted watching from the woods, but they also belonged to a beast she had known for centuries.

Krampus.

Chapter Fifteen

St. Peter's Church

Since Maggie had joined Augustus, searching for pages of Stephanus Van Cortlandt's journal, she started spending nights at Chelsea Manor. This kept her away from her parents and their occasional inquiries. She had grown accustomed to her mornings spent in Chelsea Manor's kitchen with only Grandfather Clement's servants for company. So she was surprised to find two new faces greeting her one morning.

"Maggie!" Clemmie exclaimed. He set down his cup of tea. "So this is where you've been hiding. I was starting to think I only had one sister."

Catharine was standing behind Clemmie, slicing an apple. She looked up briefly at Maggie and then turned back to the servants, Hester and Anne, who were heating some sausages.

"Are you hungry, Miss Margaret?" Anne asked. She went over to a pot and stirred what looked to be porridge. No one went hungry at Chelsea Manor.

Maggie shook her head and then gazed at Clemmie. "Why are you both here?"

"Me? Why, I go back to school in a few weeks, and I was hoping to spend some quality time with my beloved younger sister," Clemmie said in a mocking tone. After receiving Maggie's glare, he added, "I've grown tired of the Astor Library. It's becoming more crowded with each passing day. I've moved my studying to the seminary's library, which is completely empty this time of year. But I'm not sure why Catharine's here." Clemmie looked at Catharine as she took a seat next to him. "Why did you follow me here? Has the artist become too boring?"

Catharine narrowed her eyes Clemmie's direction. "No, it has nothing to do with Jervis. I just wanted to see Maggie." Catharine glanced at her sister. "You haven't been around much. Is everything going well for you?"

Maggie knew that Catharine was asking about her involvement with Poppel, but couldn't specifically mention it with Hester, Anne, and Clemmie present.

"Everything is quite all right," Maggie replied curtly. "I just prefer staying at Chelsea Manor during the summer months, as you know." Maggie joined Catharine and Clemmie at the table.

"No, I didn't know." Catharine studied her sister closely. "Have you still been spending time with Henry Livingston?"

Shrugging, Maggie picked up a roll and tore a piece off its crust. "I haven't seen him in weeks." She hoped to mask the bitterness in her lie.

Catharine arched an eyebrow as Maggie popped the bread in her mouth, trying to avoid eye contact with her older sister. Catharine would spot the anger in her eyes at the mention of Henry. She couldn't easily disguise that.

"Maggie..."

"There's nothing more to say about it," Maggie snapped. Catharine gave her a pressing stare. "Henry and I have no ties to one another. At least not anymore." Maggie stood up from the table and moved toward the back door. "I'm going for a walk."

Catharine watched her younger sister leave the Manor. She debated whether to follow Maggie, but as she stood up, taking a step toward the door, Clemmie's voice pulled her back.

"I can't blame her for not wanting to be around Henry these days. He looks terrible."

Catharine twisted her head and gazed down at her brother. Not looking at Catharine, he casually brought his teacup up to his lips, clearly unaware of his statement's impact.

"You've seen Henry?"

"Why, yes. He's staying at the seminary this summer, is he not?"

"You saw him at the seminary?" Catharine asked.

"Well, no. That's the interesting thing about it..." Clemmie took a large gulp of tea, but then nearly spit out the liquid. "Hot! Still hot!" After slapping the cup down, he fanned the throbbing tongue that dangled from his mouth. "Why do I always do that?"

"Clemmie," Catharine said sternly. She was unsympathetic to her brother's plight. "What were you saying about Henry?"

After smacking his lips until the trifling pain had subsided, Clemmie responded, "I was leaving the seminary a few evenings ago, after studying in the library. As I was walking down the street, I saw someone coming out of St. Peter's Church. It took a moment, but I recognized Henry. He looked quite awful. Thinner. Rather sickly, actually."

Clemmie stood up and grabbed a stack of books off the table. As he cradled the books on one side, he snatched a jacket from the back of his chair and draped it over his other arm.

"Grandfather Clement must have assigned him acolyte duties. That would explain his haggard appearance," he said wistfully. "I remember my acolyte days. Dreadful times."

Then Clemmie headed out the back door as Maggie had done moments earlier, leaving Catharine alone with her thoughts.

Catharine wasn't sure whether Henry could be trusted.

However, she was confident that whatever brought him to St. Peter's Church had nothing to do with Grandfather Clement or liturgy. And perhaps, it had nothing to do with Poppel as well.

"Has something upset you, Maggie?"

Augustus handed her a book as he gazed down from the ladder propped against high shelves. Once again, a day had gone by without any sign of Stephanus's journal, and they were now on their last batch of books to go through before Maggie left Poppel for the evening.

Balancing a couple of books under his arm, Augustus made his way back down the ladder. Maggie had already walked over to their usual table.

"Catharine and Clemmie both visited Chelsea Manor this morning. Catharine clearly came by to check on me. I guess I'm still bothered by it."

"This morning? But you haven't said much these past few days," Augustus remarked. "Did something else happen?"

Silently, Maggie debated whether to mention her encounter with Henry–and the kiss. She had been angry and confused ever since that night. However, she had mentioned it to no one. Although she wouldn't necessarily consider Augustus a friend, she certainty had spent more time with him than anyone else lately.

"Recently, I've been thinking about Henry," Maggie said. "I'm starting to believe that he tried to manipulate me. He knew how much I cared about him. So, he thought I would blindly believe everything he said. I used to think we were close friends, after everything we had been through. I mean, right after we arrived in Poppel we had to go into hiding when the Sister Wheel was reported missing. And even though that turned out to be a rumor…"

"That wasn't a rumor," Augustus said mindlessly. Then realizing he had cut her off, he quickly apologized. "Sorry, I didn't mean to interrupt. Please go on."

"What did you say?"

"You were talking about what you and Henry had been through…"

"No, not that." Maggie waved her hand dismissively. "What did you say about the missing wheel not being a rumor?"

"Oh, well, that actually happened." Augustus scratched his freckled cheek. "When you and Henry were discovered in Poppel, a Foundling took the Sister Wheel, believing that you two were going to steal it."

"How do you know this?"

"Because I'm the one who caught him trying to return the wheel to the horologe," Augustus explained. "Of course, we know now that those particular items were fakes. However, at the time it was a significant ordeal that it had gone missing."

"Which Foundling took it?"

"Milton," Augustus responded. "Not exactly the smartest of the Foundlings."

Maggie rubbed her forehead, trying to process the new information. "Milton? Wasn't he the Foundling who disappeared after Bickley?"

Augustus stared at Maggie as though wanting to see what her mind was thinking. Helplessly, she raised her arms and then dropped them to her sides with a sigh.

"I doubt it's relevant to what's happening now. I just had heard the name Milton before." She traced a finger along the book cover in front of her, shaking her head. "It seems more had occurred that Christmas Eve than I knew–than any of us knew."

Augustus tried meet her eyes, but she wouldn't look at him. Reluctantly, he reached down and placed a hand over the one Maggie had been moving across the book. Her hand stilled at the touch.

"We might never find all the answers." He then took Maggie's hand and used it to open the cover of the book. She finally glanced up, making eye contact with Augustus. He gave a weak smile. "But we have to try to track down at least some of them. Even the uncomfortable ones."

The pink sun had just disappeared behind the horizon of New Jersey, the land sitting on the other side of the Hudson River. In the arriving dusk, Catharine made her way to St. Peter's Church. The church was down the street from the General Theological Seminary. Like many buildings in the neighborhood, the church had been built on Clement Clarke Moore's Chelsea estate. Although the symmetrical church, with its square steeple and clock tower, stood high above the surrounding buildings, St. Peter's was unpretentious in appearance.

Even in the darkening hour, Catharine recognized the church's bright red doors and the various shades of stone in its structure.

Something about the church's aesthetic reminded her of Christmas. Catharine even swore she smelled faint hints of evergreen and cinnamon in the air. Of course, the church prided itself on being founded by the author of *'Twas the Night Before Christmas*. Although Grandfather Clement adamantly protested against it, the Christmas poem was read from the pulpit every holiday season.

Reaching into her skirt's pocket, Catharine pulled out a heavy key that had been snatched from Chelsea Manor earlier in the day. After Clemmie mentioned seeing Henry, she had stopped by the church, but there didn't appear to be anyone around. However, if Henry were using the church as his residence, she'd have better luck in the evening.

With the click of the lock, Catharine pushed open one of the church's red doors. It creaked as she slipped inside. Carefully, she tiptoed through the dark entrance. Looking to the right, she spotted the nave, dimly lit by the hauntingly beautiful stained glass windows encircling the space. From the box pews to the ornate beams, the church's wooden features were seeped in shadows. Every corner seemed to be concealing something, and Catharine questioned her decision to return at night. Possibly, Henry wasn't frequenting St. Peter's often, or more likely, Clemmie had been mistaken in his sighting.

Then she heard movement coming from the mezzanine above. The noise was too loud to be the wind, and it didn't sound like a person of Henry's stature. Catharine stepped farther into the nave, craning her neck to see if she could find the sound's origin. Squinting into the darkness, she only spotted the mezzanine's bulky pews.

"Catharine!"

Recognizing Henry's voice, she spun around to find a strange face emerging from the shadows near the altar. Although it was Henry, even with Clemmie's unflattering description, she hadn't quite expected him to look as rough as he did. Dark bags hung under his bloodshot eyes. His cheekbones jutted out from his thin face, and his usually puffy hair was flattened and greasy.

"What are you doing here?" Henry's voice was weak yet frantic as he marched down the nave toward Catharine.

"I was looking for you…"

"You need to leave!" Henry grabbed Catharine's arms.

Had Catharine not seen the fear in Henry's eyes, she would have been angry at his aggressive hold on her. But even with feigned assertiveness, his underlying energy seemed frail. However, she still wasn't leaving without answers.

"What's going on? Why are you here?"

Before he could respond, a low growl emanated from the mezzanine. Catharine watched as Henry's gaze looked up toward the rafters.

"I warned you," he whispered. His voice cracked with despair. "I warned you to leave."

Feeling another set of eyes upon her, Catharine slowly angled her neck to see what loomed above. As her vision landed on a figure perched on the mezzanine's banister, a gasp escaped her mouth.

Krampus.

Nearly three years ago, Catharine had laid eyes on the creature in the orchard outside Van Cortlandt Manor. Henry had been with her that night, but she wasn't confident they were on the same side now.

The creature's yellow eyes burned into her face while it gnashed jagged teeth. A black tongue whipped about its lips, but Catharine's attention was on Krampus's bony face and twisted horns. Chains wrapped around its hairy body, and as the creature looked ready to pounce, the rattling noise grew louder.

Not interested in becoming reacquainted, Catharine took off running toward the church's altar, the opposite direction of Krampus. A furious clanking of chains exploded through the church, followed by a loud *thump*. She knew Krampus had jumped from the mezzanine and would soon be closing in on her. But she kept her eyes focused straight ahead.

"Not her!" Catharine heard Henry bellow in the background. "She's not one that you want."

Henry's protests caused Catharine to glance back. Feebly standing in front of the creature, Henry tried blocking its path. But she knew it couldn't last long. Krampus was twice as tall as him without even mentioning its unearthly strength. She watched as the creature raised a hairy arm and then struck Henry's torso, sending the young man soaring over the pews. Reflexively, Catharine ducked between the front box pew and the altar, scurrying on her knees. When she turned another corner, she paused behind the pew closest to the wall.

Henry was groaning next to the column he had been thrown against. Although she worried he had been injured, Catharine was more concerned with the heavy footsteps headed her direction. At first, they sounded as though they were following her path to the altar, but they soon stopped. She listened to see if they would pick up again.

But there was only silence.

Carefully, Catharine pulled herself onto her knees again, and then stretching her neck, she glimpsed over the top of the pew. Exposing just her forehead, Catharine's eyes peered through the dull light. She easily spotted Krampus, balancing on top of a pew on the other side of the nave, looking the opposite direction. With its large body perched upon the wooden bench, she noted how its hairy abdomen heaved violently. The creature was angry.

She dropped behind the pew again. With Krampus turned away, she had a moment to contemplate her next move. The door leading outside was on the other end of the church but leaving wouldn't guarantee her safety. Now that Krampus had spotted her, it seemed unlikely the beast would let her go so easily.

Catharine thought back to when Krampus had cornered them in the orchard. At the time, she was able to fight the creature back using one of the Sister Wheels. But now she was empty-handed. So, whether or not escaping the church could keep Krampus away, she knew it was the best action to take. Crouching down, she positioned herself for a sprint to the doorway. But before she could make the move, a noise sounded above her head.

Breathing.

Anxiously glancing up, Catharine met a pair of familiar yellow eyes.

With a furious growl, Krampus lunged upon her.

Chapter Sixteen

A Missing Wheel

Something was wrong in Poppel. Maggie sensed it the moment she arrived the following morning. Something had changed. But she wasn't quite sure how.

As she walked through Myra Lane, a few Foundlings sauntered around, barely showing Maggie any attention as she passed. Their expressions seemed distant, and perhaps, even a bit worried. Although that wasn't completely unusual, she still felt something was off. Once she headed up the stairwell to the banquet hall, her feelings were confirmed.

The normally empty hall was plump full of Foundlings. Their voices were hushed and tense. But their attention didn't seem focused on anything particular. Within the crowd, Maggie spotted Wendell, Lloyd, and Harriet, standing in the center of the room. Pushing through the other Foundlings, she made her way to her friends.

"What happened?" Maggie asked.

None of the Foundlings were quick to speak. Instead they considered the question with tired and anxious eyes.

"Was another Foundling taken?" Maggie continued. She glanced around the hall, looking for Augustus. But she didn't see him. Instantly, she worried he'd foolishly gone after Krampus alone.

Before Maggie could ask about him, Harriet spoke. "No, all the

Foundlings are here."

"That's not what's missing," Wendell added. His voice was dreary.

Lloyd leaned over and whispered in her ear, "Poppel's Sister Wheel is gone."

Maggie's eyes widened. "Lily's wheel is gone?" The volume of her voice cut through the muffled conversations around her. Foundlings quickly glanced her way.

Not wanting the entire room's attention, she turned back to Lloyd and hissed, "Where's Augustus?"

Lloyd pushed his glasses up on his nose before nodding toward the hall's mezzanine.

"The Krog."

Without saying another word, Maggie weaved her way to the stairs on the far end of the hall. It wasn't long before she reached the Krog, located above the hall's mezzanine. The room was faintly lit by candlelight, but she still spotted Augustus sitting behind the desk. Focused on the wall adjacent to the doorway, he didn't notice Maggie entering. A fist was propped under his cheek as he slouched against the chair's armrest. His defeated demeanor surprised Maggie. She had expected to find him bustling around the Krog, considering all possibilities of where the Sister Wheel had gone.

"What happened?" Maggie finally asked.

Augustus glanced up, but he didn't make any attempt to stand. Instead he simply brought his hands down to his lap and straightened his back against the chair.

"The Sister Wheel's gone," Augustus said with little emotion. "Hostrupp discovered it missing this morning."

"Would a Foundling have taken it?" Maggie stepped toward the desk. "They now know that the Horologe hangs in Hostrupp's shop."

"Which Foundling would have done that?" Augustus sounded frustrated. "All Foundlings are accounted for, and I can't imagine why any of them would have taken it."

"Krampus," Maggie suggested. "Krampus could have taken it."

Augustus sighed. "Poppel's not a place that sleeps. Someone's always awake down here. I don't see how Krampus could have slipped in unnoticed."

"Well, it has to be someone who wants to reunite the Sister Wheels again. And since the other wheels were left to me and Henry…" Maggie's voice faded away.

Augustus stood up, but he didn't speak. The knowing expression on his face said it all.

"Henry," Maggie repeated. "He had Sarah's wheel. If he's working with Krampus, he might have stolen Lily's."

"Then that leaves only Grace's wheel," Augustus said.

But Maggie had already run out of the Krog.

Struggling to open her eyes, Catharine's head throbbed while prickly rope scratched her wrists. Moving her ankles slightly, she realized that her feet were free. But that did little to alleviate her present confusion and concern. Finally, she managed to open her eyes, blink a few times, and look around at her surroundings.

A bell.

That was the first thing she noticed. A large metal bell was suspended in the room's center, above a wooden platform. Catharine was situated below the platform, against a stone wall. Surprisingly, the room was well lit due to arched windows located on all four sides. The windows were covered in louvers, which allowed just enough morning sunlight to spill inside the space. She recognized the bell tower of St. Peter's Church. Putting together the last images of the night, she tried to make sense of how she came to be there.

Krampus.

Catharine remembered seeing Krampus before all went dark. As her head continued to throb, she concluded that the creature had knocked her unconscious, and then carried her up to the bell tower. She tried feeling thankful that Krampus hadn't killed her. But when looking around the barren tower and feeling the ache in her muscles from being situated upright throughout the night, she didn't feel too fortunate. Perhaps Krampus was planning to kill her later. The thought prompted her feet to attempt to stand, but even though her legs were free, it was still difficult to get up. She glanced down at her bound wrists. The rope was connected to a chain attached to the wall.

Leaving was not going to be easy.

Then an idea struck Catharine. Although St. Peter's bell tower stood over one hundred feet high, it was possible someone walking below on the sidewalk would hear her shouts for help. Without a moment's hesitation, her weakened voice fought to get sound through the windows. However, she had only made a couple attempts before another voice stopped her.

"I wouldn't do that."

A child's face peeked around the wooden platform.

"Violet," Catharine said, recognizing the Foundling. "You're here."

"If Krampus hears your shouting, it'll come back." Violet's voice was ominous, yet her face was calm, nearly cheerful. "It might hurt you."

When Violet stepped around the platform, Catharine could see the young girl's feet were bound. However, the rest of her body moved freely.

Catharine lifted her wrists. "Can you help me out of this rope?"

Violet hesitated. "I can't untie that kind of knot. Even if I could, I don't think it'd be a good idea. We're locked up here, and it'd be best if it didn't appear like you're trying to escape."

Catharine glanced around. "Is it just us?"

Violet nodded.

"I thought more Foundlings had been taken. Where are the others?"

Violet shrugged. "I'm not really sure. They were sent somewhere else. But Henry didn't want me to be sent away. He made sure I would remain in the bell tower."

"But why?"

Violet shrugged again. Then she gave a small smile. "He's an unusual fellow, isn't he? I don't think he always knows why he does the things he does."

A door creaked. Then footsteps could be heard coming up the bell

154

tower's stairwell. Seconds later, Henry emerged through the tower's lone doorway.

He saw Violet first, but upon noticing Catharine, his eyes widened. "You're awake," he said.

"Well, my sleeping accommodations were not ideal," Catharine shot back.

Henry walked toward her; his movements were stiff. She remembered how Krampus had thrown him across the church, and he clearly had been injured.

He kneeled in front of her. "I'm sorry I wasn't here earlier. I had to take care of something this morning."

"Oh," Catharine said. She stared into Henry's once bright blue eyes. They were now tired and gray. "Considering the circumstances, I can't imagine it was anything good."

Henry seemed saddened by the comment, but he didn't look away. "I will get you out of here as soon as I can."

"Where are the other Foundlings?" Catharine asked. Then she added crossly, "And why are you working with Krampus?"

He opened his mouth but didn't speak. He seemed to be planning his words carefully. "It's not Krampus I'm working with–at least not really."

"Then who?"

Straightening his back, Henry replied, "These answers will eventually present themselves. But I can tell you that the other Foundlings are unharmed."

"Then where are they? Why isn't Violet with them?" Catharine looked past Henry to where Violet stood nearby, listening attentively to the conversation.

Once again, Henry appeared to be choosing his words with much deliberation. "The Foundlings are no longer in the city. I was concerned about Violet's safety."

Henry didn't explain further, but Catharine knew the subtext involved the color of her skin. Although the city's black population had a rough existence, it could be even worse outside its jurisdiction.

"Why is this happening, Henry?" Catharine's voice was more

anxious than angry.

He sighed. "The wheels need to be reunited."

"The Sister Wheels? We reunited them three years ago. Have the Garrisons returned?"

He shook his head. "It has nothing to do with the Garrisons. And it goes beyond Poppel. Keeping the wheels apart is wasting their powers. Everything will eventually fall into place, and when it does, the wheels will need to be reunited again. These captured Foundlings will help move things in the right direction. Krampus is simply another tool in the plan. Krampus is at the mercy of the Sister Wheels. Nothing more."

Henry's explanation only brought more confusion. A few seconds passed before Catharine asked, "But whom are you working for?"

Pinching the bridge of his nose, Henry closed his eyes. "I've told you I can't share that information. I've already said more than I probably should."

"You should release me," Catharine snapped. "That's what you probably should do."

Her tone seemed to hit a nerve. Henry reached out and gently held her shoulders. "I promise I'll have you out of here as soon as I can. I won't let harm come to you. Or Violet." He glanced at the girl still listening nearby.

"Or Maggie?" Catharine asked.

Henry turned back to her, searching for some accusation hidden in the words. Finally, he nodded in agreement. "Or Maggie."

Catharine couldn't help but feel that Henry's promises were empty. However, he had been concerned about Violet's welfare. So maybe he wasn't as lost as he appeared.

The Chelsea estate appeared rather gloomy the day Poppel's wheel went missing. Perhaps it was the fog creeping across the lawn, or the rustling of bushes outside the nearby row houses. Maggie even heard some kind of scuffle occurring down the road. Quickening her gait, she marched toward her destination.

Chelsea Manor was bustling with life when Maggie flew through its front doors. Standing in the desolate foyer, she heard the clattering of silverware and plates coming from the dining room. The familiar voices of relatives froze her feet. She had hoped no one would be around. Looking at the library doors to the right, she pondered slipping inside the room before being spotted. But the plan was short-lived.

"Miss Margaret!" Charles appeared in the stair hall across from her. The servant held a crystal pitcher of water. "I was not expecting to see you today. Are you hungry? They're nearly finished with lunch. It would be no trouble to grab a plate for you."

Maggie reluctantly walked forward, still eyeing the library doors. "Who's here, Charles?"

Before he could reply, she saw Louis and Francis at the dining room table. From the faceless voices she heard, she suspected Uncle William, Aunt Lucretia, and their children, Gardiner and Gertrude, were with them as well.

"Is there anything particular I can serve you?" Charles asked.

"No, thank you. I'm not here to eat," Maggie replied, knowing she was now cornered into greeting her relatives. The task that initially brought her to Chelsea Manor would have to wait.

"Isn't this a pleasant surprise," said Uncle William when Maggie entered the dining room. "Here I thought I'd just have the company of my wonderful nephews. What brings you to Chelsea Manor on this day of transformation?"

Maggie looked at her uncle with uncertainty before she heard Francis clear his throat.

"Transfiguration," Francis stated flatly. "The sixth of August is the Day of Transfiguration, Uncle William."

Gardiner and Gertrude giggled from their corner of the table.

"Oh, of course," Uncle William mumbled. He wasn't used to having his normal inaccuracies corrected. "I believe I said transfiguration. You must have misheard."

Meanwhile, Aunt Lucretia gazed fondly at her nephew. "You are becoming such a great theologian, Francis. Much like your grandfather."

Her aunt looked across the room. It was then Maggie noted Grandfather Clement sitting stoically at the end of the table. Not even pretending the guests held his attention, an open book was spread out next to his empty plate. Louis was seated near Grandfather Clement. Maggie caught her cousin's eye. He gave a lopsided smile, which she did not return. Louis narrowed his gaze, correctly sensing that something was amiss.

"Would you like to have a seat, Maggie?" Aunt Lucretia gestured to the chair next to her.

She shook her head. "I wasn't planning on staying. I actually came by to…" She searched her mind for a reason. Then she spied the scenic oil painting hanging behind Grandfather Clement's head. "I came to see if Jervis was still painting the neighborhood. I wanted to observe."

"You wanted to observe?" Aunt Lucretia repeated.

"I've always had an interest in art."

Maggie tried to speak with some conviction, but Louis choked back a laugh before covering it with a cough. Meanwhile, the rest of family shot her curious looks.

"You have an interest in art?" Uncle William inquired with a skeptical tone.

Keeping her expression unreadable, Maggie nodded slowly. "Yes. Yes, I do."

The room remained silent until Grandfather Clement arose from his seat. "I'm going to my bedroom to rest." Clearly, he had done enough entertaining for the day. A moment later, he left the dining room, barely acknowledging Maggie as he passed.

The other relatives hadn't stopped eyeing her questioningly. Spying Grandfather Clement's empty spot at the table, she saw the chance to slip away.

"Oh, Grandfather Clement left his book behind." Maggie went around the table and snatched up the forgotten item. "I'll return it to the library. Louis, could you please help me?"

"Help you?" Louis asked in disbelief.

Maggie shot her cousin a piercing gaze, intended to halt further questioning.

Reading her expression, Louis quickly agreed. "Yes, of course. I can help you with that book. I am much better at all matters involving the library... and books."

He followed Maggie out of the dining room.

"What's happening?" Louis hissed as they entered the stair hall.

However, he didn't get a response as Maggie dashed toward the library. By the time he entered the room, she had already pulled out a thick book from the shelves. After slamming it down onto the desk, she opened its large cover. Her face immediately dropped.

"No," she murmured. "No, it can't be gone."

"What's gone?" Louis approached the desk.

"The Sister Wheel," Maggie whispered.

Louis stopped walking. "The Sister Wheel?" he repeated.

"I hid Grace's wheel in here." Maggie stared down at the hollow space formed from the carved out pages of the book. "But it's gone."

"Perhaps it was moved," Louis said with feigned optimism. "Grandfather Clement always complains about things being rearranged around Chelsea Manor."

Maggie shook her head. "Lily's was taken from Poppel as well. Henry already had Sarah's. So now it seems Krampus has them all."

"By the look on your face, I am guessing that's not an ideal situation," Louis said. "Still, the Sister Wheel could have just moved. It's happened before."

Maggie arched an eyebrow. "What do you mean by that?"

"Well, three years ago when I watched you and Henry disappear down the ash pit, I didn't notice a wheel. However, I hadn't been looking for one. So it could have been there initially. Soon I fell asleep on the sofa waiting for you to return. Later that night, I woke up momentarily, thinking I heard a sound coming from the fireplace. So, I investigated it more closely. Once again, I didn't see the Sister Wheel. This time I remember more specifically, because I had really studied the fireplace, believing you were trying to return and couldn't get back inside. However, nothing more happened, so I went back to sleep. Then you sent sugarplums. That's when Catharine and

Clemmie awoke, and Catharine spotted the wheel in the ash pit. I couldn't believe I had missed it. But when I try to remember, like really remember, I'm certain there hadn't been a wheel hours earlier. At least when I woke up the first time..."

"What did you say?" Maggie cut off Louis's rambling.

She had never asked what had happened after the sugarplums arrived at Chelsea Manor. A lot transpired once Louis, Catharine, and Clemmie made it to Poppel, so there never had been a good opportunity.

"Which part?" Louis asked.

Maggie thought carefully. Events from that Christmas Eve hadn't always been clear. But Louis's story sparked some insight.

"Did you notice anyone else in the ash pit?" she asked.

"Like who?"

Maggie paused. "A Foundling, perhaps."

Louis furrowed his brow, apparently trying to retrieve insignificant memories of a rather significant night. He finally shook his head. "No, it was Clemmie, Catharine, and myself. I don't remember any Foundlings down in the ash pit or tunnel. We didn't see anyone until we ran into the Garrisons." His eyes widened. "Why do you ask? Was someone else down there?"

"I'm not sure," Maggie said. "Milton and Bickley were the first Foundlings to disappear. From what I've learned about that Christmas Eve, Milton stole Poppel's fake wheel before returning it later that night. And while you slept in the Great Room, Bickley had the opportunity to take Chelsea Manor's wheel. He also could have returned it before you awoke."

"Why would they take the Sister Wheels—real or fake—only to put them back shortly after?"

Maggie stared at Louis, a realization dawning upon her. "Because it hadn't been time to reunite them. But now it is." Her grip tightened on the large, empty book. "Krampus didn't take Milton and Bickley. They left willingly."

Chapter Seventeen

The Ancient Deceiver

Krampus slid through the window frame with ease. The creature's raspy breaths shattered the silence previously held within the tower's chamber. Looking upon its frightening grayish body with its horned bony head and sharp, curved teeth, Lily was taken back to the time when she had first encountered the beast.

If Krampus recognized Lily as well, it gave no indication. Instead the creature moved across the room with little regard to the young woman watching him. Hastily, it lurched the door open with its claws, leaving deep gashes in the wood. And then it vanished down the hall.

Many years ago, Lily had come across the creature in the woods outside of Poppel. Grace and Sarah had been afraid to go near it, but Lily trailed Krampus through the trees, desperately wanting to know more. The beast had led her far into the forest while night approached. Still, she had carried on as the rattling of bells filled the darkness.

Upon reaching a moonlit clearing, Lily paused to examine her surroundings. She knew she had lost her way. The rattling had stopped, so she believed the creature was gone. However, something rustled in the branches above. She looked up and once again laid eyes on the curious beast. Its yellow eyes scanned her face. But before the creature decided what to make of the girl, it leapt off the branch and disappeared into the woods.

"Do not follow."

Lily turned to locate the voice behind her. It was one she knew too well.

"Nicolas," she said. "You found me."

The man lingered in the shadows.

"Krampus is a deceiver. It has been around for ages, and will continue on for years to come," Nicolas said. "You must not look for it. However, when it does find you, there will be a reason. So be aware. And be wary. But do not ignore it."

Lily could hear Nicolas's words in her mind while Krampus disappeared out her tower's door. Ignoring the creature seemed impossible. After taking a deep breath, she crept out of her room, intending to follow Krampus throughout the castle. Or wherever it planned to go.

The tower steps were dark, but Lily still spied Krampus's enlarged shadow moving along the stone wall. She tried to stay back while not losing sight of the beast. Lily knew Ficzko could be lurking nearby, so she kept her eyes out for any sign of him or the other castle workers. Surprisingly, she didn't feel anyone watching in the darkness. Perhaps everyone had been given Christmas Eve off.

Krampus led Lily down corridors she had never seen before. The creature never looked back, but it seemed aware of her trailing it. She partially believed that its destination might be meant for her to see. That would explain why Krampus had entered her window. She didn't believe that was by accident.

Step after step, Lily descended farther within the castle. She had lost sight of Krampus, but she heard a faint rattling of chains somewhere in the distance. The cold air caused her breath to solidify into misty clouds, and it occurred to her that she no longer was underneath the castle. The tunnel extended past the castle grounds, probably leading to a secret location. That seemed like something the mysterious Bathory family would have constructed, Lily thought.

Suddenly, pain flooded Lily's body as her knee collided with a hard surface. Grabbing her leg, she looked down at the wooden box. The long tunnel was an odd place to store a single nondescript crate. However, Lily soon noticed there were other similar boxes stacked along the tunnel walls. With her curiosity piqued, she touched the top of the box. As she started to lift its rather heavy lid, a foul stench infiltrated her nose. Quickly, she dropped the lid back down, and brought her hands up to cover her face. She recognized the rotten smell.

Death.

The crate was filled with death. Lily didn't need to open it again to confirm what she already knew. If even a portion of what she had heard and witnessed regarding Countess Bathory were true, the remains of former handmaidens likely resided inside the crates. Although Lily should have felt horrified at such a realization, over the past weeks she had come to terms with the less than honorable acts committed by the Countess. She understood Countess Bathory's situation, and the motivation prompting her actions.

Of course, Lily would never admit this to anyone else. Not that it was a struggle to keep her thoughts to herself. Besides occasional interactions with Thorko, Darvulia, and the Countess, Lily spent all of her time alone. And it's what caused her mind to keep returning to Laszlo.

There were some moments–many moments–when her thoughts wondered about the young man. She imagined things would have been different had he lived. Certainly, Laszlo would have convinced her to leave Cachtice Castle, even with his mother's promises of eternal life. Discovering a method to avoid aging had plagued Lily for many years, but when faced with a lonely future, she felt less passionate about obtaining what she had sought.

Lily missed Laszlo. She truly missed him. Sometimes in the evening when the darkness further illuminated her loneliness, her chest actually constricted as though closing in on the abyss his death had created. During some moments, when the blackness lingered, Lily wished to leave Cachtice Castle behind. However, these feelings were swiftly pushed away. She needed Cachtice. As much as she hated to admit it, she really did need the castle, and all that pertained to it–both the hope and the darkness.

The wooden crates extended far into the tunnel. But Lily didn't turn back. If anything, their presence made her more determined to reach the end. Krampus didn't lead her down there to escape–the creature wanted to show her something.

And then it happened. A familiar feeling overwhelmed her senses. Laszlo.

Lily wasn't sure how, but she knew he was alive. She could see their moments together at Lockenhaus, and the unusual comfort his presence had started to provide. Then she knew–Laszlo wasn't just alive, he was near.

Picking up her pace, Lily scurried down the tunnel, which seemed darker than before. But, strangely, it was brighter as well.

The terrors only happened at Cachtice. Laszlo never experienced them at Lockenhaus or Sarvar, and certainly not at Katterburg. During his years at Cachtice, the shadows would come to him at night. They were always near, always waiting. Laszlo claimed his mother's activities in the dungeons were what kept him away from the castle. But it had been more than that.

Since being locked way in the cellar below the church, Laszlo had yet to experience the terrors that had visited him as a boy. Initially, when arriving at Cachtice Castle to help Lily escape, he worried he had sensed the shadows. However, there had been no further sign of them, and for a while, he foolishly believed the terrors had ended. But that night they unexpectedly returned.

The chills were first. Cold tremors, spilling over his body, were always the harbinger of the shadows. Laszlo immediately recognized the icy sting, and he clenched down his eyelids in response. But he couldn't escape through sleep. Nothing ever kept them away.

With chattering teeth, Laszlo stiffened his jaw to control the shaking. Then he heard a rattling of chains as the cellar door screeched open. Although he kept his eyes shut, he knew a shadow moved across the space. A moment later, heaviness formed across his body as the shadow approached. Soon it became difficult to breathe.

Finding some strength, he muttered, "Be…be gone." The words were barely louder than a whisper. "Be gone," he choked out again. "Leave me."

As expected, nothing changed. The shadow continued toward the helpless young man. Instinctively, Laszlo curled up on the floor, even with his hands and feet uncomfortably chained. His current circumstances made him more vulnerable than he'd ever been when confronted with the terrors.

However, the terrors never had a name. Not until that moment.

"Kram…" Laszlo murmured. "Kram…"

He had little control as the words left his mouth. The shadow had reached Laszlo's coiled body while cold tremors pounded him harder than ever. With shaky breaths, Laszlo continued to mumble the foreign sounds.

"Kram… kramp. Krampus."

The word was ugly. It tasted violent. But Laszlo couldn't stop saying it.

"Krampus. Krampus."

Loud ringing filled Laszlo's ears, obscuring all the noises of the cellar, including his own voice. But a few moments later the ringing ceased. And he felt alone once again.

Slowly, Laszlo opened his eyes. The cellar was dark and empty with no shadow in sight. He pushed himself up into a sitting position. Something was different. After a couple of seconds, Laszlo realized what had changed. His hands were free–as were his legs. During all the confusion, his body had broken free from the chains.

Or perhaps, he had been released.

Krampus.

The word played over and over in his head. No, not simply a word, Laszlo thought. It was a name. Maybe naming the terror had been the key to his release. And as he looked to the other side of the cellar, one thing was clear.

The door was open.

On any other night, Lily would have thought it was a ghost. The pale figure stood on the snow outside of the church, but he didn't see her. However, she recognized his blond hair, even if the rest of Laszlo was harder to distinguish.

The underground tunnel had finally terminated. Distracted by the seemingly empty chambers she passed, Lily nearly ran into a wall, marking the tunnel's end. Momentarily, she worried there was no way out, forcing her to turn around and return to the castle. But then she spied a wooden ladder leaning against the wall. After climbing the ladder and pushing through a hatch in the ceiling, Lily mustered enough strength to pull herself up. The trapdoor had led to the antechamber of a church.

The moonlight filtering through the stained glass windows afforded her enough glow to see the new surroundings. The small church was empty. The lingering remnants and smells of the Christmas Eve service could still be sensed. Although she had only seen it from the outside, Lily knew it was the church she had stumbled upon earlier that day.

Why did a tunnel connect Cachtice Castle with the church? More importantly, why were crates–likely containing human remains–stored in it? Unfortunately, the only way for Lily to uncover those answers could possibly result in her demise.

Feeling uneasy in the church, Lily ran to the front door. However, she didn't have to struggle to unlock it. The plank barring the door from the inside had already been lifted, and the door's latches had also been unfastened. As she heaved the thick door open, she instantly breathed the chilly air. And that's when she saw the young man.

"Laszlo," Lily hissed. She didn't want to draw the attention of anything lurking in the darkness.

Hesitantly, the young man turned around. Now facing her, Lily could confirm it was Laszlo. However, he looked gaunt and weak, and she worried he would collapse any moment. But his lifeless eyes brightened significantly at the sight of her.

"Lily!" He staggered her direction. "Lily," he repeated, as though questioning her existence. Or perhaps, he believed his words kept her alive, and if he stopped speaking, she would disappear completely.

Stretching her hands out toward his fatigued body, Lily took a few eager steps and quickly wrapped Laszlo in her arms. He was notably thinner than last time she saw him, and he also smelled of death. She wanted to ask what had happened. But she knew it was more important to get away from Cachtice Castle.

Laszlo's gray eyes searched her face. He still seemed to doubt that she was really in front of him. When he rubbed his bony hands along her arms, trying to erase the goose bumps sprouting up from the cold, he spied the scars and bruises on her skin.

"They were going to kill you," Laszlo murmured. "What happened? How did you escape?"

Lily was puzzled by Laszlo's comments. She wondered what he knew. At that moment however, it didn't matter. Seeing Laszlo returned all the apprehension she had felt at Cachtice. Suddenly, things she thought had been important no longer were worth surrendering so much.

Lily led Laszlo back into the church where they were out of the cold. Before either of them could speak, another voice cut through the silence.

"I'm sorry. I am so sorry."

Out of the darkness emerged the minister, Istvan. His frail white hair looked disheveled while his eyes were heavy with grief.

"It started with just a couple dead," he said. "Workers at the castle. I don't even know who they were. But they needed to be buried. Young girls. Then the numbers started to grow. More and more dead came from Cachtice. I couldn't take on that many bodies. It was too much death. It would cause too much suspicion. The villagers were already starting to notice. So I refused. I refused the Countess. But no one refuses her— no one. Eventually, the bodies were stored in crates down below. Others were hastily buried around the castle grounds. I don't even know who they are."

Then Istvan slipped back into the shadows without saying another word.

Lily turned to Laszlo. "We need to leave Cachtice. I don't care where we go. I just want to be far away from the castle. And with you."

The corners of Laszlo's mouth started to turn up. But then his eyes darkened. "They'll find us. No matter where we go. Thorko and my mother–they'll come after us."

"So what do we do?"

Laszlo had a look of determination on his face Lily had never seen before.

"We must make sure that they can't."

Laszlo hadn't planned to return to Cachtice on Christmas Eve. Actually, he'd hoped to never see the castle again, and the way Lily's solemn expression remained unchanged as they crept along the underground tunnel, it seemed like she also had no intention of going back.

Upon returning, they slipped into one of the castle's largest halls. As Laszlo stood in the middle of the room, which was covered in murals and tapestries he knew by heart, he realized something. Cachtice Castle was full of evil and suffering, where more unmentionable acts had occurred than any other place he had known. Yet it was his past, and in many ways, it was his foundation. He had come back that night with thoughts of murdering Thorko and his mother. But now he felt differently.

Lily jumped as Laszlo took a chair and smashed it against the ground. Then he took another chair and threw it on top of the first.

"What are you doing?" she asked as Laszlo walked over to one of the tapestries displaying Ferenc Nadasdy in battle. He tore it down from the wall and tossed it upon the growing pile.

"It's not enough to kill." Laszlo took a flickering candle from its holder on the wall. "The castle needs to burn."

Before Laszlo could bring the flame to the kindle, Lily reached out and stopped him. "No, you must not. There could be others imprisoned in the dungeon. We'd need to get them out first."

With a reluctant sigh, Laszlo nodded in agreement. However, another voice spoke from the doorway.

"Allow me to help you with that."

A small glowing silhouette moved along the ground as Ficzko entered the hall with a torch in his grasp. Darvulia followed closely behind. As Ficzko neared the tapestry hanging by the doorway, a menacing look gleamed in his eyes.

"Stand down, Ficzko," a deep voice bellowed on the far end of the gallery.

Thorko emerged from the shadows. However, the old man was not alone. Countess Bathory also stepped forward, her hands clasped together, and her face impossible to read.

"There is no need to burn anything," she said. "Laszlo and Lily are not going anywhere."

The light from Laszlo's candle caught its reflection off a long blade in the Countess's hand. He noticed Ficzko and Darvulia were armed as well. Lily seemed uncertain about what to do next; but Laszlo's only concern was getting her away from Cachtice. Her blood was far more valuable than his.

In one swift motion, Laszlo threw the candle down upon the tapestry. Flames rapidly burst across the fabric. Then he grabbed the legs of a burning chair and hurled it toward Ficzko and Darvulia. The sinister pair ducked out of the way, granting Laszlo and Lily an opportunity to escape. Hand in hand, they ran toward the door, but their path was blocked by a group of men storming inside. Laszlo recognized Emperor Matthias's assistant, Melchior, and Elizabeth Bathory's cousin, Count Gyorgy Thurzo, leading the charge.

While the fire continued to burn across the tapestry, Melchior pronounced, "Countess Bathory, from the highest order of Emperor Matthias, you are under arrest for the murder of hundreds of Hungarian children."

169

Chapter Eighteen

An Odd Fellow

Still imprisoned in St. Peter's bell tower, Catharine struggled to stay conscious throughout the day. She had lost Violet as a companion. The Foundling was now allowed outside of the tower. But the girl would occasionally visit, dropping off meager meals of bread and cured meats.

When the day's light slowly died away, Catharine finally resigned herself to sleep.

"Do not struggle." The voice was cold. "You'll remain here until you learn not to interfere."

Shackles rattled, and another voice muttered a protest.

"If you do not cooperate, your father will not return," the icy voice spoke again. "It is your choice to make. Decide wisely, Henry."

Henry.

Catharine wondered how Henry had managed to infiltrate her dreams. But as night departed, she realized it hadn't been a dream. Opening her eyes, Catharine spotted yellow bands of sunlight adorning the tower's old floor. She visually traced the streaks until she spied a pair of feet resting on the other side of the huge bell. Catharine blinked a few times, allowing her eyes to adjust to the morning. However, even with full vision, she had a hard time believing who sat across from her.

With his arms bound and legs shackled to the wall, Henry sat on the ground, looking like a seasoned prisoner. His blank expression appeared unconcerned as he stared off into nothing. Seeming to have accepted his current predicament, he didn't even notice Catharine studying him. She wondered if Henry really the same bold individual was who had been full of life years ago when he bombarded Chelsea Manor, confronting Grandfather Clement over the Christmas poem. Yet memories of him as anything other than a deathly pale and haggard young man were hard to conjure now.

"What happened?" Catharine finally addressed her new companion. "Why are you in the bell tower?"

Slowly, Henry's eyes drifted over to her, but they didn't carry any emotion.

"I was disobedient," he whispered with no urgency to explain further.

"Disobedient to whom, Henry?" Catharine felt that by speaking his name, she could possibly retrieve him back to the land of the living.

He shook his head. "It doesn't concern you."

With a scoff, Catharine deliberately shook her arms, which rattled the chains attaching her bound wrists to the wall. "I would politely disagree."

She received nothing but silence in response.

"Henry, who were you disobedient to?" Catharine's tone was less patient. "If it's not Krampus, there's something else controlling you."

"I'm not being controlled," he snapped. "I make my own decisions."

"Then what decisions have you made?"

Catharine expected him to once again ignore the question, so she was surprised when he spoke after a few quiet moments.

"The situation's not as nefarious as you may believe."

"A violent creature running loose in the city does not help quell my fears."

"Krampus shouldn't be your concern," Henry said pointedly. "That creature, while no doubt unsettling, is nothing more than an instrument. It did little more than guard Sarah's wheel at Van Cortlandt Manor. And it continues to be of similar use."

"So this has to do with the Sister Wheels?" Catharine asked. "Will we ever escape those cursed heirlooms?"

"They aren't curses," he replied. "The wheels are gifts. Once the rift has occurred and the blood properly shed, the transfiguration will be fulfilled."

Catharine raised her eyebrows in alarm at the prophetic claim. The words seemed foreign coming from Henry's mouth. It was as though he was simply repeating incantations he'd previously heard from a suspicious source.

"What are you saying, Henry? What rift?"

But he didn't respond. A minute passed before he spoke again.

"I miss my father. Every day I miss him," he admitted sincerely. "Don't you wish you could bring your mother back?"

"Back?" Catharine repeated. "My mother's been dead for nearly two decades. And your father, Sidney, has been deceased for three years as well."

"But if they could return, wouldn't you see it to completion?"

Henry stared into Catharine's eyes. His expression was surprisingly desperate, as though pleading for her to understand. For the first time since the infamous Christmas Eve, she felt connected to the young man from Poughkeepsie.

"It depends on what such a magical feat would cost, Henry. I imagine it is more than either one of us could offer."

Footsteps sounded on the stairs leading to the bell tower. They were too heavy to be Violet's, and far too human to belong to Krampus. As a cloaked body moved through the tower's entrance, Catharine struggled to identify the figure standing in front of her. While not quite familiar, he was also not a stranger.

"It's nice to officially meet you, Catharine. Even in these less than ideal circumstances, you understand."

Near Jefferson Market, a new structure stood along Tenth Street. The three-story brick building, simplistic yet inspired by French architecture, looked out of place on the New York City block.

Maggie paused outside its front doors, admiring the large windows.

Since the studio apartments housed artists, natural light was a necessity. The beauty and smell of new construction almost made her forget why she'd traveled down to Greenwich Village.

Catharine was missing, Maggie reminded herself.

No one in her family had seen Catharine in two days. Although it wasn't a significant length of time, Catharine had never disappeared for more than a day her entire life. Also, considering the situation in Poppel, Maggie had more reason than usual to be concerned.

As Maggie entered the building, her eyes were immediately drawn to the two-story main gallery and its glass ceiling. Although the room now stood empty, with the exception of gaslights, she imagined the building's residents would soon fill the grand foyer with art.

Surrounding the gallery was a series of doors, apartments belonging to the resident artists. Due to Clemmie's wealth of knowledge, which came from deliberate attentiveness and prying ears, Maggie not only knew Jervis McEntee lived in a studio, but she also knew which one.

After two quick knocks, Jervis's door swung open. The artist looked surprised to see Maggie. Dried paint dotted his white tunic, and a brush was snuggly tucked behind his ear.

"Maggie!" Jervis gave a startled smile. "This is quite a surprise. What brings you here?"

"Hello, Jervis," Maggie greeted as she peered over his shoulder. She wanted to see Catharine somewhere in the studio, but she only spied easels, paintings, and an old paint-speckled tarp. Her hopes of Catharine being involved in a scandalous elopement were dashed.

Jervis stepped aside, allowing Maggie entrance into the studio.

"I was looking for Catharine," she said. "Have you seen her recently?"

He shook his head. "No, I haven't seen Catharine since the other week when I ran into her outside Chelsea Manor. I've been very occupied as of late." Jervis gestured to a dozen paintings leaning against the wall. "Is everything all right?"

Disregarding Jervis's question, Maggie stepped toward an easel. "Are these your paintings of the Chelsea neighborhood?"

His eyes instantly lit up. "They are! I was just finishing this one before you arrived. As you can see, it's the General Theological Seminary." Jervis bent over and picked up a painting that had been propped on a chair. "And here is the Manor."

After studying the painting, Maggie agreed that it was certainly Chelsea Manor. From the rooftop's multiple chimneys, which she knew only too well, to the sycamore tree positioned near the west porch, Jervis had masterfully captured the nuanced character of the mansion.

"It's lovely, Jervis. Truly. Grandfather Clement will adore it."

Beaming at the compliment, Jervis turned to retrieve other paintings. As he busied himself with the collection of canvases, Maggie glanced at the General Theological Seminary painting still prominently displayed on the easel. Like the painting of Chelsea Manor, Jervis had also managed to convey the particular charm of the building in his art. However, a detail not seen in the previous painting caught Maggie's attention. The scenery in Chelsea Manor didn't contain any people, but the seminary painting had various crowds walking along the sidewalk, with the exception of one lone figure standing in the shadows of the building.

Leaning closer to the painting, she stifled a gasp.

Although the facial details weren't precise, Maggie still recognized the individual. She looked down at the rest of the collection lined up against the wall. The paintings included St. Peter's Church, the well-known row houses of Chelsea, and the distilleries along the Hudson River. And in each painting, she spied the same person.

"Jervis," she said with a shaky voice. "Why is this man in all of your paintings?"

His eyes widened. "Oh, you noticed him." Jervis stepped toward the painting of the seminary. "For some reason, I kept spotting him throughout the neighborhood. Something about the odd fellow stuck with me, and his presence made its way into the art. It's hard to explain. I don't even know him, but there was something about the man I found impossible to forget."

Jervis leaned forward to study the stranger. His nose nearly brushed the paint on the canvas. Then he turned to Maggie. "Do you know him?"

"Not exactly," Maggie mumbled, trying to gather her thoughts. "Where did you see him specifically? Was he coming from any particular building? The seminary, perhaps?"

With a furrowed brow, Jervis looked to the wall, seeming to search his memory.

"No, not the seminary." Maggie gave a defeated sighed at Jervis's response. But just as she felt like her search for Catharine was going nowhere, he added, "However, I did see him around St. Peter's Church. Quite often, actually. I even noticed him entering the church a few times."

A second later, Maggie had slipped out of the studio without another word uttered to Jervis. She wanted to immediately head to Poppel and find Augustus. She needed to tell him what she had discovered. But Maggie worried that there wasn't much time.

Catharine was at St. Peter's Church–and likely Laszlo as well.

Augustus had become accustomed to Maggie's constant presence, so when she didn't visit the following day, Poppel seemed eerily empty. This feeling struck him as odd, since he was a creature of habitual loneliness. He had been that way for as long as he could remember.

Over a decade ago, young Augustus McNutt had traveled with his father across the Atlantic Ocean. He left behind his mother, Laetitia, and sister, Jane, in Ireland. The plan was for Augustus and his father, Gideon, to settle in New York City before writing home, instructing the rest of the family to join them. But Laetitia and Jane had both died not long after Gideon and Augustus left Ireland. Soon Gideon was imprisoned in Ludlow Street Jail for debt. He died a year later.

Having nothing and no one, Augustus McNutt became a Garrison in Poppel.

As Augustus glanced around the quiet Boeken Kamer, Maggie's absence was strangely loud and glaringly apparent. However, he forced his attention back on the pile of books stacked in front of him. It was the last batch to look through before he retired for the evening.

With a defeated sigh, he lifted the top book off the pile. Mechanically, he flipped through the pages, looking for something that didn't belong. Minutes ticked by before he finally reached its back cover. Nothing of interest had been discovered, which had become the common result. After setting aside the examined book, Augustus reached for the next one.

He had only rustled through a handful of the book's pages before a discolored paper caught his eye. He swiftly paused his hand. If Maggie had been present, he would have made a small gasp to catch her attention. But alone in the Boeken Kamer, he internalized his shock while picking up the loose paper. Having read many pages of Stephanus Van Cortlandt's journal, Augustus instantly recognized the cursive handwriting. While he skimmed the journal entry, specific words seemed to radiate off the page.

Lily.

Laszlo.

Krampus.

Without reading the page again, Augustus folded the delicate paper and gently slid it into his breast pocket. Then he rushed out the Boeken Kamer door. His only thought was on finding Maggie and sharing what he had discovered. But where could she be? Perhaps Chelsea Manor. However, he couldn't imagine visiting her grandfather's mansion unannounced.

While debating the next course of action, Augustus ran down the banquet hall's staircase. Upon reaching Myra Lane, the sight of a familiar young woman halted him in his tracks.

Maggie was walking down the cobblestone road. Judging by the expression on her face, Augustus had a feeling she had much to tell him as well.

Night had arrived once again to St. Peter's bell tower. And even though their guest had left hours earlier, Catharine and Henry remained bound inside. Knowing the identity of the individual behind her capture had left more questions than answers.

"How were you disobedient?" Catharine asked quietly.

Her lethargic body already seemed to resign itself to an infinite sentence of confinement in the tower, but her mind sought more clarity to their predicament.

"Henry, how were you disobedient?" she repeated.

Once again, her question was met with silence. She wondered if Henry had already drifted off to sleep. But before she could ask again, she heard his broken voice reply.

"After Laszlo got hold of you, he wanted to capture Maggie. She was heading to Chelsea Manor around noon the other day. No one else was around. But when the moment presented itself for Krampus to take her, I interfered. I'm not even sure why. I just remembered the promise I made you about not letting any harm come to your sister."

Catharine could see Henry's eyes across the darkened tower. For the first time in quite a while, she spotted a glint of blue. She couldn't help but feel that part of him had returned.

"I don't understand," she said. "After you left Chelsea Manor that Christmas, Maggie had given you Sarah's wheel. When we were at Van Cortlandt Manor, I was able to scare Krampus off using the same wheel. How did it overpower you? Why were you not protected?"

Henry made a sound that almost resembled a chuckle. "You forget that my family married into the Van Cortlandt line. I carry no actual Van Cortlandt blood. It seems that's why both you and Maggie are able to exert some control over the creature with the wheels at hand. Which is why Maggie poses a threat and Laszlo wants her captured. He knows about how she's trying to uncover the truth behind the Foundling disappearances. And he's correct in fearing that she might be the only person who can stop Krampus. That's why..."

Henry's voice trailed off, but Catharine pressed him to finish.

"Why what?"

Henry sighed, possibly louder than he intended. For whatever reason, his previously guarded façade had faded, and he nearly resembled the young man Catharine had remembered. It was the version of Henry capable of surprising vulnerability and honesty. In

177

that moment, she spotted a rare opportunity, and she planned to take full advantage of it.

"Henry, what's happening? How did you get involved with all of this?" Catharine took in her surroundings again as she lightly rattled her chains. "And how did it get to this point?"

He sighed again. Catharine worried that he would pull away, but a few silent moments later, he seemed to acquiesce. "After that Christmas Eve, Krampus found me in Poughkeepsie. It followed me to my family's home at Locust Grove. I didn't see it right away, but I felt its presence." Henry's voice was faint. "With the passing months, my resolve weakened. It seemed to gain some power over me. I was no longer myself. It's difficult to recall specifics during this time. However, at some point, Laszlo came to visit me. Or maybe I went to him. Again, I'm not really sure."

"What did Laszlo want?" Catharine asked, but she wasn't expecting his response.

"He wanted to help me," Henry said. "Although I never discussed it with Laszlo, he somehow knew the suffering my father's death had caused me. He said he could make it go away, for he understood the loss I felt."

"That's why you came back here?"

"The Sister Wheels are paramount to the plans. Laszlo feared that the construction of Central Park would put Poppel's existence in jeopardy. And therefore, threaten the safety of Lily's wheel."

Catharine's eyes widened. "So you did start the fire at Crystal Palace. I knew that you had."

Henry shook his head. "I was there to make sure it went as planned. But I did not start it. Krampus was responsible for that portion. Laszlo had other assignments for me. I was to keep an eye on the Sister Wheel at Poppel. I already had surrendered Sarah's wheel over to Laszlo. And he was also able to obtain Grace's. A Foundling named Bickley stole it from Chelsea Manor. Finally, I was given the order to remove Lily's from Poppel. And so I did. However, preventing Krampus from nabbing Maggie greatly angered Laszlo. He said such disloyalty would hurt all that we'd wished to achieve. And Laszlo's right. But I didn't want him to hurt Maggie. She scares Laszlo. I didn't know what he would do to her."

Squinting through the darkness, Catharine studied Henry's face. "I find it difficult to trust your story. Why are you being so forthcoming with all of this information? You claim to be under Krampus's spell, but then suddenly, you are questioning both Krampus and Laszlo."

Chains rattled as Henry sat up straighter against the tower wall. "I've always questioned the means Laszlo uses. For the most part, I recognize them to be necessary in reaching the end goal, which is the most imperative part. Unlike Laszlo, however, I do not see any reason that Poppel and the Van Cortlandt descendants need to be viewed as obstacles in the quest. Your family could benefit in the same manner as I can. You and Maggie should join me in helping Laszlo."

Catharine couldn't help but to scoff. "Ah, so that's it. You aren't imprisoned up here as punishment. Laszlo put you in the tower to try and persuade me into joining your cause, whatever that may be."

Henry's expression dropped. Any small light it had recently contained was washed away by sadness. "No, not at all," he said warily. "Actually, Laszlo has been very insistent that the Van Cortlandt descendants not be involved again."

"And why's that?"

A cold voice spoke from the doorway. "Because they will only get in the way." Laszlo stepped into the bell tower. "Since you are so willing to share valuable secrets, Henry, it seems you are also getting in the way–and will have to be disposed of as well."

Chapter Nineteen

Manna

A gray cloak flapped in the air as Laszlo paced about the room.

"I do not understand. How could she not be forced to stand trial?"

The faces of Emperor Matthias, Melchior, and Count Gyorgy curiously watched the young man.

"As I've already explained," Count Gyorgy said, rubbing long fingers down his dark beard. "Considering her level of nobility, it would not be advisable to make the Countess testify. We still have the reputation of the Nadasdy and Bathory families to consider."

Abruptly, Laszlo stopped walking and twisted toward the other men. "She viciously murdered hundreds of girls. Surely, that deserves some public scrutiny."

Count Gyorgy sighed. "We are not able to confirm how many there were. Did young women die at Cachtice? Yes, that much is clear. Possibly murdered? Most likely. But the precise numbers are still hard to prove."

"I am not sure what more you want, Laszlo," Melchior interrupted. "Her assistants, Ficzko and Darvulia, were tortured and promptly executed. Elizabeth Bathory will be locked away in one of Cachtice's towers for all of her remaining days. Of course, this mystical man, Thorko, has not been found. But he likely fled, never to return again. As far as I see it, justice has been served."

"Also, I can't imagine that you would want Countess Bathory killed," Count Gyorgy added. "Regardless of everything she may have done to others, she is your mother after all."

Laszlo's face turned to stone. Speaking softly, he tried to maintain a steady voice. "What I want is for my mother to no longer have the opportunity to hurt anyone again. Locking her in a tower will never guarantee this. You clearly don't understand her abilities."

"What's done is done," Emperor Matthias said after a few quiet moments. His tone was calm and rather detached. When he stood from the table, Laszlo could see in his eyes that the conversation had ended. "It's over, Laszlo," he continued. "I suggest for everyone's benefit including yours, that you move on."

Laszlo gave a slight nod. "Very well. But I must know one last thing. If you had no intention of truly punishing her, why bring any judgment at all? Many in the area had already known about my mother's crimes. Why bother to act now?"

"There was a handmaiden named Ilona. She was from a noble family," Count Gyorgy explained simply. "It was different when Countess Bathory targeted those whose disappearances would go mostly unnoticed. But Ilona's could not be ignored."

Laszlo knew that the Count's story only offered one reason for their storming of Cachtice Castle. For in addition to Ilona's death, Emperor Matthias was in no hurry to pay back the debt owed to Countess Bathory. Also, with the Countess's imprisonment, Count Gyorgy would be next in line to receive Ferenc Nadasdy's land and inheritance. However, the motives of the other men meant nothing to Laszlo now.

Lily's safety was his greatest concern, and until Thorko was captured, it was something Laszlo could not promise.

The weeks of freedom following Countess Bathory's arrest had been wonderful for Lily. Not only had her body begun to heal after nearly a month of abuse, but she also started to feel more at peace than she had in years. But the feeling of contentment didn't last forever.

Laszlo had been hiding mirrors. She didn't notice right away. Since they had to remain in the area for the trial, Istvan had allowed them to stay at his home. Lily had been thankful for his hospitality, especially after learning that the minister had been alerting the authorities of Countess Bathory's crimes for years. A few weeks later, however, she found it odd that Istvan's home did not contain a single mirror. In fact, any reflective surfaces were hard to come by in his residence.

One afternoon while Laszlo was away, Lily broached the unusual topic. "Istvan, why doesn't your home have mirrors?"

The old minister seemed surprised by the question. "Because Laszlo had them removed before you arrived. He said it would upset you to see the abuse you suffered at the hands of Countess Bathory."

Lily was well aware of the scars and bruises, for they were not easily hidden from view. Since Laszlo knew she didn't need a mirror to see them, she found Istvan's explanation odd.

"Where are the mirrors kept now?" she asked.

Istvan led her to the far end of his modest home. He stopped in front of a lone door with a padlock.

"Laszlo was very adamant that you were not allowed in here." Shaking his head, Istvan took a key from his pocket and unlocked the door. "He insisted that it would be too upsetting."

"Laszlo can be a bit protective," Lily replied. She forced a smile. "But I will be fine."

With a nudge, the door swung open. Istvan stepped back to allow Lily inside. The room was small, so it didn't take much for the space to feel crowded. As she entered, she saw at least a dozen reflections of herself staring back. From a large full-length mirror to a small circular one, the room was covered in framed glass. At that moment, she knew Laszlo's intention wasn't to avoid shocking her with the damage caused by Cachtice Castle. For when she gazed upon her reflections, Lily instantly became less concerned about the lingering marks on her body. She was too captivated by her eyes.

Something was missing in them. Youth, she realized. Youth had left her eyes.

When Laszlo returned to Istvan's home that evening, he immediately spotted Lily. Almost in a hypnotic trance, she sat alone near the fireplace, watching the flames wildly dance. She didn't look up at Laszlo, even though the floor loudly creaked, as he approached.

"Everything will be fine, Lily." Laszlo kneeled next to her. "Ficzko and Darvulia have been executed. Meanwhile, the Countess will be locked up in Cachtice forever."

Lily sighed but did not look at Laszlo. When she spoke, her voice was surprisingly cold.

"And what about Thorko?"

Now it was Laszlo's turn to sound removed. "There is still no sign of him. He's gone." Laszlo reached out and gently grabbed Lily's hand that had been resting in her lap. "We can leave, too. We can go anywhere you want and never come back."

Finally, Lily looked down at his hand upon hers as though just noticing the touch. She slowly brought her eyes up to meet Laszlo's.

"If the Countess is kept at Cachtice Castle, Thorko will not be far away," Lily said firmly. "You've known the man your entire life. You must be aware of places he resides outside of the castle."

Laszlo's eyebrows lifted at the suggestion, indicating to Lily that she had guessed correctly. Unexpectedly, she placed her hand on top of Laszlo's.

"Where? Where is Thorko?"

Laszlo stared at Lily's hand covering his own. The small display of affection caused his breath to hitch.

"The cave," Laszlo whispered. "There was always the cave."

North of the village of Cachtice, through dense forests and over a stream, a deep cave hid within a low mountainous ridge. Carved from ancient water now dried away, the natural formation was essentially a narrow crack embedded in limestone. Mostly ignored by all creatures, except for various kinds of bats, Thorko had long ago established it as his home outside of Cachtice Castle.

During his childhood, Laszlo had often wondered where Thorko disappeared to when he wasn't at Cachtice or Lockenhaus. The old man never mentioned his travels, which only added to his mystery. Laszlo would secretly watch from the highest tower as he left the castle grounds. Thorko would walk along the path connecting the castle with the village, and then vanish somewhere before the trees enveloped the road.

Since he traveled without a horse, Laszlo assumed Thorko never went far. Still, he needed to know more. One day, he followed Thorko down the road, always maintaining a reasonable distance. Eventually, he lost sight of the old man. Before he dejectedly headed back to the castle, a voice called to him.

"Were you going somewhere, Laszlo?"

Laszlo turned back toward the road and saw Thorko leaning against a tree. He didn't remember answering, but Thorko was soon leading him away from the castle. Before night fell, they had arrived at the cave. Laszlo watched Thorko approach the entrance, but upon noticing that the boy wasn't following, he gestured for Laszlo to join him.

Even with all the horrors Laszlo witnessed at Cachtice, the idea of entering a remote cave still frightened him. Walking only a few yards into the darkness, he stopped. His feet refused to move. But Thorko continued on, leaving the boy alone. Laszlo spent the night curled on the ground, waiting for morning to arrive. He could hear bats fluttering above his head. But their presence wasn't what made him want to leave. Although Laszlo was miles from Cachtice Castle, his nightly terrors had accompanied him.

A shadow could be felt moving through the cave and soon Laszlo's body was hit with chilly tremors. In an instant, Laszlo rushed from the cave, trampling over the rocky terrain, just as the pink morning sun peeked over the mountainous horizon. He never again mentioned the cave to Thorko. And he never went back–until he returned with Lily.

Although the event with Thorko had been many years ago, Laszlo remembered the path to the cave. Before the sun was hanging low in the sky, Laszlo and Lily arrived at its ominous entrance.

"Are you sure this is it?" Lily asked. "It would be unfortunate to come all this way and end up at the wrong cave."

"Yes, I am sure." Laszlo turned to face her. "Allow me to go inside first. Alone. I don't want you near Thorko. If he's still around, it's in order to stay close to the Countess so they can finish what they started. You will not be safe."

Reluctantly, Lily agreed. While placing a kiss on his cheek, she affectionately squeezed his hand. Although Laszlo couldn't quite name the look on her face, it seemed like uncertainty about whether she'd see him again. It was almost enough to make him stay back with her.

After kissing her forehead in return, Laszlo headed into the cave as he did once as a boy. Except now he was alone–at least as far as he knew. As he walked deeper into the cave, and farther away from the entrance, the darkness became impenetrable. He wouldn't be able to continue on without the assistance of light. However, he soon spotted a tiny glow in the distance. Moving closer, he discovered a small torch situated within a holder on the limestone wall. Although he eagerly grabbed the torch with his hand, Laszlo felt apprehensive about the much-needed light. Its existence meant that Thorko was already there.

Laszlo's suspicions were confirmed more quickly than he had anticipated. After walking a little farther, he saw an illuminated space up ahead.

A silhouette greeted the intruder.

"After your first visit, I thought you would never come back." Thorko didn't bother turning to face Laszlo, as usual. "However, I am pleased that you have."

He watched as Thorko fiddled with the various liquids and powders stationed on a stone table in front of him. He seemed unconcerned by Laszlo's presence.

"Why didn't you leave?" Laszlo asked. "Ficzko and Darvulia are dead. And the Countess will be imprisoned at Cachtice for the rest of her natural life."

A rather alarming and jovial laugh escaped from Thorko's mouth.

"Natural life," Laszlo heard Thorko mutter under his breath. Then the old man chuckled again.

"So I'm correct in assuming that you're still here for the Countess."

Thorko finally turned around to look at Laszlo. A small smile played at the ends of his lips.

"She still needs to eat." Thorko held a vial between his fingers.

"How are you still providing her with tonics?" Laszlo snapped. He felt a surge of familiar anger sweep through him.

"Certainly, you don't expect me to give away all of my secrets," Thorko said. "Although trust that no matter what I tell you, I will still see to it that the Countess is well-supplied. Locking her away in the castle will not prevent her from aging." Thorko nodded to a vat of golden liquid bubbling in a cauldron. Its color matched the tonic in the vial.

"I should be on my way." Thorko started to walk toward the passage leading outside, but Laszlo aggressively moved to block his path. "Now, now, Laszlo. There's no reason to be hostile, especially toward your own father–your own blood."

The last comment hit Laszlo harder than expected. Before he knew what had happened, he brought up his fist to strike Thorko. However, the old man was surprisingly fast, and in one swift movement, he grabbed Laszlo by the neck, slamming him to the solid ground.

Laszlo groaned in pain as Thorko maintained a firm grip on his neck, rendering the boy motionless. Thorko's strength was unimaginable, not just for his age–but for anyone.

"What did I tell you?" Laszlo had never heard Thorko's voice so menacing. "Do not threaten your own blood. Not only can I destroy you just as easily as you were created, but I will also destroy those you care about most."

Lily.

With renewed energy, Laszlo reached up and grabbed Thorko's forearm, using all of his power to lessen the man's hold on his neck. Finally, Thorko released him.

"Do not interfere," Thorko calmly said as he stood back up. "Or you will meet your end."

Laszlo remained on the ground, listening until the sound of the man's footsteps disappeared into the distance. Slowly, he sat up and touched his neck. He imagined a bruise forming with each passing moment. And even though Thorko's threat still echoed through his mind, Laszlo looked over to the vat of liquid simmering in the center of the room. He didn't question what he needed to do next.

Laszlo recognized a container labeled *Manna*. Years ago, he had mistakenly tried stealing it from Thorko's chamber while attempting to concoct a sleeping serum. The potion was to help with his nightly terrors. Upon realizing what he was taking, Thorko had stopped him.

"Do not use manna," Thorko warned. "It would kill you."

"What is it?" Laszlo asked curiously.

"It comes all the way from Sicily. A special poison that leaves behind no trace of color or taste. Contains arsenic, lead, and a little bit of belladonna, among other things."

"Why do you keep such a poison in your cabinet?"

Thorko scoffed. "Not everything is meant to heal, Laszlo. Occasionally, death is the merciful choice. Sometimes death is needed."

The conversation came back to Laszlo as he studied the clear container of gray powder. *Sometimes death is needed.*

Silently, Laszlo opened the bottle. Not wanting the powder's absence to be conspicuous, he dumped only a portion of its contents into the golden liquid. His movements had been discreet on the chance that Thorko was lurking in the shadows. But Laszlo didn't sense the old man's presence like he often did.

After the manna was secretly poured into the vat, Laszlo expected the mixture to hiss or sizzle, giving some kind of indication that the ingredient worked. But the potion did not react. Laszlo worried it possibly wouldn't have the desired effect–Countess Bathory's death.

However, trusting the poison to perform like it should, Laszlo returned the container to the stone table. Then he swiftly headed back down the passageway, anxious to get back to Lily. Nearing the front of the cave, he was struck with worry that Thorko had found her. The fear was heightened when he came outside and didn't see her.

"Lily," Laszlo whispered into the early evening air. A mist had settled over the area, and he craned his neck, desperate for any sign of her. "Lily!"

Had Thorko taken her? Or perhaps, Lily even went willingly. Her disposition had recently changed, returning to a more depressed state. Undoubtedly, she was feeling the effects of aging again, and Thorko might have offered her the tonic...

The tonic.

He knew where Lily had gone, and it hadn't been with Thorko. Laszlo spun around and ran back into the cave. He didn't have much time.

Tired of being told what to do, Lily didn't heed Laszlo's instructions. Instead of remaining outside, she slipped into the cave, following him at a distance. While he confronted Thorko, she waited in the shadows. As suspected, the old man was still making sure Countess Bathory received her tonics. When she witnessed Thorko tackle Laszlo to the ground, Lily felt compelled to help him. However, she remained pressed against the wall of the cave.

Thorko brushed past Lily on his way out. She was confident that he had spotted her. But he didn't stop if he had. Instead she watched him disappear into the darkness. When she looked back to where Laszlo had been slumped on the ground, she saw him standing near the vat filled with the golden potion. He seemed to be staring at it intently, but from her position she couldn't get a clear view of his face.

Soon Laszlo bolted from the cave as well. Lily was now left alone—with the tonic. She wasted little time. After weeks of the torture she had experienced in Cachtice, she felt owed at least a drop of the infamous tonic, for it did contain her precious blood as an ingredient.

Taking a ladle from Thorko's supplies, she dipped the utensil into the glowing brew. After a few stirs, she brought the spoon up to her lips. A warm sensation trickled down her throat as she consumed a rather large quantity of the potion. Instantly, she felt it start to work.

The sensation began in her hands. A strange tingling rushed through her fingers. Then her chest constricted as the cave began to blur and shake. It must be effective, Lily thought.

But soon her vision went black. As her legs buckled and collapsed, Lily wondered if the severe pain was just the body's reaction to getting younger.

"Lily!" Laszlo screamed. But the only sound was his voice echoing off the limestone walls. "Lily! Are you here?"

When Laszlo reached the end of the cave, he thought he had been mistaken. Perhaps Lily hadn't ventured inside after all. Then he saw a body slouched on the ground. An empty ladle rested near the young woman's feet.

Immediately, Laszlo fell to Lily's side.

"Wake up." Laszlo cradled her in his arms. A soft groan escaped her lips, and his hopes were momentarily lifted. "Lily, please open your eyes."

Turning her face up toward him, he saw a mixture of blood and saliva dripping down her chin. The poisoned tonic had worked quickly on her system.

"Lily," Laszlo whispered into her ear. "It will be all right. I'll... I'll fix this. I promise."

Her pale hand clutched her chest, gripping something hidden beneath the clothes.

"Poppel" she murmured. "Poppel."

Then releasing an unsteady breath, Lily was gone.

"Well, if that isn't the saddest story I've ever heard!" Houten popped a final borstplaat into his mouth.

"Terrible, terrible," Hostrupp said. He wiped the back of his hand across his moist eyes. "Poor Lily. Poor dear, dear Lily."

"Shh, you fools," said Susanne. "Let Laszlo finish telling us what happened."

The group turned its attention back to the strange man who seemed unmoved by his own tale.

"There really isn't much more to tell," Laszlo said with a sigh. "To honor Lily's last words, I went to the village of Poppel to find Grace and Sarah. There I discovered that the daughter of Grace, Annette Loockerman…"

"My mother," Stephanus interrupted.

"Yes, your mother," Laszlo said curtly. "I discovered that Annette had gone off to New Amsterdam with the two remaining Sister Wheels. Hoping to reunite the wheels at last, I also made the long journey across the Atlantic. Upon arriving, I learned Annette had married Oloff Van Cortlandt, and I made it a point to seek out their eldest son." Laszlo nodded to Stephanus.

"So you have Lily's wheel?" Stephanus asked.

Laszlo's face darkened and he shook his head. "It was tragically taken from me before I could contact you."

"Taken?" Susanne snapped. "By whom?"

Laszlo hesitated. He didn't seem to want to reveal much more. But looking around at the pressing stares urging him to continue, he acquiesced.

"Krampus," Laszlo said. "The creature called Krampus followed me across the ocean. During one fateful night when wandering the city alone, the beast overpowered me. And it took the wheel. I have now sought you out to help me recover Lily's wheel, so all three may once again be reunited. I imagine such a reunion would be needed for the underground village you are attempting to build."

"How do you know about the new Poppel?" Houten asked. However, his question not only went unanswered–it was drowned out by Stephanus's voice.

"How are we to know that this Krampus creature is real?"

A peculiar look crossed Laszlo's face. His lip twitched slightly as he locked eyes with Stephanus. "I can show you."

Chapter Twenty

Altar Altercation

Laszlo led Catharine and Henry down from the bell tower. With their hands still bound in front of their bodies, they weren't able to struggle–even as Henry defended his case.

"We should have the Van Cortlandt lineage involved." Henry tried not to stumble as they hurriedly descended the steps. "You're worried they could prevent your plan from being fulfilled. Inviting them to join will eliminate that concern."

Stopping on the landing, Laszlo tugged on Henry's unkempt hair, jerking the young man's head back. Menacingly, Laszlo twisted his face near Henry's and hissed, "Or you and the others may just as well be eliminated. That seems like the simpler option."

"Me?" he gulped. "But you can't get rid of me. I've contributed a great deal."

Laszlo cackled. "Oh, Henry, you are the most arrogant boy. My plan has been in the works for over two hundred years. It has existed before you and will continue on after you're gone. Your purpose is now complete, so there's no more use for you."

Finally, they reached the bottom of the winding stairs. With a sharp shove, Henry and Catharine were hurled down into the foyer. They landed solidly upon the hard floor, not far from the church's entrance. Showing little regard for their wellbeing, Laszlo stepped around the pair, and then gestured toward the nave of the church.

"In here," Laszlo ordered.

But Henry ignored the command. "What do you mean I'm no more use?" He sat up on his knees. "What about my father?"

Meanwhile, Catharine spied the front doors. Within a second, she ran over to them, rattling one of the handles with her bound wrists. But the locked door didn't budge. Henry and Laszlo's argument continued behind her as though they weren't even aware of her failed attempt to escape.

"You promised!" Henry's voice shook angrily. "You promised you would bring him back!"

"That was before you interfered in the girl's capture, you understand," Laszlo said calmly. "It was also before you decided that defending your character to a beautiful woman was more important than secrecy. Now, please, make your way inside the church."

In the distance, a clattering of chains could be heard. Three years ago, Catharine and Henry had heard the same sound in the barren orchard of Van Cortlandt Manor.

Krampus had arrived.

Catharine mumbled something under her breath, which Henry asked her to repeat.

"Run!" Her voice echoed through the hall, shaking the building's skeletal structure. A moment later, Catharine sprinted down the nave while Henry chased after her.

"Catharine," Henry huffed. "Not this way. It's where Laszlo wants us to go."

"Well, you can try breaking down the front door with your fists. Or fight Krampus head on," Catharine snapped. "Those are the only choices." While Henry pondered the options, Catharine grabbed the golden processional cross standing near the altar. She hoisted the crucifix in her arms, looking ready to fight a battle.

"Fine," Henry agreed. "This way is better." He glanced around, hoping to find something useful. The best alternative to an actual weapon appeared to be a candelabrum. He quickly snatched one off the altar.

Catharine and Henry turned back toward the doorway where Laszlo stood watching them. As usual, his expression was hard to read, but he seemed unconcerned that the prisoners were now somewhat armed.

Then the rattling sounded again. It wasn't coming from the hall where Krampus had been expected to emerge. Instead the noise came from the mezzanine. Although Catharine and Henry didn't want to look up, it was impossible not to see the piercing yellow eyes glaring down, ready to attack.

The ash pit opened with a screech and a freckled hand reached out into the empty chamber, grasping a handful of air.

"Remember the time you asked how we were going to get into St. Peter's, since everything's locked up for the evening?" Augustus suppressed a smile as he crawled out of the fireplace hole.

"When you don't spend most of your life traveling on underground sleighs, it's easy to forget," Maggie said defensively. She climbed up into the room after him.

Augustus looked like he was about to retort, but instead he took in the sights around them. They had entered the church's sacristy where vessels were stored in cupboards and the dressers held vestments. Moonlight illuminated the chamber with a bluish tint, and Maggie felt relieved to find neither Laszlo nor Krampus lurking in the shadows. But the initial calmness was short-lived. Noises erupted on the other side of the chamber door, prompting Maggie and Augustus to crouch on the ground.

"Remind me again why we didn't bring any weapons?" Maggie asked.

"I'm not exactly sure what you think will work against Krampus," Augustus whispered. "It's a beast–not a Garrison. We just need to find Laszlo and hope Krampus isn't nearby."

A moment later, a scream came from somewhere within the church.

"That sounds unlikely," Maggie said.

Approaching the door, Maggie rested her hand hesitantly on the handle. She pressed her ear to the wood, but even Augustus, standing a few feet behind her, could hear the events happening outside of the room. She recognized the voices of Catharine and Henry, and she heard the ominous rattling of chains.

Turning back to the chamber, Maggie immediately began opening drawers and cupboards. Augustus watched anxiously as she pulled out sacred items, and he hesitated when she handed him the chalice.

"Why are you giving this to me?" Augustus asked with wide eyes. He looked at the religious cup in his hands like it was a fragile infant.

"We are a little limited with what we can use from here." Maggie handed Augustus a pouch containing vials of holy oils. Once again, he hesitated taking the items. She raised an eyebrow. "I think in an emergency it's all right. I won't tell anyone."

Reluctantly, Augustus grabbed the pouch while tightly gripping the chalice in the other hand. Meanwhile, Maggie picked up a stack of golden patens and a wine flagon.

"I think anyone worth telling already knows." Augustus stared up at the ceiling with a guilty expression.

Maggie realized that she had no idea if Augustus was religious. But it would have to be a conversation for a later time. Feeling only slightly more armed than when they had arrived, Maggie headed toward the door, momentarily looking back at Augustus to make sure he was following.

The sounds in the church had yet to stop, so rather than enter quietly, Maggie swung the door open and charged into the darkness. Her extended arms were positioned to fight.

"Maggie!" Catharine shouted.

Her sister and Henry were crouched behind the pulpit. Maggie had no trouble figuring out what they were hiding from.

In the center of the aisle, Krampus paced between the pews, growling and shaking its chained body. Resembling a caged animal, unable to feel settled within its walled surroundings, it took no time for the creature to spy Maggie and Augustus. Krampus's temperament instantly shifted. A black tongue angrily clicked while its clawed hands clenched.

"Run, Maggie," Catharine yelled. "Run!" But Maggie disregarded her sister's instructions.

Instead she moved near the altar, directly in Krampus's path.

"Laszlo, get rid of your beast," she called. "Face us yourself."

But Laszlo did not appear. And Krampus did not stop making its way toward Maggie.

"You're not wanted here, Krampus." She tried to keep her voice from trembling. A second later, she heaved the wine flagon at the beast. The glass vessel shattered against its body, sending crimson liquid spilling down its gray hair. The wine almost looked like blood upon its drenched body, but the flagon did little actual damage.

Next Maggie held up the patens in her left hand and began flinging them toward Krampus like discs. One by one, the spiraling plates created a golden streak in the air. When they rhythmically clattered against Krampus, the creature seemed more annoyed than injured.

Knowing that the creature was about to launch an attack, Maggie turned to Augustus. Grabbing his shirt, she tugged him behind the altar.

"What do we do now?" Augustus gasped. "You just made it angrier."

Maggie eyed the contents in his hand. She considered distracting the creature with the chalice, giving Catharine a chance to escape. But as she was about to grab the cup, she reconsidered. Instead she took the pouch from Augustus. She lifted its flap and pulled out one of the vials of oil. Before Augustus could stop her, she ran back around the altar where she nearly collided with Krampus's thick chest. Gripping the cork with her teeth, Maggie opened the vial, and in one motion, she tossed the oil onto the beast.

Gnashing its sharp mouth, Krampus angrily released a deep howl. Maggie was sure the creature's claws would soon shred her skin. Before she attempted to slip away, Krampus stepped back from her. Still wailing as though in pain, the beast retreated to the middle of the nave. She watched Krampus leap upon a pew and then hurdle its body to the mezzanine. The creature's howls soon faded into the shadows as it disappeared from view.

The church turned eerily silent. Catharine and Henry came out from behind the pulpit, joining Maggie and Augustus near the altar.

"Is it gone?" Catharine whispered.

All eyes turned to Henry who seemed surprised by the attention. "I don't know," he said. "I've never seen it act like that before."

"What have you done?" The voice echoed throughout the church. Maggie turned to see Laszlo trampling down the aisle. "What did you do to it?"

Even Maggie wasn't quite sure what had happened. Staring down at the empty vial in her hand, she noticed the word *Bari* scribbled across the glass. But she didn't have the opportunity to consider what it meant before the clicking of a gun barrel brought her attention back to Laszlo.

"Unfortunately, it seems I must dispose of you all myself." Laszlo pointed a pistol their direction. "It was not how I intended this to happen, you understand."

"Wait!" Henry shouted. "The Sister Wheel! I removed Lily's wheel from Poppel, as you had requested. But I never told you where it's hidden. If you shoot me, or any of us, you'll never see it again."

Laszlo actually seemed to consider Henry's threat before shaking his head. "A clever attempt, Henry." Laszlo sighed. "However, I am quite confident that I would be able to track it down. You underestimate my connection to the wheel. It'd be no trouble at all to find it, you understand."

"I don't believe that," Henry replied. "You'd never find it. Your head's too hollow."

"Really, Henry?" Laszlo said. "Petty name-calling, after everything we've been through. I thought you were better than that–or at least capable of producing better insults." He once again lifted the gun toward the group. "Now, please, stop distracting me. This will be over soon enough."

"Wait!" Augustus stepped forward. "There's one more thing."

Laszlo let out another frustrated sigh. "You are really trying my patience."

"It's about Lily," he said. "I know where she is."

Maggie looked at Augustus out of the corner of her eye, trying to predict where he was going with such a proclamation.

"Oh, really," Laszlo replied doubtfully. But his eyes glowed with interest. "What makes you say that?"

Augustus reached into his breast pocket and pulled out a frail piece of paper.

"Were you aware that Stephanus Van Cortlandt scattered pages of his personal journal throughout the Boeken Kamer? In great detail, he writes about meeting you for the first time, and your history involving Lily."

"Interesting," Laszlo said listlessly. "Quite interesting. And why should I care about this?"

"Because I know where you are keeping Lily. I told the Foundlings that if we do not return to Poppel this evening they are to get rid of the body. Then it won't matter what you do to us. You would still not be able to bring her back."

The church filled with silence. Laszlo didn't speak and his face offered little indication of his thoughts.

"So you should allow us to leave," Augustus said, and then added, ominously, "Perhaps you can still make it to Lily in time."

Maggie stared Laszlo, wondering if Augustus's threat would work. As his grip tightened on the pistol's handle, it seemed he wasn't going to back down. However, before Maggie could grab her sister and dive behind the pulpit, Laszlo turned on his heels and ran back down the aisle. Then he disappeared out of sight.

"Is he gone?" Catharine asked.

"Difficult to say," Maggie replied. "But we shouldn't wait around to see. Let's get to the ash pit..."

An animalistic shriek sounded throughout St. Peter's Church, signaling to the group that Krampus wasn't too far away. While Maggie and the others considered their options, Henry seemed concerned for his own wellbeing. Without saying a word, he bolted toward the sacristy. He didn't look back once. A moment later, Maggie heard the ash pit open and close. And then silence.

Henry had left them– perhaps forever.

"Henry can't just leave," Augustus spat. "He hid Lily's wheel. We'll never get it back to Poppel now."

Before Augustus could start after him, Maggie grabbed his arm. Henry's insult to Laszlo echoed through her mind.

Your head's too hollow.

"I know where to find Lily's wheel," Maggie said.

Chapter Twenty-One

The Island

How are you so confident Henry took the wheel here?" Augustus asked, crawling out of the refectory's ash pit.

Maggie dusted ash from her shoulders as she stood in front of the fireplace. "Because," she replied, "I told him about how John Pintard's bust was hollow. He was trying to let me know where he'd hid Lily's wheel without Laszlo realizing."

Maggie looked up at the marble statue. Although the sculpted face was angled to the side, the fixated eyes seemed to be looking right at her. With Augustus's help, they were able to slide the heavy bust over a few inches. It was enough to reveal a small golden wheel sitting peacefully upon the mantel. She reached up and grabbed Lily's wheel.

"Turns out that you know Henry pretty well," Augustus remarked.

Maggie scoffed. "Actually, I've only recently come to realize how little I do know him. You understand Henry just as well as me." She thought for a moment. "Apparently, you know Laszlo, too. Where was he keeping Lily's body in Poppel? I don't recall reading that in Stephanus's journal."

"That's because there wasn't anything written about it. It was just an assumption," Augustus admitted sheepishly. "I never found journal pages that went beyond what Laszlo told Stephanus in the cellar of Lovelace Tavern. However, Laszlo was clearly as obsessed with Lily as she was with immortality. I'm quite certain that everything is happening in order to bring her back to life. If the story about Countess Bathory is any indication, Laszlo would need lots of death to accomplish that."

Maggie's eyes widened. "So that's why he's taking Foundlings? To kill them for some kind of immortality spell?"

Augustus shook his head. "If that were the case, he would have destroyed Poppel long ago. Instead he needs the Foundlings to help execute his plans. Since he likely hid Lily's remains in Poppel, he was concerned about the village's safety. No, Poppel's not big enough to bring about the kind of death he needs. It was only a tool to help achieve his true goal."

"And what do you think that is?" Maggie asked.

He hesitated before replying. "War. A war greater than any of us can imagine. With more blood spilled than all previous wars before it and all the wars to come."

"Then I know what we have to do," Maggie stated. Augustus looked puzzled, so she continued, "We need to find out what happened after Stephanus's journal ends."

Augustus appeared even more confused. "I'm not sure how we could possibly come to know that. Stephanus has been dead for centuries, and Laszlo doesn't seem like a willing storyteller this time."

"Don't you remember reading about the others present in the cellar?"

"Sure, Stephanus mentioned some Foundlings. Their names were Casparus, Gerhard, and Susanne, I believe. But no one in Poppel has those names now."

"Are you sure?" Maggie asked. Something bounced around her mind. She had heard one of those names somewhere before…

"Gerhard Hostrupp!"

"Hostrupp?" Augustus repeated.

"His first name's Gerhard. Wendell told me," Maggie explained. "Perhaps Casparus is Houten and Susanne is Madame Welles." Unexpectedly, she let out a chuckle. "Strange. It's possible that others in Poppel had the information we were desperately trying to find this entire time."

"Then we should return to Poppel and see what they know," Augustus said before adding quietly, "Perhaps it's time to include the Foundlings as well."

He didn't appear excited at conceding to Maggie's original plan. But she had no intention of gloating. Her mind was too occupied.

"I wish we would have found Violet," she said with a frown. "Henry left before I could ask about her. Where do you think she could be?"

The steamboat glided up the Hudson River with more ease–and yet more urgency–than it had for some time. The morning sun appeared in the east, sending a sparkling glow across the water, and Violet wondered if the river always seemed so peaceful.

She had never been on Poppel's steamboat. Feeling some excitement, she momentarily forgot the chaos and confusion leading up to the boat's departure. Violet knew something had happened at St. Peter's Church with Catharine and Henry. At the time, she'd been locked away in a nearby chamber. However, she had heard Maggie's voice as well as the others.

After the noise died down, Laszlo's assistants, Bickley and Milton, arrived at the church. They didn't explain what had happened. But in a strange turn of events, they said they were taking her back to Poppel.

And then things only got stranger.

Bickley and Milton took Violet straight to Poppel's steamboat–Stoomboot. They instructed her to load some supplies, mainly bags and small crates, onto the boat's deck. It wasn't until Laszlo appeared did she finally receive any insight to the plans.

"Is everything ready?" Laszlo asked. The man, who was usually apathetic in nature, now gave off a fearfully impatient energy.

Bickley nodded. "Everything's packed. Captain Noble says he can leave as soon as we want."

"Is–you know–taken care of?" Milton asked.

"Yes, yes," Laszlo snapped. "That was done first thing."

Without saying another word, Laszlo swept toward the steamboat and boarded. He didn't even look at Violet as he passed. When Bickley approached, she attempted to pry answers out of him.

"Why is Captain Noble taking us? I thought he was loyal to Poppel."

Bickley chuckled. "Captain Noble will assist anyone who can pay him. He's been helping Laszlo for years. Laszlo or Poppel–it makes no difference so long as he's paid."

Feeling hopeful by Bickley's casual exchange with her, she pressed for more details. "What needed to be taken care of?"

Bickley draped a lanky arm around Violet's shoulder, guiding her further onto the deck of the boat. "Don't concern yourself with anything else. We will be departing soon."

Violet watched Bickley start to walk away. He'd always been the tallest boy in Poppel while his blond hair looked nearly white. Both of these traits had made him self-conscious. Since he'd always been reserved with the other Foundlings, Violet had never talked with him until Krampus abducted her.

"Where are we going?" Violet asked. "Or can't you tell me that either."

Looking back, Bickley gave her a mocking smile. "We are going on the Hudson River, of course."

Violet had been left alone for most of the trip. As the boat continued up the river to an unknown destination, she sat patiently in the middle of the deck. Although she would have preferred to stand near the railing, watching the landscape pass by, she worried the others would assume she was trying to escape.

"We're almost there," Milton announced as he walked over to Violet.

In many ways, the boy was the opposite of Bickley. He was stout with dark hair and a thin mustache. Milton had been Harriet's Foundling pair, so Violet had spoken with him often enough to know he wasn't particularly bright. Therefore, he was her best chance at obtaining information.

"And where is that?" Violet asked innocently. "Bickley didn't know. Laszlo doesn't seem to think very highly of him, so he won't tell him things. But I bet Laszlo trusts you, Milton."

His eyes widened and he looked around the boat to see if anyone was nearby. Laszlo and Bickley were in the hull, and Captain Noble remained in the wheelhouse.

Since the surroundings were clear, Milton kneeled next to Violet.

"An island," he whispered. "That's where we are going."

Violet's ears perked up with interest. "Is that where the other Foundlings are kept?"

"Some of them. Others were sent on secret missions," Milton explained. "This island has been Laszlo's for a long time. He's been constructing a fortress on it for centuries. And now it's finally ready."

"Ready for what?"

"For an army!" Milton's voice grew with excitement. "There are great things in store. All of Laszlo's plans will soon be fulfilled."

Violet's mind buzzed with even more questions, but something kept pulling at her.

"What's in the hull? Laszlo seems very protective of that area."

Milton was quiet for a few seconds before finally whispering, "Lily's down there. He's bringing her to the island."

"Wonderful, wonderful!" Hostrupp greeted Maggie and Augustus upon their return to Poppel. "And you brought back Lily's wheel as well. Van Cortlandt descendants always have a way of hunting those wheels down."

Maggie handed the wheel to Hostrupp who headed into his shop where the Horologe still hung. Meanwhile, Madame Welles cornered the pair on Myra Lane, eager to hear more about the wheel's whereabouts.

"Henry took it," Maggie said. "I'm not sure where he is now, or if he'll ever come back. He was working with Krampus and Laszlo."

Madame Welles seemed shocked by the news. However, Maggie barely had the chance to explain how the events unfolded at St. Peter's Church before Houten came wobbling down the cobblestone road.

"Something's happened in the Horologe Hall!"

Without further explanation, Houten led Maggie, Augustus, Madame Welles, and Hostrupp, down to the Horologe Hall. Maggie hadn't been to the large hall, located deep within Poppel, since the fateful Christmas Eve. Containing the decoy horologe and its fake wheels, the hall had been successful in misleading the Garrisons.

When they arrived at the Horologe Hall, it was still not clear what had happened to warrant the journey down there. As the group shuffled down the wide aisle, situated between rows of tall columns, Maggie felt that something was different. Peering toward the far end of the hall, her mind was flooded with memories of the men from Furnace Brook being slaughtered by the Garrisons. The men had been left to die across the very floor they now walked. But as they neared the fake horologe, the ghosts from the past were pushed aside as the mysteries of the present appeared.

The gigantic fake horologe, built into the wall of the cavernous room, was cracked open.

"When did this happen?" Madame Welles asked.

"Couldn't have been too long ago," Houten replied gruffly. "I have Lloyd coming down here a few times a week. He said he didn't notice the horologe open until this morning. I didn't believe him. I hobbled all the way down here to see it for myself. But sure enough–it's open!"

"But what's inside of it?" Maggie asked.

"Nothing," Augustus said, climbing down the metal ladder that led to the horologe. While Houten had been talking, he had gone up to have a look inside. "At least there's nothing in there now. I'm not sure what was stored inside before."

"Don't look at me," Houten grumbled. "I never even knew the stupid thing opened. It's simply a decoy. I thought building the fake horologe was a ridiculous idea when Laszlo suggested it. And I still do."

"The horologe was Laszlo's idea?" Maggie asked.

"Oh, yes," Hostrupp answered. "Laszlo was most insistent about it–most insistent. He tells the Van Cortlandts that there needs to be a fake horologe in Poppel. It was the only suggestion he made–the only one. He was most insistent."

"That's true," Madame Welles said. "The best chance of discovering what was inside the horologe would be to ask Laszlo. However, that seems unlikely to happen, considering what occurred at St. Peter's Church."

Augustus shook his head. "There's no need to speak to Laszlo. It's clear why it had been built." He turned to Maggie. "Laszlo was keeping Lily up there. Since we knew about the body, he had her moved."

"But now the question is to where," Maggie added.

They looked back to Madame Welles, Hostrupp, and Houten, all of whom seemed visibly surprised at the mention of Lily.

"How do you know about Laszlo's connection to Lily?" Madame Welles asked.

Augustus explained the pages of Stephanus's journal. "It ends with Laszlo trying to convince Stephanus that Krampus was real. Since all of you were present in the tavern's cellar, you must know what happened after that."

"Perhaps," said Houten, placing his cane between his feet. "But it hardly seems relevant now. That was two hundred years ago."

"All that really matters is that Stephanus and Laszlo fought the beast," Hostrupp said. "They captured Lily's wheel. And it was brought back to Poppel. Of course, Laszlo wanted no part of the lore, insisting that any retelling of the story should say it was the Foundlings who fought Krampus those many years ago."

"Afterward, Krampus disappeared for a while," Madame Welles explained. "Likely moving around the Hudson Valley before settling at Van Cortlandt Manor, in order to stay close to Sarah's wheel. Now it appears the creature is back in New York City."

"Where did Laszlo and Stephanus fight Krampus?" Maggie asked.

"The island," Hostrupp said. His voice squeaked with excitement. "Laszlo took Stephanus to the island. And ever since that day, Stephanus believed Laszlo. Oh my, how he believed him."

Maggie locked eyes with Augustus. It was the first time they had heard any mention of an island other than Manhattan. She sensed the detail should not be ignored.

"Tell us more about this island, Hostrupp." Then looking over at Houten, Maggie added, "Although many things change over the centuries, it seems Poppel, Laszlo, and Krampus, do not."

Epilogue

A breeze swept over the East River, sending a much-welcomed mist into the warm summer night. As instructed, Stephanus waited on the dock in front of City Hall. The earlier crowd had long ago departed, leaving the streets empty. The night's stillness made it easy to hear Laszlo's arrival when he rowed up to the dock in a small wooden boat.

Without so much as a greeting, Laszlo said, "Get in."

Stephanus hesitated. He still did not trust the strange man, so he certainly had reservations about joining him unaccompanied. However, he eventually stepped into the bobbing boat, and Laszlo dipped the oars back into the river, rowing them away from shore.

The lights of Manhattan faded into the distance as the boat moved out of the East River into the open waters of the bay. Laszlo steered them around the southern tip of the island.

"Where are you taking me?" Stephanus asked.

Traveling up the Hudson River, the boat now fought against the current.

"Rest your eyes, Stephanus," Laszlo said evenly. "We will be there by morning."

Alarmed, Stephanus twisted about to face Laszlo. "Morning? Return me to the city immediately. I did not agree to travel so far."

Although he spoke sternly, Stephanus was unable to mask the fear in his voice.

"There's no need to be nervous," Laszlo replied. "The trip will be worth the distance, you understand."

Stephanus reached for the oars, but before he could grab one, Laszlo extended a hand to the man's forehead. A sharp burning sensation penetrated his skull, as the world around him grew dark.

The next thing Stephanus heard was the soothing sounds of birds at dawn. Although his eyes remained closed, he knew he was still in the boat. He could hear the oars lapping the water and feel the occasional bumps of the river. Slowly, he peeked through his eyelids.

"We are almost there." Laszlo's voice was quiet as though trying not to cause a disturbance.

Stephanus wanted to ask where they were going, but his throat had yet to wake up. He could barely release a grunt. However, Laszlo seemed to read his thoughts.

"You wanted me to prove that Krampus is real. So I am taking you to the creature."

Upon nearing an island, Stephanus peered toward a cluster of trees swaying without a breeze. He looked back at Laszlo for an explanation, but the pale man's expression remained stoic, and he said nothing. When the boat finally landed on the island's rocky shore, Laszlo still remained silent. With a simple nod, he directed Stephanus out of the boat.

Carefully, Stephanus disembarked. Taking tentative steps, he walked about twenty yards before turning around. He was afraid to find Laszlo rowing away, leaving him alone on the island. But the boat remained stationary. Laszlo once again nodded, encouraging Stephanus onward. However, when he looked back at the shadowy trees, a pair of yellow eyes met his gaze.

Emitting a growl neither animal nor human, the creature lunged off a branch. From its hairy form to its twisted horns and sharp teeth, the creature was a nightmare embodied. Without hesitation, Stephanus ran back to the boat. Laszlo seemed unmoved by the beast.

When Stephanus leapt into the wooden craft, he shouted, "Move the boat. Go now, you fool!"

But Laszlo remained motionless. "Have no fear," he instructed. "You will only scare it."

"Scare it?" Stephanus stammered. "That seems unlikely."

Reaching into his jacket's pocket, Laszlo pulled out a tiny item attached to the chain he had showed Stephanus earlier. The man immediately recognized the gleaming emblem.

"Lily's wheel," he whispered. "You said it had been taken."

Ignoring Stephanus's comment, Laszlo remarked, "You are the grandson of Lily's sister, Grace. Krampus will not harm you–so long as it knows you intend on protecting the wheels. And protecting Lily."

"Protecting Lily?" Stephanus spat. "Lily's dead."

Laszlo's mouth curved. "Only momentarily."

Before Stephanus could ask what he meant by that, a loud growl shook the boat.

"Prove to me that Krampus means no harm." His voice trembled. "Prove that to me, and I'll help you with whatever you need."

As though waiting to hear those exact words, Laszlo stepped out of the boat and confidently marched up the rocky beach.

When Laszlo reached Krampus, he held out the wheel toward the creature. Even in the face of such a beast, Stephanus noticed that Laszlo's arm never once wavered.

After Lily died in his arms, Laszlo fled from the cave and into the night, clutching the wheel within his hand. His legs moved fast, but it wasn't clear where they would take him. The feet just obeyed his heart, which wished to get away from the pain. However, as swiftly as his legs had started running, they quickly came to a crashing halt. He had heard a monstrous growl from within the forest, and he knew it was the beast from his dreams.

Looping Lily's chain around his neck in order to free his hands, Laszlo picked up the pace again. However, he was weighed down by the heaviness spreading across his chest. With the pain of Lily's death feeling insurmountable, Laszlo was helpless facing the creature that hunted him. So when his foot collided with a tree root, sending his body soaring to the hard ground, Laszlo knew he would soon meet death. Yet he embraced his fate with surprising calmness.

The thumping of footsteps neared his prone body. He dug his hands into the dirt and scurried toward the base of the tree. He didn't want to die lying face down on the ground. Twisting about, he sat up against its trunk, and that's the first time he saw the creature.

The beast towered over Laszlo, its massive body propped up on muscular back legs. The moonlight reflected off its twisted horns, causing them to glow. Meanwhile, sharp teeth jutted out of its mouth, threatening to violently gnaw anything that got too close.

In one swift movement, the beast crouched to Laszlo's level. A black tongue nearly licked his face. The creature's claws reached toward Laszlo's chest where his heart beat rapidly, waiting to be slashed out. As the claws neared his body, Laszlo closed his eyes, bracing for his skin to burn in pain. A sharp talon grazed his shirt, hooking itself around the collar. Hearing a soft clink and no longer feeling the pressure of the claw against his skin, Laszlo opened his eyes. With surprising ease, the creature had pulled the chain out from underneath his shirt.

The creature's yellow eyes were fixated on the small wheel as though the item had been what it sought. But it didn't rip the chain from Laszlo's neck. Instead it released the chain from its claw, dropping it back to the young man's chest.

"Kraaaa," it growled. "Kraaamp. Krampus."

As Laszlo stared into the fearsome face of a creature that had haunted his dreams for an entire lifetime, he recognized the power it offered. Then Laszlo knew what had to be done.

ABOUT THE AUTHOR

Sonia Halbach was born in Minnesota, raised in North Dakota, and attended college in South Dakota. So naturally, a week after graduating from Augustana College, she hightailed it east to try New York City on for size. And it turned out to be pretty big. But with a passion for history, Halbach soon became infatuated with New York City's rich collection of stories.

When Halbach's not trying new flavors of bubble tea, civilizing her cats, or conjuring up schemes to get locked inside The Morgan Library & Museum for a night, she can be found researching forgotten stories on the island of many hills, which inspired her to write *The Krampus Chronicles*.